"ANY ANSWER FROM STARFLEET?"

"Just static, sir. I think I'm getting feedback from Beta Argola, though." Ina's hands did a coordinated dance over her console. "It's possible they got the first message, but I can't confirm it."

"We need to reach *them*, if no one else," Gold said, pacing toward the command chair, then motioned Gomez to his side. "Commander, assuming we didn't get through to Starfleet, how can we increase the damage we're doing to their ships? If we can just disable them long enough to repair warp drive, and we can break away long enough to be out of jamming range, we can call for reinforcements and head for Beta Argola."

Gomez's brow knitted in thought. "Yes, sir. Increase the damage, hm?"

"I have a ship full of engineers here," Gold said with a wry smile. "Surely we can put them to use. What materials do we have aboard that could be used defensively or offensively?"

"Nothing that I can . . ." She paused. Gold knew that look in her eyes: drip-drop, drip-drop. Engineers didn't often have a flood of ideas. Their genius was in gathering the dew from leaves of intelligence and experience. "Mining equipment," she said, finally. "The cargo bays are filled with it. They're overflowing, in fact."

"Can you use it?"

Probably not yet quite s̶ Gomez nodded anyway

STAR TREK®
S.C.E.

BOOK THREE

SOME ASSEMBLY REQUIRED

Greg Brodeur, Scott Ciencin,
Keith R.A. DeCandido, Dave Galanter,
Dan Jolley, and Aaron Rosenberg

Based upon STAR TREK® and
STAR TREK: THE NEXT GENERATION®
created by Gene Roddenberry
and STAR TREK: DEEP SPACE NINE®
created by Rick Berman & Michael Piller

POCKET BOOKS
New York London Toronto Sydney Singapore Maeglin

This book is a work of fiction. Names, characters, places and incidents are products of the authors' imaginations or are used fictitiously. Any resemblance to actual events or locales or persons, living or dead, is entirely coincidental.

POCKET BOOKS, a division of Simon & Schuster, Inc.
1230 Avenue of the Americas, New York, NY 10020

Star Trek® S.C.E. #9: The Riddled Post copyright © 2001
by Paramount Pictures. All Rights Reserved.
Star Trek® S.C.E. #10: Here There Be Monsters copyright © 2001
by Paramount Pictures. All Rights Reserved.
Star Trek® S.C.E. #11: Ambush copyright © 2001
by Paramount Pictures. All Rights Reserved.
Star Trek® S.C.E. #12: Some Assembly Required copyright © 2002
by Paramount Pictures. All Rights Reserved.

STAR TREK is a Registered Trademark of
Paramount Pictures.

This book is published by Pocket Books, a division of
Simon & Schuster, Inc., under exclusive license from
Paramount Pictures.

ISBN: 0-7434-6442-7

First Pocket Books paperback printing April 2003

10 9 8 7 6 5 4 3 2 1

POCKET and colophon are registered trademarks of
Simon & Schuster, Inc.

For information regarding special discounts for bulk purchases,
please contact Simon & Schuster Special Sales at
1-800-456-6798 or business@simonandschuster.com

Printed in the U.S.A.

These titles were previously published individually in
eBook format by Pocket Books.

CONTENTS

THE RIDDLED POST

Aaron Rosenberg

CHAPTER
1

"*Starfleet, come in! Emergency! We've got cata-strophic systems failure, equipment down across the board, we need help! Please respo—!*"

Captain David Gold switched off the audio recording and glanced around the observation lounge. As always, Sonya Gomez admired his ability to stay calm at a time like this.

But then, he had heard the distress call already, as had Sonya, his first officer, and second officer Lt. Commander Kieran Duffy. Around the table, the rest of the S.C.E. team on the *U.S.S. da Vinci* looked more startled at the urgent cry for help.

Gold turned his blue eyes on Sonya. She nod-ded, and began filling in the gaps.

She tugged absently at her shirt cuffs and looked around the table at her team. "Okay, first off, a bit about the planet." She pressed a control on the console in front of her, and an image of a planet appeared on the viewscreen. "We're looking at BorSitu Minor—anybody heard of it?" No one responded. "Right, that's not surprising. It's got only the one outpost on it. But BorSitu Minor does have something worthwhile—dilithium, some of the richest deposits ever found. The outpost is geared toward mining operations, and tends to rotate staff every year or two. Most of the work is automated, so the staff is pretty small."

"How small?" asked Dr. Lense from the other side of the table, though Sonya noticed the doctor didn't make eye contact with anyone as she spoke.

"Less than a dozen, according to their latest records."

Lense nodded. "We should be able to handle any casualties, then, but I'd like to know if there's a ship with a bigger sickbay nearby that we can call on just in case."

"Both the *Fearless* and the *Sugihara* are in the area," Gold said. "I'll have McAllan contact them."

"Thank you," Lense said quietly.

Gomez went on. "The biggest issue with BorSitu Minor is the atmosphere. It's highly ionized, and the charge blocks normal transporters, communicators, and sensors. In addition, it has a high acid content—it's dangerously corrosive. The outpost has a transporter pad, heavily shielded and with extra signal boosters. They've even got a matter/antimatter plant on-site for power, to give them enough to cut through and to shield against that atmosphere. But, based on that distress signal, the transporter probably isn't working, so the away team will have to take a shuttlecraft down there. And when they get there, the shield may be down as well."

"In which case," Kieran said, "we'll have to rig up a portable shield generator. The team can activate it as they open the shuttle door, and use it to move around."

"It'll have to be quick," Fabian Stevens said from his seat next to Duffy. "Those portables only last about an hour or so."

From her modified chair at the far end of the table, P8 Blue said, "For an outpost of that size, an hour will be enough."

Sonya smiled. "Glad to hear you say that, Pattie, because you're on the away team, along with Corsi and Soloman. From you, I want a structural analysis, and any first guesses as to what happened." Turning to the short Bynar, she said, "Soloman, check the computer files and make sure the systems are repairable." Finally, she gazed upon the tall human security chief sitting next to Lense. "Corsi, assess the safety level—I need to know if we can all go in, and if we need security with us." All three nodded. "Meantime, Fabian, I want you to prepare possible attack scenarios for us—"

Fabian frowned. "We're going to attack the outpost?"

"No, but somebody may have. I want to know who could have done it from orbit, and how. We'll compare those to Pattie's assessment and see if we get a match." She glanced at Gold, who nodded. "Okay, that's it. Let's get to work."

The meeting over, people began rising from their seats. Corsi was the first to her feet and out the door, as usual. She seemed eager to prepare, and Sonya repressed a smile. Corsi was always enthusiastic about security, and she was probably thrilled to be playing a major part in the first portion of this expedition. Gold was out next, back to the bridge and the business of running the *da Vinci*—including having the other two ships notified that they may be needed for medical backup. Soloman also wandered out, chatting with Bart Faulwell and Fabian. Carol Abramowitz and Pattie were right behind them—Sonya was glad to see that the two roommates were on speaking terms again, after a tiff they'd had over Carol's musical choices—as was Dr. Lense.

That left Kieran and Sonya alone in the observation lounge.

"Gee," Kieran said, "you and I not on the away team on the day we were supposed to have lunch. Coincidence?"

Sonya stood up and put on her official face. "Commander Duffy, I am shocked—shocked—that you would accuse me of putting personal preference before duty." Then she broke into a smile. "Besides, those three really are the best ones to go on the team—especially Pattie, with her tough hide, in case there are problems with the atmosphere."

"Fair enough," Kieran said, with a smile of his own. "Shall we go to the mess hall, the mess hall, or maybe the mess hall?"

"Actually, I was thinking my quarters," Sonya said.

Kieran's smile widened.

CHAPTER
2

"Entering BorSitu's atmosphere," Blue reported from the *Franklin*'s co-pilot seat. "Shields holding, systems fully operational."

"Good." Corsi was piloting, blue eyes narrowed in concentration, and her steady hands held the shuttle-craft on course. This, despite the sudden buffeting of the ever-present electrical storm, not to mention her hands being gloved, since both she and Soloman wore atmospheric suits. Blue's chitinous hide and Nasat physiology made such an encumbrance unnecessary for her.

Behind her, the Bynar sat quietly, absorbed in his own thoughts. He had come a long way in dealing with the loss of his mate, but she'd noticed he still disappeared into his own head when there wasn't work to do. That was dangerous if something came up suddenly, but she already knew better than to rely on him in combat.

The shuttle rocked a bit, its stabilizers fighting to compensate for the lightning and wind, but

Corsi kept them on target and within a minute they could see the outlines of the outpost up ahead. It grew rapidly in their view, and Blue glanced down at her readouts.

"Matter-antimatter readings normal," the insectoid announced, and Corsi allowed herself to relax just a little. That had been their first concern. If the power plant had been bled off or jettisoned, they would have needed to reinstall and recalibrate it before they had any hope of getting power again. With the generator's matter-antimatter chamber intact, they just had to worry about finding the problems and restoring functions.

Just. Corsi realized she'd been hanging around with engineers for too long.

"The bad news," Blue continued, "is that I'm not getting any shield readings. It's down like we thought, so we'll need to use the generator and hope the damage isn't too severe."

Then the station came fully into view, and Corsi actually let a soft curse escape her. That distracted Blue enough to look, and even Soloman glanced up, then stared in shock.

The outpost was not that large—a dozen buildings, perhaps, all clustered together—and without its shields Corsi could clearly see each building even through the haze of the acidic atmosphere. The buildings were weathered, the air obviously having worn away edges and pitted surfaces once the shields had dropped.

But what had evoked the curse were the holes. Everywhere she looked, the buildings were riddled with them, drilled right through the walls at various angles. It was as if a giant needle had pierced the outpost, time and again.

"Approaching shuttle bay," Corsi announced, and she was angered that her voice shook slightly. At least her hands were steady. She shouldn't have been so affected by this. "Get the shield generator ready."

A minute later, the shuttlecraft settled to the deck of the shuttle bay—which, being exposed to the atmosphere, was also pitted and warped in spots. The *Franklin*'s engines shut down with a whine, and they all unbuckled. Corsi had insisted on everyone strapping in before they left the *da Vinci*, which had proved necessary in the turbulent ionization they had just flown through. As Blue set up the generator, Corsi drew her phaser as she stepped toward the exit hatch.

"Is that necessary?" Soloman inquired, gesturing toward the weapon. "Anything dangerous would have been killed by the outside air."

"Maybe, but I can't chance it," she replied, wishing in retrospect that she'd requested that Gomez let her bring another one of her own team down. "If it's safe, fine. But if there is something out there, something built to survive this stuff or prepared to handle it, I'd rather not have to waste time reaching for a weapon." The little Bynar seemed at a loss for a reply, and all three of them were silent as they gathered around the hatch. She looked at Blue. "All set?" The eight-armed blue insectoid nodded. "Okay. On three I pop the hatch, you hit the shield, and we step out. One, two, three!"

It worked perfectly, especially for a nonsecurity

team. Corsi opened the hatch, Blue already extending her arm and the generator, and the shield formed just beyond the shuttle door, protecting them from the atmosphere. Blue stepped out first, being careful to keep the shield just overlapping the hatch, and Corsi followed, then Soloman. The Bynar shut the hatch behind him. Then Corsi took the lead and led the other two quickly over to the nearest building. The doors were inoperable, of course, but she knew where the manual override was and it took only a minute for her to flip the lever, pop the doors, and usher the other two inside. She noticed the head-size holes in the door and the walls, but set that aside for now—she'd examine them more closely later.

Once inside, Blue set the generator down on the floor. She and Soloman turned to the consoles, while Corsi examined the rest of the room. It wasn't a pleasant sight. There were bodies on the floor, all of them largely decomposed—the air had done the same to them as to the walls, only far worse. The air felt alive even through the shield and their suits, as the charge transferred to every surface. Details seemed to waver slightly—Corsi knew it was a side effect of the current in the air, but it made her nervous, and she tightened her grip on the phaser for reassurance. At least the area seemed secure—no lifesigns, no movement beyond that shimmer, and no other entrances beside the door they'd used. So once again Corsi forced herself to wait and watch while the two engineers did their work.

"Systems all check out," Blue announced after several minutes, and Soloman nodded in agreement. "The shields are functional, at least on this end."

The next step was back outside and around the front of the building, to the emitter array. Once there, it was obvious even to Corsi what the problem was—the array had a hole the size of a hover-ball through it.

"Could you give me a hand here, Commander?"

Corsi did as Blue requested, setting the generator down beside her and the phaser on top where she could reach it quickly, and among the three of them they managed to wrestle the damaged piece off the array. Then they trundled it back to the *Franklin*. Once inside, it took less than an hour for the two engineers to repair the damage, and only ten more minutes to restore the piece to its place. Soloman then rebooted the system and restored the shields over the outpost—Corsi always found it creepy to hear him speaking in computer language, interfacing directly with the systems, but she couldn't argue with the effects. It was another hour before the filtration system had removed all contaminants from the air, replacing corrosives with breathable elements—she insisted they spend that time safely inside the shuttlecraft, to be sure. Finally, the *Franklin*'s sensors indicated it was safe to step outside, and they did so, this time without the portable generator.

Without the haze of BorSitu's atmosphere, the devastation was even worse. Every hole was clearly defined, and the buildings looked like ancient ruins, ready to crumble at any moment. But the damage was less than a day old, and

Corsi knew that clues were often time-sensitive, so she didn't waste any time. Once she was sure the air was safe she allowed her two companions to go about their assigned tasks, although she kept a close eye on them. She also scanned for lifesigns—and got a surprising response.

"We've got survivors!" she said. Soloman looked up, and Blue did as well. "Two lifesigns, human, over there." Corsi waved her phaser across the square. "Ten meters distance." She glanced up. "That's only half the size of this square. They're not on the other side—they're at the center." She turned toward the squat building in the middle of the open area, as did the others.

"That's the power station," Blue confirmed.

"Makes sense," Corsi admitted, leading them toward the building. "You said the generator was showing as normal. And there aren't any holes in this building. So these two, whoever they are, were in the only safe place when it happened. Whatever it was."

Stepping inside, she marveled at the difference. The power station hadn't been hit by whatever had caused the holes, and so although its outer walls had been worn down by the air, the inside was fully intact. It was like stepping out of a sandstorm and into a gleaming steel playground. Corsi wasn't an engineer, but she recognized several pieces of equipment around the area—before her eyes were drawn to the two figures slumped on the floor.

"Damn!" She slapped her communicator out of habit, and was surprised when Gomez responded.

"I linked our badges in through the *Franklin*,"

Soloman explained. The little Bynar actually sounded apologetic. "This way they have enough power to get through the atmosphere."

"I wish you'd told me," Corsi muttered.

"Told you what? Corsi, what's your status?" Gomez sounded worried.

"Sorry, not you. Status is good—we've got the shields restored, and the air breathable. And we've got two survivors, though they're both in bad shape. I'll get them to the shuttlecraft, and then bring them up. Have Lense standing by."

"How does the station look, Corsi?" Gomez asked. *"Any idea what caused the systems failure?"*

Corsi paused in the act of hoisting one of the figures—a stocky middle-aged man—onto her shoulder, and glanced out through the open door at the holes decorating the other buildings. "Oh, I've got a pretty fair idea."

CHAPTER
3

Back on the *da Vinci*, Duffy waited in the shuttle bay with an impatient Sonya Gomez. As soon as the *Franklin* had cleared the atmosphere, they had beamed the two survivors directly to sickbay, where Lense was working on them.

Corsi's call had come just as they were finishing up lunch. Sonnie had instructed the computer to route any calls from the away team to her. It was her way of justifying them indulging in their date.

And it was a date. Just like the old days on the *Enterprise*. In fact, it was almost exactly like their dates on the *Enterprise*, even with all the water that had gone under the bridge in the seven years since they broke up following her transfer to the *Oberth*. Duffy chose to view this as a good sign for the renewal of their relationship.

The *Franklin* soon settled in next to the *da Vinci*'s other shuttle, the *Archimedes*, and the hatch closed. Sonnie turned her attention to Corsi as soon as she exited—Duffy wasn't surprised that the tall blond security chief had a full report ready for them.

The content of the report was a bit surprising, though, and more than a little alarming. As soon as Corsi finished, Sonnie called a meeting of all staff, excepting the good doctor.

"We've got a problem," she informed the others when they'd all reached the observation lounge— Gold was there as well, but he'd deferred to her. "Apparently something took out this outpost by holing the buildings and letting the outside atmosphere leak in. But the shields themselves weren't damaged."

"I thought Pattie said they'd repaired part of the shield," Carol said.

"No, we repaired a piece of the array that was damaged," Pattie replied. "The shield itself was fine." The cultural expert still looked puzzled, and Pattie explained. "Usually, when a shield is hit, the shield itself absorbs the damage. It may cause feedback in the controls or the array, shorting out circuits that have been overloaded, but the shield integrity is what gets hit the most. If you reduce a shield to half its normal strength, then shut it down, when you turn it back on it's still at only half-strength until the integrity has been fully repaired. I replaced part of the array, which had a hole in it, but when we switched the shields back on they were at full strength. No damage at all."

Fabian cut in. "So the only thing that knocked them down was that hole."

"Precisely."

"Which means something got through the

shield itself and then damaged the array," Carol said. "Okay, yeah—that's bad. What can ignore a full-strength shield and then do physical damage to things on the inside?"

"Nothing. At least, that's what we thought." Sonya glanced around. "Which is why we have a problem. Sure, you can tune a weapon to the same frequency as a shield, and bypass the defenses that way—if you know the frequency for that particular shield. But that only works with energy weapons, most of which wouldn't work in this atmosphere. If someone's got a way to physically penetrate a shield, without affecting the shield . . ."

"We're talking a major impact on starship combat tactics," Corsi said. "Shields would be functionally useless."

"*If* that's what this is," Duffy said. "I recommend we investigate with a full team."

"Agreed," Sonnie said. In fact, she'd already decided on this course of action before the meeting started, but she also suggested that Duffy make the recommendation and have her agree with it to present a united front. Duffy had to admit to liking the new Sonya Gomez—after her ordeal on the planet Sarindar, she had become more sure of herself. Duffy liked the change, especially if it meant more lunches like today. . . .

She turned to Fabian. "Did you have any luck with those attack scenarios?"

Fabian shook his head. "None so far. I mean, there are ways to hit the outpost from space, although that atmosphere's like a natural defense grid—it'll dull or even stop most attacks from penetrating through to the surface. But I don't know anything that can do what Corsi described. I'll need to get a firsthand look at the damage."

She nodded. "That'll be your job. Soloman, did you have a chance to work on the computers?"

The little Bynar shook his head. "We were concentrating on the shield controls, Commander. I volunteered to remain behind to examine the rest of the station's systems, but Lt. Commander Corsi felt the team should stick together."

Corsi smoldered at that, but Sonnie defused that quickly. "That was the right choice. We don't know the terrain well enough to leave someone there alone. When we head back down, you'll get to work on that. First priority is the transporter—if we can get that running again it'll make all our lives easier. Then check on the station logs, see if you can get any idea what happened. Duffy, give him a hand— you're better at sifting through entries."

Kieran groaned—he hated research, and Sonnie knew that—but he nodded anyway.

"Pattie, you and I will check out the power station—I want to know why it wasn't hit. There's got to be a reason, and I have a feeling it's important somehow." She glanced at the others. "Corsi, continue what you were doing before—give us a full sweep of the place. Not just possible dangers, but see what their security systems were, and how they were bypassed. Carol, I want you and Bart to do some digging. See if you can find anything out about this place, both the planet and the station, and any reasons why someone might want to put it out of commission. Everybody clear?"

She glanced around once more. Corsi, to Duffy's total lack of surprise, spoke up. "Commander, I want a full security team this time."

"That's fine. Everyone else, gather what you need—we'll meet at the shuttle bay in fifteen minutes."

As everyone got up, Gold said, "Be careful down there, people. We still don't know a damn thing about what happened here."

"We will, sir," Sonnie said with an encouraging smile.

CHAPTER
4

Fabian's first comment, once Pattie had remotely opened a window through the shields and the *Franklin* had landed in the shuttle bay, was "Damn!" The others voiced similar sentiments—even the three who'd already been down seemed a little stunned by the sight before them. But they were all professionals, and after a minute they shook themselves, unhooked their safety harnesses, grabbed their gear, and set about on their various assignments. They broke into teams of three, mostly—two S.C.E. team members and one security guard—with Corsi taking the remaining security guards to do their sweep.

Fabian was the first one out, and he went straight to the nearest hole, running his tricorder over it. Behind him stood Frnats, a Bolian security guard.

"It's not a beam, that's for sure." He was talking more to himself than any of his teammates, recording first impressions to be checked over later. "Not smooth enough. The corrosion accounts for some of that, but not all. Not a laser, either—the edges are hot, probably from friction, but the rest of the metal is cool, and the material's been stressed, not just melted away." He glanced at the hole again, then out and away, eyeballing the angle, then down at the tricorder, then back at the hole.

"The angle's all wrong," he muttered.

"All wrong for what?"

Fabian looked up to see Commander Gomez, Pattie, and another security guard, Hawkins, standing nearby. "For an attack from space. It would have to be at least fifteen degrees sharper for a ship to make this hole from orbit, unless it's firing from the side, almost on the horizon. And with BorSitu's atmosphere there's no way a shot like that could penetrate this far." He glanced over at Sonya. "This was done from the ground, Commander, or near to it. We're looking for something on the surface, not something in space."

Gomez nodded. "Well, that'll narrow it down a lot. Good work, Fabian. Keep at it. Come on, let's get to the central core."

The slender woman, the short blue insectoid, and the tall man set off together for the power station, leaving Fabian and the Bolian woman standing by the hole. He ran his fingers around the edges again, then dug into his belt pouch and pulled out a small emitter, which he affixed to the top edge. After that he moved on to the next hole and placed an emitter there as well.

*   *   *

Duffy had located the transporter pad on the schematic before heading down, and he, Soloman, and Lipinski from security made a beeline for it as soon as the *Franklin* had landed. There were two full-size transporter pads, and although one of them had been shattered by two different holes, the other was still intact. The controls were another matter.

"This one's shot," Duffy pointed out, studying a console that had taken a direct hit through its front panel. He deliberately overlooked the body slumped half out of the console chair—it had been hit by the same blast or whatever, and even with the decomposition Duffy could see a gaping hole in what had been the woman's chest. He quickly moved to another panel.

"We've lost readouts, but I think the main controls are okay on this one." Then he stepped to the final station. "And this one's got readouts, and half the controls. Okay, let's perform a little surgery here." He opened up the console and removed the display panels, then transferred them to the second station. Next he wired them in, replacing any damaged components.

Soloman had been rooting through the room's power relays, chattering in that odd chirpy computer language of his, bypassing damaged areas and routing systems through backup lines. A minute or two after Duffy reassembled the control panel, Soloman flipped a last switch and the panels lit up.

"Great! Now let's see." Duffy accessed the system and ran a diagnostic. "Yes!" He tapped his combadge. "We've got transporters online, Commander!"

"*Good work, Duffy,*" Sonnie replied. "*Fully operational?*"

"Running the first test now," Duffy replied. He entered a quick command, and the pad hummed, as bluish-white light filled the air above it. Then the light and the humming faded away, leaving a small toolbox resting on the platform. "First test successful. I'll set the console to handle the rest at timed intervals, but judging from the readings, I'm betting we're good to go, Sonnie."

"*Great. Once the last test finishes, link the system in to our combadges so we can hightail it if we need to. And Kieran? Don't call me Sonnie on duty.*"

Duffy grinned at that—he could hear the smile in her voice, even through the combadge.

"*Okay, you and Soloman get over to the command center and start accessing those files. Gomez out.*"

"Well, you heard the lady," Duffy said to Soloman, as they turned toward the door. "Command center, here we come."

Sonya, Pattie, and Hawkins were in the power station, examining the power plant and its surroundings. What they'd found so far was—nothing, aside from the structure itself.

"Why leave this building intact?" Sonya wondered aloud as they walked the floor. There were no holes here—Lense's preliminary report was that the two survivors had suffered from oxygen deprivation but nothing else, so they hadn't been directly attacked. But why would someone leave the power station unharmed, and even unopened?

"Perhaps they feared the possibility of explosion," Pattie suggested.

That would make sense. If the generator had been breached, the matter-antimatter would have caused an explosion, obliterating the outpost and everything in it. But that meant whoever did this hadn't wanted the station destroyed, just out of commission. She tapped her combadge.

"Gomez to Corsi."

The response came immediately. *"Corsi here, Commander. Do you need me?"*

"Just a question, is all. If you wanted the people in this outpost to be out of the way, how would you do it?"

"Gas. Because of the atmosphere outside, the station's constantly filtering its air, all from central tanks. The scrubbers clean out any contaminants, but they're programmed to look for certain conditions and elements—that's something that can be reprogrammed. Drop gas into the tanks and everyone within the shield gets it. They'd be out—or dead—in a few minutes, and the only way to stop it is to flush the tanks completely, which is risky in this environment."

Sonya repressed a chill as she listened to the explanation—it was a bit frightening that their security chief had so quickly hit upon such an effective method for poisoning an entire outpost. She realized it was probably a question of forewarning—difficult to guard against a danger you couldn't imagine yourself—but it still spooked her. And it did nothing to answer her questions.

"But these people weren't gassed—the shield was knocked down and the buildings holed, and they were suffocated by the planet's air. So if you're going to attack with something that can put holes right through the walls, why not hit the power station as well?"

This time it was Fabian who answered—Sonya had deliberately put her call on an open channel, in case anyone else had some insight. *"Too risky,"* her tactical expert replied. *"You could detonate."*

"What, the generator? But that's only a problem if you want the outpost intact."

"Not just the generator," Fabian corrected. *"The planet."* There was a moment of quiet, then he continued. *"Think about it. BorSitu Minor's got dilithium deposits everywhere, right? And its atmosphere has a high electrical charge to begin with. So if you blow up the station's power plant, it could set off a chain reaction, cascading through the air itself, and the dilithium would simply augment that, adding additional charges spread across the planet. Do it the wrong way—or the right way—and the whole planet could go boom."*

"Great." Sonya repressed another shiver. "Thank you for that cheery thought, Fabian."

"Sure, no problem." He even sounded cheerful. Then again, there was a big difference between hypothesizing explosions and actually planning them—for Fabian, this was probably just a theoretical exercise. But at least it had answered the question. Now they knew why the generator was

untouched. It also meant the attackers—whoever or whatever they were—had probably avoided this building altogether. So there wouldn't be much to go on here. Sonya hesitated, trying to decide what to do next, when her combadge beeped.

"Commander, this is Lense. My patients are awake, if you'd like to talk to them."

"On my way, Doctor." Sonya headed toward the door, glad for the sudden distraction. "Duffy, care to talk to some people? Pattie can help Soloman."

"Sounds good to me," Duffy replied. *"I'll take people over log books any day."*

"Good. Corsi, you're in charge until we get back."

"Will do, Commander."

"Hey, Commander," Duffy said, *"last one to the transporter buys drinks!"*

Sonya shook her head, but she broke into a light jog nonetheless.

Fabian, meanwhile, was examining the holes riddled throughout the camp. He had found a long pipe, a replacement piece for part of the filtration system, and now he inserted it through a hole in one of the building walls. Glancing through the pipe, Fabian saw a hole in the next building over. The walkways were not that wide here—everything was built close together to conserve space and energy—and by pushing the pipe out a bit farther he was able to reach the next hole with it, linking that one with the hole he was standing next to. Then he ran his finger along the edge of the hole, right above the pipe. There was a faint ridge there, and he filed the information away to examine later, but for now he was curious about something else. He took out his tricorder again. The wall was several centimeters thick. He measured the hole, then stepped outside and around to the next building, and examined that hole. It was the same size.

Fabian smiled.

"What do you have to smile about?" Frnats asked.

"Patterns, Frnats, patterns. That's what it's all about."

"The only pattern I'm seeing is that you're doing the same boring thing over and over again."

Laughing, Fabian pulled out another emitter, typing a frequency into it before setting it in place.

CHAPTER
5

"This is Alex Volk and April Rictor." Lense introduced them when Sonya and Kieran stepped into sickbay. "They're engineers, both assigned to BorSitu Minor. Alex was there for two years, April for six."

The two survivors were sitting up in their beds, and they were pale but alert—Alex was heavyset, with dark hair and a full beard, and April was slight, pretty, and blond. Both of them immediately struck Sonya as friendly, reliable people, the kind she'd have on her own team.

"I'm Commander Sonya Gomez. This is Lt. Commander Kieran Duffy. I know this is all pretty horrible for you, but anything you can tell us could be helpful."

"I'll help if I can," April replied, "but I don't really know how. Acid Camp—that's what we called it—was a pretty quiet place. We only had about a dozen people at any given time, sometimes less." She stopped for a moment, tears welling up, but managed to continue. "It was mostly miners—Alex and I, along with Carol and Tina, were there to keep the systems running, Price and Geoff broke up the occasional fight, and we always had a couple scientists around running experiments on new mining methods."

Sonya felt terrible for her—she wasn't sure she'd have been able to speak so calmly if the *da Vinci* and its crew were killed like that—but she forced herself to continue with the questions.

"Did you keep a large supply of dilithium on hand, or anything else that might be worth stealing?"

Alex shook his head. "Why bother? We had more dilithium coming through every few days. Most of our equipment's too specific for nonminers to care, or too heavily modified to be worthwhile—like our transporter pad. Sure, it's souped up, but just to cut through interference, and it's a lot more unwieldy and a much bigger power drain than even a cargo transporter."

"Had anyone new come in recently?" That was Kieran. It was a good question, but Alex shook his head again.

"No, the last new arrival was almost eight months ago—two new miners to replace ones who'd shipped out. And they never caused any trouble, really—okay, maybe Cortez kept bugging the scientists, but just out of curiosity. He never hurt anyone. No one did."

"What about new supplies, new equipment, anything?"

"We get supply shuttles every few months—last one was almost two months ago. It didn't have anything unusual on it, just some replacement gear."

Sonya tugged her shirt cuffs, then forced herself to stop. "What about the day this all happened? What can you tell us about it?"

Neither of them spoke for a moment, but finally April answered. "We were on shift, Alex and I—it's pretty boring, really, just keeping an eye on the matter-antimatter readings, doing general maintenance. We were chatting, and then suddenly we heard people screaming, and this weird sound, like a giant bee or something." Her voice was soft, so low Sonya had to strain to hear her, but she didn't ask the woman to speak up—this was hard enough on her.

Kieran glanced at Sonya, and she could tell he was thinking the same thing about what April had just said. A bee? Could this have been a native of the planet, attacking at random?

"Yeah, it was a hum, but low and sort of gravelly." Alex shook his head. "We opened the door to see what was going on, and saw people running and holes in the walls—and the shields down. So we slammed the door again and hid. I know we should have helped the others . . ." he faltered, and Lense patted his shoulder.

"There was nothing you could have done," she reassured him—Sonya was used to Lense's bitterness, and a bit surprised at how well the doctor projected sympathy and understanding. "You were right to save yourselves."

The engineer shrugged. "Honestly, we weren't even thinking that clearly—I think we both just panicked and hid. Whatever was attacking never bothered us, but without the filters we had only the air in the power station, and after a while we both passed out. Next thing we knew, we'd woken up here."

Lense glanced at her charts. "You were both lucky. Even another twenty minutes and you'd have had brain damage. As it is, your lungs will feel a little weak for a month or so, but you'll be fine."

"I wish we could do more to help," April said. "I—I want to help. They were our friends, and now they're all gone." She didn't cry, though it looked as if she might, and Lense patted her arm as well.

"You've been a big help already," Sonya told her, "even if it's just by eliminating possibilities. We'll let you know if we think of any more questions. In the meantime, you should rest and get your strength back. Thanks." She stepped back out into the hall, Kieran right behind her.

"Well, I'm running out of ideas," she admitted, heading toward engineering more out of habit than anything. "So far, there's no explanation and no real reason behind whatever attacked."

"One of the others may turn up something," Kieran pointed out, which was true. As always, this was a team effort, and everyone played a part. Sonya just hated feeling like her part was useless.

"We can head back and see how they're doing. But first, I think I owe you a drink."

That brought a smile to her face. "Yes, you do, don't you?"

He returned the smile. "One Earl Grey, coming up."

CHAPTER
6

Fabian was at one of the outlying buildings of the little outpost—he had just set an emitter on the hole that perforated its back wall. Now he moved over to the building on the left, and studied the hole there. Similar height to the last one, and the same size. Running his finger along the inside edge, he felt that slight ridge again, although before it had gone from front to back, inside to outside, in a clockwise motion—now it ran counterclockwise. Fabian frowned, and inserted his handy length of pipe through the hole—there was a supply cabinet against the wall, also pierced, and he passed the pipe through there as well, so that it rested at the angle of the attack. Glancing back at the other building, he tried mentally extending the line from its last hole, and then extending the line from the pipe. They didn't line up, at least not right here—perhaps farther out they would. But he'd deal with that later. Sighing, Fabian retrieved his pipe, set an emitter on the hole by the supply

cabinet, and trudged back around the building to
find the point on the opposite side.

Frnats continued to follow him, keeping a
bemused eye on things.

"Okay, Fabian, what are all these for?"

Sonya and Kieran had returned to the surface
after their quick drink. While Kieran had gone to
check on Pattie and Soloman, Sonya had joined
Fabian and Frnats in the outpost's center square.
There were tiny emitters attached to the nearest
holes, and glancing around she noticed that every
hole in sight had one, which was an impressive
feat in and of itself.

"Well, I've got these on every hole in the camp,"
Fabian explained, tapping a series of commands
into his tricorder. "I noticed that several of the
holes line up perfectly—they had to be made by
the same shot passing right through several buildings in a row, or else the angles wouldn't have
matched so precisely. So I've linked the emitters
that line up, each line to a separate frequency." He
hit a key, and a small map appeared on the screen.
"Soloman found a schematic of this place, and the
computer extrapolated it into a 3-D model. Now
I've linked the emitters into the model and—
voilà!" He handed her his tricorder—on it was a
model of the outpost, with colored lines crisscrossing it. Some of the lines ran through a single
building, others through two or three, and a few
on the edges pierced four or more locations.

"Acid Camp with straws," she muttered.

"Sorry, Commander?"

Sonya shook her head. "It just looks like it's got straws sticking out of it. And 'Acid Camp' is what the two survivors referred to this place as."

"With that soup out there, it fits. Anyhow, this tells us a few things. First of all, this wasn't done by a single ship." Fabian took the tricorder back and pointed out one side of the image—the end points for the lines on that side ranged from centimeters apart to full meters away from each other. "See how far apart these are, and how the angles are different? The only way a ship could have done this is if it were shifting positions, rotating around and firing almost continuously. Even then, it should be more consistent—the angle should be changing by a set amount each time, as the ship pivots to face the center of the outpost. Plus," he pointed to where one line started, not far from the square, and pierced through two buildings farther out, "lines like this aren't starting on the outer edge, they're near the center. That'd take either a guided missile of some sort, or a shot that came down from above and leveled out—anything else would have to hit the buildings on the opposite side of the square, and the holes there don't line up. An attack like this, with all these variables, could take hours."

"That doesn't match up with what the two survivors said." Sonya let out a long breath. "They said the attack only took a few minutes."

"There could be multiple attackers; otherwise, I don't see how we could wind up with this many lines. But I'm still working on it."

Sonya nodded. This was definite progress. "Okay, what's next?"

Fabian grimaced. "Now I get to the fun part. I can run an analysis on the holes, comparing the stress on the materials and the amount of corrosion on the inner edges. That'll tell me which holes were made first. Using that, I can turn this image into an actual blow-by-blow, showing the attacks in order. The first and last will probably be the most important."

"So you've got to go to each hole and get readings?"

"Yep." He grinned at her. "Want to help?"

Sonya laughed. "No, thanks." She turned to the Bolian security guard. "Frnats, want to do a little legwork?"

"I thought you'd never ask, Commander. What do you need me to do, Stevens?"

Leaving them to it, Sonya went to the command post to get a report from Kieran and Soloman.

"What have you two got for me?" Sonya asked as she glanced around. Corsi and her people had started clearing away the remains of the former inhabitants. It helped significantly. Sonya thought the holes that passed through one wall, through various consoles, chairs, desks, doors, and cabinets, and then out the opposite wall were still ominous, though.

Kieran and Soloman looked up from the console they'd been huddled near. "Well, Soloman's tapped into the station logs," Kieran said, "and he's already sorted through them a bit. It's pretty much what we'd heard from those two in sickbay—just a couple of miners, a few scientists and engineers, and two security officers. Nothing worth stealing, no major fights, no threats or strange occurrences. Nothing."

"There had to be something," Sonya said, glancing down at the logs herself. "Unless this was a random event, and I don't buy that—not with the power station so obviously left alone. What about swiping a shipment of dilithium?"

"Unnecessary." Soloman didn't even look up, although he did shift over to let her see the console more easily. "There are several dozen remote mines on this planet, fully automated. They have no real defenses, and could easily be robbed by anyone equipped to reach this planet undetected."

"Okay, so if you wanted to rob the place you'd hit one of those instead, not have to worry about witnesses or interference, and have a lot less trouble doing it. Got it. But if it's not the dilithium, and it wasn't the people, what was it?"

"Well, there is one possibility," Kieran admitted, although he looked a bit embarrassed.

"Spill it."

"Well, I was thinking—we've got scientists here working on new mining methods. What if one of them had come up with something really spectacular? Enough so that someone else wanted it?"

"Badly enough to kill for it? Sounds a bit far out, but right now we don't have anything better to work with." She thought for a second, then nodded. "You'll probably need to find personal logs or scientific records, though. I doubt the command post kept track of every device that got worked on."

Kieran stretched. "Great, more research. I thought this job was supposed to be exciting."

"It is—you're researching how an entire outpost got wiped out." She turned and headed back toward the door. "Soloman, keep checking the logs in case we missed anything. Duffy, get to work." She stepped out quickly, before he could find anything to throw at her.

The next person Sonya checked with was Corsi, who only had more negatives to tell her.

"The good news is, this place is safe," the security chief admitted. "The shields here are strong enough to withstand anything short of heavy bombing, and the *da Vinci* would see any ship or missile attack coming. The bad news is, I can't find any traces of attack beyond the holes themselves. There's no forced entry anywhere, no signs of fighting, no missing or damaged ships—nothing. If people did this, they weren't interested in looting the place, and they didn't even want to kill everyone—I think that was just an unfortunate side effect. There aren't any bombs or booby traps anywhere, and no signs of someone searching for anything hidden, whether in personal quarters or workspaces or cargo bays."

Sonya was impressed with the other woman's thoroughness. "I didn't realize you'd look for all that," she admitted. "I thought it would just be whether someone was lying in wait for us, or had left us a trap of some sort."

"There's a lot more to security than that," Corsi pointed out. "Part of it is anticipating your opponent, which means figuring out what he, she, or they want and then how they will try to get it. And I can't figure out what anyone could have wanted that would have caused this, unless they just hated this place and wanted to see it wrecked."

"Great, so we might be dealing with a revenge-crazed killer." Sonya sighed and shook her head. "Well, keep me posted."

Fabian and Frnats were going from hole to hole, checking the readings on each one. They'd entered one of the buildings now, sidestepping a body Corsi's team had not yet reached—Frnats paused to alert Eddy and Friesner that they'd missed one—and were entering those rooms that had been holed. The doors in this building were all blackened by phaser fire where locking mechanisms had been—Corsi's work, most likely. Except for the one Fabian had just tried, which was undamaged.

"Stevens to Corsi." He glanced around the room as he entered. It looked much the same as the others in this building—cabinets along the walls, their surfaces half-eaten by the corrosive air, and several workbenches strewn about with machine parts covering them. Another workroom.

"Corsi here. Go."

Fabian wondered if he imagined the hitch in Corsi's voice. She hadn't spoken two words to him since their little one-nighter before the mission to Empok Nor. "Did you enter every building when you did your sweep?"

"Affirmative."

"Did you enter every room?"

"*Of course.*" Now she sounded annoyed.

"Any problems getting in?"

"*Only in one building—all the doors were locked. So I had to open them.*"

Fabian grinned—he could hear the shrug in her voice. "And you opened them by blasting the locks?"

"*Look, mister, my job is to make sure this place is safe so nobody gets hurt. If that means wrecking a few locks—*"

He'd already thrown up his hands in surrender, then realized she couldn't see the gesture. "Whoa, Commander, I'm not attacking you—you did what you had to. I'm just asking a question. I'm in that building now, and there's one door that doesn't have blast marks on it. I just wanted to know why."

"*Oh. Well, that door was already unlocked—no sense wasting a phaser blast on it. Anything else?*"

"No, that was all I wanted. Thanks. Stevens out."

Behind him, Frnats was chuckling as she took out her tricorder. "Core-Breach doesn't like to waste phaser beams."

"Or time," Fabian said, trying to keep from laughing out loud.

"Corrosion reading shows at seventeen point five eight percent," Frnats added, examining one of the holes.

"Same as all the others." Fabian shook his head. "Okay, what about the temp?"

"Metal temperature along the edge of the hole reads at thirty-seven point eight nine degrees."

"Okay, now we're getting somewhere. That's point two-five degrees lower than the hole in the building facing this one. So this hole came first." He stepped over next to her, and ran his fingers around the edge of the hole, encountering the same ridge he'd felt in every other hole. This one ran clockwise, though, and the ridge on the hole opposite had run counterclockwise.

Fabian stepped back and glanced around the room again, taking in the walls, the cabinets, the tables, the two low stools, the various parts and pieces of equipment, the tools—then he stopped and looked at the walls again.

"Frnats, take a look at this." He put his back against the outer wall, right beneath the hole, and gestured at the wall opposite. "What do you see there?"

His companion looked where he'd directed. "Nothing. Why?"

Fabian simply grinned at her. "Nothing. Exactly."

CHAPTER
7

An hour later, the team had reconvened in the observation lounge on the *da Vinci*, this time at Fabian's request. Sonya had never seen the tactical expert so excited—he was like a little kid with a new toy.

"With Frnats's help, I was able to analyze each hole in Acid Camp."

"Acid Camp?" Gold asked.

"That's what the locals called it, sir," Sonya quickly explained.

Nodding, Gold said, "Fine, go on."

Fabian put up an enlarged image of one of the holes. "First off, we know what did this—at least, what kind of thing."

Gold leaned forward. "And what, you were just saving this information for a rainy day?"

"No, sir. We just found out and I'd already requested this meeting, so I figured I might as well tell everyone in person." Fabian pointed at the image onscreen. "Notice the edges of the hole itself. I've had the computer remove the corrosion damage, so all we're seeing is the hole the way it first looked. The edges are slightly jagged, which means they were torn rather than burned or even cut. But the metal beyond the immediate area is barely stressed, not bent or bowed at all, so whatever tore through was moving so fast it didn't affect the surrounding area. And if you look very closely," he magnified the image along one edge, "you'll see a slight ridge running through the hole, at a diagonal. Whatever did this was rotating."

"Like a drill bit?" That was Carol, and Fabian smiled at her—it reminded Sonya of a teacher who'd just gotten the right answer from a favorite student.

"Exactly. Which makes sense—this is a mining camp. Now, it would take an enormous drill to do these, far too big for a person to lift, and some of these holes are in places no drill rig could reach, not to mention the fact that these lines go all the way from one end of camp to another, which would require a drill bit some two hundred meters long. But it's a start."

"And every little bit helps," Sonya said. "Good job, Fabian. But you were going to call us together anyway, so I'm assuming you have something else to tell us." She already knew he did—Fabian wasn't the type to get all worked up over something minor.

She immediately saw that she'd been right, as the eager look returned to Fabian's face. "Not to tell you, Commander—to show you. Like I said, Frnats and I analyzed each hole in the camp. Now,

the corrosion levels proved to be a dead end—
they're the same for every hole."

"So they were all caused at the same time?"

"Either that or the shields didn't drop until after
the holes were made. So no help there. But it's
only been a day since the attack, and something
moving that fast generates a lot of heat. When we
first went down there those holes were still hot to
the touch. So we measured the temperature of the
metal around each edge—minute variations on
some, but enough for the computer to organize
them." Fabian hit a few keys on his padd, and the
model of the camp came up, with the crisscrossing
lines he'd shown her before. "Now, when we factor
in those variations, and tell the computer to display each hole as it occurred, in order—"

The lines disappeared, leaving the model
untouched for a moment. Then a hole blossomed
in one building, on the outer rim of the camp. A
line formed from that hole to the next building in,
continuing until it had passed through the center
square and then through several buildings on the
opposite side. A second line began an instant later,
angling back in toward the center and across.
Everyone watched silently as line after line
appeared, and Sonya noticed several shudders as
her team thought about what it must have been
like with those holes sprouting all around them.
She fought down the shivers herself, determined
to present a strong front to her team. Then Kieran
leaned forward.

"Computer, freeze sim!" The line stopped in
mid-formation, and everyone turned toward him,

but he gestured at the screen instead. "Sorry, but look! That line isn't straight. A lot of them aren't."

"Right," Fabian said triumphantly. "Good catch, Duff. I did a computer simulation of the lines before, but only linked the holes where the lines matched angles perfectly, so I had lines starting and stopping within the outpost. That was my mistake—the temperatures showed they were continuations of other lines, just not perfectly straight ones. Whatever did this was veering away every time it came near the power station. So either we had an operator directing things, or programming to avoid the risk of explosion." He resumed the simulation, and they watched again until the last line was formed.

"Okay," Gold commented, rubbing the bridge of his nose. "Maybe I'm just an old man, but what does that tell us?" He frowned. "No, scratch that— I'm just slow today. There's only one attacker, isn't there?"

Sonya shot him a surprised glance, as did several of the others, but Fabian just grinned.

"Got it in one, Captain. Each new line doesn't start until the previous one ends—no overlaps. So we've got a single object here, not multiples. And I know how it did all this so quickly." He keyed in another command. "Watch the screen. I've extended each trajectory beyond the first and last hole, until each line touches the one before and after it." The pattern became a single unbroken line, with sharp reversals at each end. "Notice that those connections all happen the same distance from the buildings."

"It's the shields!" That was Corsi, and she looked abashed at her own outburst, but kept going. "This thing was inside, and ricocheting off the shields!"

"Exactly. Until it holed the emitter array here—" Fabian pointed to a hole midway down the last line segment, "and the shields dropped. Then it just kept on going, out past the station."

"So this thing didn't bypass the shields, after all," Sonya commented, fighting an insane urge to giggle—it was a response to the sudden stress release, and she managed to keep it down this time. "It started out inside, and just kept bouncing around. We don't have a shield-killer on our hands." Everyone slumped a bit. That had been their single greatest fear—finding out that something or someone had learned how to ignore their shields. Whatever had done this was still dangerous, and still a major threat, but at least it wouldn't nullify Starfleet's primary defense.

Fabian was still fiddling with the screen. "It did start inside, Commander—and I can even tell you where." The screen now showed two holes side by side. "Both of these are shown from the outside— they're the first and second holes, respectively. Notice the scoring on the inside edge—that diagonal ridge I mentioned."

Bart Faulwell spoke up. "They're mirror images, not matches, so it's reversed on one of them." Leave it to the linguist to catch the visual cues, Sonya thought. And, of course, that was why Bart and Carol were both in most briefings—they sometimes caught things the engineers didn't.

Fabian was already agreeing with Bart's assessment. "Right, it's spiraling in the opposite direction. Which means this first one isn't an entrance hole—it's an exit. And there aren't any other holes in that room, so whatever did this came from inside there."

Soloman, who had already downloaded all the station's records, spoke up. "That's a workroom for one of the scientists, V'reet D't Madl'r. He's a Syclarian and has been assigned to BorSitu Minor for eleven months."

"One of the bodies was a Syclarian," Lense said. "They've got a distinctive digit structure, tentacles rather than fingers—even after the decomposition the computer identified that."

"He's the only one on-station," Soloman said, "so that would be him."

Sonya stood up, feeling a warm glow of pride for her people. "Nice work, Fabian. Okay, troops, now we know where it came from and almost what it is. Kieran, get down there and tear that room apart. I want to know anything and everything about this guy, and about what he was working on. Soloman, I want anything and everything you can learn about V'reet D't Madl'r, both from station records and from our own library. Fabian, you and Pattie put your heads together—tell me how large an object we're looking at. Go down with Kieran and take a look at this guy's notes and equipment. That should help narrow the field." She smiled. "Let's get to work, people!"

*   *   *

Fabian, Duffy, and Pattie stood in the workroom, glancing around.

"It was unlocked?" Duffy was asking.

Fabian nodded. "The only one in the building that was. I checked with Corsi. She blasted her way through the others."

His friend grinned. "That's our Core-Breach." Then Duffy sobered. "This was Madl'r's private workroom, judging from the records. Those locks on the doors, they've got codes keyed in by who-ever's assigned the room. The central computer doesn't have access to them, except in an emer-gency situation, when it can lock or unlock the entire building, depending on what's necessary." Duffy shook his head. "I mentioned to Sonnie before that someone could've been after what-ever the scientists were working on. Well, we'll worry about that later. Let's see what we can find here."

The three of them began combing the room. Fabian took one of the worktables and Pattie the other, while Duffy checked the cabinets.

"I have something," Pattie announced after sev-eral minutes. She was studying an object on the table, and Fabian joined her, as did Duffy. The object was roughly three meters on a side, square but mostly open—a hollow half-sphere formed the center.

"Notice the surface," Pattie indicated with one claw. "No breaks or gaps. This is a finished piece."

"Okay, but what is it?" Fabian ran a finger along the inside of the ring, searching for tactile clues. "Looks like a cradle of some kind. I'd guess these

are power couplings, for recharging." He pointed
to several small linkages he'd felt near the top.

Pattie was holding her tricorder. "Two meters
exactly—the same size as the holes."

"So we've found the holder of the thing. That'll
help." Duffy glanced around again. "But blueprints would be better, or a log, or something." He
frowned. "What's missing here?" Fabian and
Pattie both looked around the room.

"The device?" Fabian offered, but Duffy waved
it off. It had been the obvious answer, of course,
and Fabian had known it wasn't what Duffy was
thinking, but he'd wanted to eliminate every possibility.

"A computer?" Pattie suggested, and Duffy nodded. The minute she said it Fabian knew she was
right.

"That's it—no computer. What kind of scientist
works without a computer?" On a hunch, Fabian
stepped back over to the other worktable, rum-
maged again through the objects piled haphaz-
ardly on top, then noticed the shallow drawer
slung underneath. "Aha!" he announced, pulling it
open and hauling out several large sheets of paper.
And, amazingly enough, a book.

"I'll bet night duty for a month that this is what
we're looking for." Neither Duffy nor Pattie took
him up on the offer, as he hit his combadge.
"Commander?"

CHAPTER
8

"*Well, I've got good news and I've got bad news,*" Fabian said to Sonya over the comlink. "*The good news is, this Madl'r was a typical scientist, kept notes on everything. We even found a journal.*"

"And the bad news?"

"*He didn't write it in anything we can read.*"

"Write it? He didn't record his notes?"

"*Of course not—that'd be too easy.*" Even on the combadge Sonya could hear Pattie and Kieran chuckling in the background. "*This guy actually handwrote his journal—on paper!*"

"Great, a Luddite." Sonya leaned back in her chair and tugged absently at her cuff. "Well, bring it up and we'll set Faulwell on it. What about diagrams, schematics, blueprints?"

"*That's the other bad news. We've got what are probably engineering diagrams, but we can't make heads or tails of them—they're written in whatever he did the journal in, and it's more scribbles and little sketches than anything else. We know this thing is round, at least."*

"Which we'd already guessed. He had nothing on the computer?"

"Just the same basic personnel record everyone had—he was either really paranoid or really old-fashioned. Or both."

"All right, bring up what you can. How are Commander Duffy and Pattie doing?"

Kieran came on the link. *"We've found some of his tools—odd-looking things, must be because of those digits Lense mentioned. And Pattie found a cradle for the device itself—about two meters in diameter. And those diagrams. But not much else."*

"Well, keep looking—something may turn up. Send that journal up here on the double. Fabian, you're pretty sure this thing doesn't have the power to punch through shields?"

Fabian spoke up again. *"Not a chance. It would have drilled its way through right from the start, if that were the case. No, even if it's still active and hopping around out there we're safe from it. And I'd be willing to bet it doesn't have enough propulsion to exit the atmosphere, so the* da Vinci's *fine, too."*

"Some good news, anyway. Okay, keep me posted. Gomez out." Sonya rubbed a hand over her face and sighed. The bigger threat was gone, at least, but their job wouldn't be done until they knew exactly what this thing was, why it had wrecked the outpost, and how to prevent any repeats in future. And now it was sounding like that information was all locked away in a book—a book!—that none of them could read. Well, maybe one of them. She hit her combadge. "Mr. Faulwell, please meet me in the observation lounge."

Bart Faulwell was excited. He enjoyed his time on the *da Vinci*, but usually his only involvement was lending a hand in research matters, and sometimes offering suggestions when they were puzzling over the wording of journal entries. To be given the chance to decipher a journal—a handwritten one!—was thrilling. It was like the old days of the Dominion War when he worked for Starfleet Intelligence decoding enemy communications.

A little less thrilling was the fact that the entire S.C.E. crew was waiting on his results. Which meant that—like his superiors at SI—they kept checking on his progress.

"This sort of thing takes time," he reminded Commander Gomez after her third visit back to the observation lounge. "This isn't a common language, so it's not something I can simply translate."

"No, we don't have a Syclarian dictionary," he answered Duffy on his second trip. "The Syclarians are reclusive, first of all, and they tend to use communicators and padds like everyone else. This is actually the first time I've seen their written language—and it may be the first time anyone has."

"Yes, they have an alphabet," he replied to his roommate Fabian Stevens, on his second time checking in. "Every written language has *some* kind of structure. But some are for letters, others are for words, others are for images or phrases or even whole ideas—it can vary widely. The first step is to determine what the alphabet is by looking for repeating patterns. Then you figure out what each symbol stands for. Then you can assemble a working translation program, and actually convert the writing into usable information. But it all takes time."

Privately, in between these little visits, Bart admitted the truth—he had no clue where to begin. Oh, he'd translated languages before, certainly. But usually they were on a tricorder, or in a computer system. He would copy over the files, then run them through his translation programs— the programs would search out any patterns, and compare those with all the languages on file. Often that was all it took—the computer would then recognize the language, and proceed to translate it. Sometimes it would find near-matches, languages with similarities, and Bart would then tweak the match, analyzing the files and extrapolating variants of the ones they'd found until he had a cohesive root structure that fit every instance in the file. Then the computer ran the program. But this! He'd scanned the pages into the computer, of course, but even familiar languages could vary widely between handwriting and programmed text, so he was unsurprised when the computer found no matches. They had very little on the Syclarians to begin with, and what contact they'd had was through standard channels, which meant it was already in their own language and format, not that of the Syclarians.

He stared down at the journal again. It was a handsome book, actually, fashioned of dark leather worn smooth over time, with a single swirl embossed into the front. The pages were thick and velvety to the touch, with just a bit of crinkle to them. Held up to the light, they showed a faint tracery through them, golden-brown and speckled like an egg. To Bart, who preferred writing letters to his beloved Anthony on paper and who generally preferred the tactile aesthetics of ink on paper, it was a glorious sight.

But the writing! Bart wasn't even sure he could call this writing, in the normal sense. It looked more like painting, or perhaps stamping. Each page was covered in dark blotches, overlapped as if ink had spilled repeatedly and then spread. It was like staring at an old Earth inkblot test, with the dark color forming odd patterns on the paper. It was at once fascinating and frustrating.

"No, I haven't—" he started, as the door behind him slid open, but he stopped when he saw who was standing there. Carol Abramowitz was one of his closest friends on the *da Vinci*—as the other non-engineer in the S.C.E. crew, she understood the frustration of being useless in technical situations. And, as a cultural specialist, she knew as well as he did that some problems took time to solve.

"Sorry, I just wanted to see how you were, and if I could help at all." She slid into the seat next to him.

"No, I'm sorry. Everybody else keeps poking their heads in to see if I'm done yet, and I thought it was one of them again." He sighed. "To be honest, I don't have a thing yet. This one's completely new to me, and not like anything I've seen before. Plus it's on paper, which means the computer's almost useless."

"I know. What little I've been able to glean about the Syclarians is that they kept a lot of their old heritage but moved it to the background, and adopted Federation standards on the surface. So we don't see their language at all, because they only use it for private things now. But you probably found that yourself."

Bart smiled at her. "Yes, but it's nice to hear you confirm it. What else can you tell me about them?"

Carol pulled out her padd. "Not much, really. Humanoid, but with tentacular digits on hands and feet and eyestalks on their head—most likely evolved from cephalopods. Vestigial gills, and a strong cultural interest in aquatic sports and activities." She smiled. "That ink is probably from an *h'stirip*, their equivalent to an octopus—they're favored pets, and the ink is popular for personal letters and greeting cards."

"I thought it looked like real ink, judging from the blotting." He held up a page to show her. "And he used a real pen, too—if you run your finger across the surface you can just make out the scratches."

Carol set her padd aside, though she toyed with the stylus. "So it wasn't a stamp? That's what I thought when I saw it, what with those big circles."

"No, it's a pen—the circles were made deliberately by a smaller instrument." Bart spun the book around slowly. "To be honest, I'm not entirely sure which way is up. Especially on the inner ones—they leak over to the ones around them, so it's hard to tell exactly where they start." He glanced up at Carol, who was absently making circles on the table. "If we—"

"What?" Whatever she'd been thinking of was lost as she realized he was staring at her.

"That's it!" Bart laughed, and spun the journal around, a little faster this time. "Carol, you're a genius!"

"I am? Well, of course. What did I do?"

Bart was staring at the journal again. "The Syclarians have tentacles—small ones in place of fingers." She nodded. "And their eyes are on stalks. So they can rotate around." Carol nodded again. "Look at this." He flipped the book shut and pointed to the whorl on the front. "I thought this was just a design, but it's not. It's his name! Or the word 'journal,' or something like that—but it's writing! They write in little swirls!" He opened the book again, to a random page, and stabbed at one of the blotches. "I don't know if they're words or sentences, but I'm guessing longer because of all the scratches involved. Each swirl holds a lot of information. It could even be a whole paragraph, one discrete thought per circle. They start in the center, then spiral outward. When that thought's done, they start a new swirl. If the two are related, the new one starts where the old one stopped, which is why they overlap!" He tapped on the screen, and pulled out his own padd. In an instant he had one of the swirls displayed, magnified several thousand times.

"Look there, that's the actual marking." Bart pointed out the lines within the larger swirl. "Also circular—they don't have sharp angles themselves, so they think in circular patterns instead. My God, the sheer amount of information they can fit on one page—it's staggering!"

Bart set to work, and it was only after he looked up and saw that Carol was gone that he realized that she'd left.

Making a mental note to apologize to her later, knowing full well he'd forget to, he dove back into the work.

CHAPTER 9

"It's a journal, all right," Bart explained a few hours later. They were all back in the briefing room again, and the slight linguist was standing for once, looking like nothing so much as a professor Sonya had had back at the Academy. "Once Carol and I figured out how their language worked, it wasn't that hard to isolate symbols and break them into patterns. The cover symbol is his name, V'reet D't Madl'r—it means 'Swimmer in Deep Waters,' by the way. That gave me a key to work from. Each swirl is an entire thought made up of smaller swirls for sentences, which have smaller ones still for words or objects or actions." Kieran rolled his eyes. Bart noticed the response and smiled. "Sorry. I get a little excited. Anyway, Madl'r was a scientist-miner, and he was working on a new device to help find dilithium more easily. It's a sensor, really—it's attracted to dilithium right through the rock."

"So why wasn't it drawn to the power station in the camp?" Kieran asked.

"It was," Fabian said. "But Madl'r was smart." He gestured at his roommate. "Once Bart cracked the language, he translated those diagrams for us, too. They tell the real story." He looked at Bart, who sat and gestured for him to continue. "Madl'r's device is round, with sensors inset on all sides, and self-propelled. It's built to rotate at high speeds, like a drill—leave it to a race that thinks in circles to design something like that. Dilithium is hard to find because it tends to be deep underground, and that much rock interferes with sensor readings, and it's worse here because of the ionized atmosphere. So you've got to get closer, almost right on top of it, before you know it's there. Madl'r's device has all these sensors linked in together to create a stronger array. It can pick up dilithium a little farther away than most, and it's built specifically to work through rock and metal. What happens is the device locates a dilithium deposit and zeroes in on it. It drills its way right through the surrounding rock—not a big hole, we all saw the size, but enough to put equipment through and enough that miners could easily expand them into real tunnels. It rings the deposit, but doesn't touch it—that could risk an explosion, which could lead to a series of bigger ones. So the device is programmed to skirt the dilithium itself, and just make tunnels close by. It's small enough and fast enough that it can switch direction quickly, so it's got ample time to change course and avoid hitting the deposit. It was meant as a labor-saving device."

"How's the design?" That was Gold asking, and Sonya hid a smile as Fabian, Kieran, and Pattie grinned at each other. Give an engineer a diagram and he'd show it to other engineers, so they could all pore over it together—she'd wanted to take a crack at the thing herself.

Pattie actually answered the captain's question. "Very good, actually. There are many failsafes, several redundancies, and the sensor array is clever, as is the general design. He managed to protect the sensors from damage while making the device strong enough to drill through solid rock, and it's highly maneuverable. I think miners will find it very helpful."

"So what went wrong?"

The change in the room was obvious. Gold had, sensibly, let the engineers finish going through their explanation, knowing that he wouldn't get anything useful out of them until they finished talking about the new toy. Once that was done, though, it was time to get down to the business of why this miraculous device wiped out an entire outpost.

"We're still working on that, Captain," Sonya said. "We think it must have gotten turned on accidentally, and not by Madl'r—Corsi found his body in the commissary, nowhere near the device. There may have been a tremor—BorSitu's atmosphere has electrical storms all the time, and when they hit the shield they can cause a slight shudder—or the cradle had a power surge, or a cleaning 'bot bumped it somehow. We don't know yet. But the device switched on, and its programming kicked in. It set out to find dilithium. And the nearest source of that—"

"—was the power plant," Gold finished. "Okay, so it rings the station, drilling its way through everything, thinking it's making paths to the deposit. Every time it hits the shields it bounces back and makes another pass. Then it holes the shield array, and on its next pass it goes outside the boundaries of the camp. So why didn't it come back?"

"This thing was built to make enough holes for miners to use, and then to move on to another location," Fabian explained. "It had already provided plenty of tunnels—if not for the shields it probably would have moved on long before. So once they dropped, it set out to search for another deposit."

"Did it find one?"

"Probably not." Pattie glanced down at her padd. "The rock is thick here, and the sensors don't work as well aboveground—too much electrical interference. Once beyond the camp, the device probably decided it couldn't find any more deposits, and shut down."

"Is it still out there?"

Pattie and Fabian glanced at each other, then nodded. Fabian explained. "Like I said, Madl'r was smart. He built this thing with enough protection to withstand the atmosphere's corrosive effects. If left out there for a week or two, it'd eventually get worn away, but right now—yeah, it's still out there."

It looked like Captain Gold was done with his

questions, so Sonya leaned forward. "Okay, good work. We know what did this, and how. The why sounds like pure chance—crazy, but it can happen. So the question is, do we retrieve it?" She glanced at Gold—as captain, it was really his call.

If she was hoping for a decisive answer, though, she was disappointed, as he shrugged. "The mission was just to find out what had happened, which you've done. Then it was to make sure this wasn't some 'shield-killer' weapon, which it isn't. So, do we need to go get that thing? Probably not. But it just doesn't sit well with me to leave it out there."

"Actually, there's a very good reason for going to get it," Kieran put in. "I'm assuming this place will be restored and restaffed, right?"

"It'd make sense," Pattie said. "BorSitu's too valuable to leave unattended, and this outpost is already established and easy enough to repair. In fact, we've already done most of the repair work ourselves. Why waste the effort to build a new one?"

Kieran nodded. "Okay, so they're going to put more people down here. Now, we're guessing that device is still active somewhere. What if it winds up near the camp again?"

"It'd get stopped by the shields."

"Sure—if it came at them from aboveground. But this thing's built to go belowground—let's say it burrows in at some point. It could wind up under the outpost."

Sonya froze as what he was saying sank in, and she silently berated herself for not catching it before. The shields were built to provide a protective dome over the camp. They didn't extend far belowground.

"Right, we go get it." She tugged at her cuff and forced herself to take charge. "Pattie, look into boosting the shuttle's sensors—I want some way to see what we're doing out there. Fabian, project the device's exit trajectory, and see if you can approximate storm movement so we know if it's been knocked out of its flight path. Kieran, I want you and Soloman to go over the device's schematics again—Bart, help them if they need it with the translations. See if there's a way to contact it remotely, some frequency it responds to. If so, set up something that can reach it through that mess down there. Let's do it, people."

"Well, I'd say you have things well in hand, Commander." Gold stood up, smiling. "Good. Let me know when you need the shuttlecraft."

"Yes, sir." Sonya watched him walk out. For a moment she'd worried she'd overstepped her bounds by essentially dismissing everyone, but once again Gold had made it clear that he didn't stand on protocol much. As long as the job got done. And she was confident they'd get it done.

CHAPTER
10

"We've boosted the sensors," Pattie reported a few hours later. "Actually, we borrowed from Madl'r's design, and built several smaller sensors into a larger array. The results are . . . impressive. We should be able to cut through the atmospheric disturbance without any difficulty now."

Sonya nodded at Pattie, who was standing next to her in the docking bay. "Good job, Pattie." She turned to her tactical expert, who was discussing something with Kieran. "Fabian?"

"I've plotted its course. I also tapped into the outpost's sensor logs—got the weather patterns right up until the incident. Then I had the computer extrapolate them, and merged that in with the readings once the sensors were back online." Fabian was grinning, clearly proud of his work, and Sonya didn't blame him. "I've got the weather for the entire period, and I factored that in. I'd be willing to bet I've got the thing placed within two meters of its actual location."

"Impressive, Fabian. We'll have to see how close you came. Kieran, any luck?"

"Well, we did find a frequency—Madl'r built it with a retrieval switch, and if it picks up the signal it'll retrace its path until it reaches the original drop-off point. Only problem is, that would be the workroom inside the camp, and it can't backtrack to there because we've got the shields back on. We could drop them again, at least long enough for it to come in—"

"But that means exposing the outpost to the air again, which I'd rather not do if we can avoid it."

"Actually," Kieran gave her a sheepish grin, "I was going to say we couldn't because it would rip right through the shield array again. Unless we lowered the shields, unhooked that segment, recalled it, then reassembled that portion and raised the shields again, all while using the portable generators to keep ourselves alive."

"Right. Sorry, I should have let you finish." Sonya mentally scolded herself—trust your team and don't second-guess them so much. "Okay, so the recall's out for now. Good to know we have it, though, if we wind up needing it." She frowned. "I suppose there's no chance of just locking onto its location and beaming it back to the base?"

"Doubtful," Kieran replied. "The transporter down there can cut through that soup to get us up here, and it could probably reach a little ways out-side the camp, but not too far—and based on Fabian's calculations, I'd say it's well out of range."

"Okay, so we do it the hard way—we shuttle down, land right next to it, put up a portable

shield, and drag it inside. Messy, but it'll work."
Sonya made sure her team were all paying attention—she hated having to repeat herself. "Fabian,
you're with me. Corsi, you've got the helm. The
rest of you, stay put—we shouldn't be too long."
And she climbed into the *Archimedes* and started
strapping herself in.

"Sonnie, pull out!"
The ride down had been uneventful, Corsi holding the shuttlecraft to a tight descent and riding
out each storm front they encountered, and Sonya
had started to relax a little, sure this mission was
almost over. The sudden shout through the comm
systems made her start, and she winced as the
straps cut into her skin.

"Kieran? What the hell—?" but he cut her off
before she could finish.

"Tell Corsi to break off, now!" She wasn't sure
what was going on, but the panic in his voice was
unmistakable, and she nodded to Corsi, who
frowned but immediately changed their flight
path.

"All right, Lieutenant Commander," she said,
reminding Kieran who was first officer here,
"we've veered off. Now what's this all about?"

"Set down at the outpost—it's closer than the da
Vinci. *I'll beam down and meet you there."* And he
cut off.

"Dammit, Duff, if this is some sort of joke it'll
cost you," Fabian muttered from the backseat, but
Sonya could tell it was an empty threat, and a
glance from Fabian confirmed it. Kieran did like

to joke around, but they both knew he'd never do it in the midst of a mission, especially under such conditions.

Besides, she knew him more than well enough to know that something had him spooked.

Twenty minutes later they had reached the outpost. Kieran had obviously transported down and beaten them there, because the shield opened for them before they even requested it. Sonya was already undoing her harness. By the time the shuttle-craft's engines switched off, Sonya was standing by the door.

"All right, what's this all about?" she demanded when the door slid aside to reveal Kieran waiting.

"Sorry to startle you, Commander—we had to get your attention fast, before you got into range." Kieran's hand reached for her, but he visibly fought down the impulse and turned instead, leading her and the others to the outpost's control room. Pattie and Soloman were already there when they arrived.

"It's the device," Pattie explained as they entered. "It really was well-built. Even down to a standby mode."

"Okay, so it's got a standby—so what?" That was Corsi, who didn't look too happy at having her mission aborted. "What difference would that make to us?"

"Quite a bit, actually," Fabian admitted, wincing. "I should have thought of it myself. Damn! We almost got ourselves killed back there."

Corsi whirled on Fabian. "Killed? I thought we were just retrieving the damned thing!"

"That was the plan, but we forgot about the standby." Kieran didn't look as overwrought now, but his hands still clenched tightly to the back of the chair he was standing behind. "The device shuts itself down if it goes a certain amount of time without finding a deposit—eight hours, to be exact. It conserves its power until either it does detect a deposit or it's retrieved. It destroyed this place almost fifteen hours ago now, so it's been inactive for seven. But the minute a sufficient quantity of dilithium comes in range, it'll wake back up and home in on that source."

Corsi winced. "And the shuttle's got a warp engine." Both the *Archimedes* and the *Franklin* were warp-capable.

"Well, I'm glad you called, then," Sonya admitted, shaking her head to hide the shakes in her hands. "But what do we do now? We can't go after it in the shuttle, obviously."

"We could eject the warp core," Fabian pointed out. "It'd take a while, but we could do it—then we grab it with the shuttlecraft the way we'd planned, bring it back, turn it off, and reinstall the drive."

Sonya was glad he'd given her something to focus on instead of their near-death. "Workable, but not optimal. Ejecting the core's easy enough, but it will take time to put it back in, and we'd probably have to do it at a starbase. I don't think Captain Scott would appreciate our taking the time. It's an option, but I'd rather save it for a last resort."

"We could recall it," Kieran pointed out. "We'd have to set up shield generators."

"I know, but it's dangerous. If something goes wrong we could wind up without any shields here, and that means more time to refabricate them and then rebuild them."

"Suits are out?" Corsi asked.

"Absolutely," Fabian said. "This atmosphere'd shred them in a matter of minutes."

"Can we beam it back?"

Shaking her head, Sonya said, "We already thought of that, but it wouldn't work—the transporter on the outpost isn't made to reach that far across this interference. It can go up and out, especially with another transporter on the other end, but this is too far and too one-sided. And the *da Vinci*'s transporters couldn't cut through the atmosphere."

After she finished, Sonya noticed Fabian was staring off to the side. She'd seen that look before, usually in the mirror. "Fabian, you've got an idea?"

"Maybe," he admitted. "It's a little crazy, but I think it'd work. Only thing is, I need someone who's good at targeting—a lot better than I am. Someone who can pick off a small, high-velocity target without hesitation."

They all turned to look at the tall blond security chief, who actually grinned in return.

"What do you want me to shoot?"

CHAPTER
11

"**E**verybody ready?"

"As I'll ever be."

"Ready here."

"*Affirmative.*"

"All set."

"*Let's do it.*"

Sonya smiled with pride. This was her team. "All right, here we go. Kieran, hit it."

At the communications console, Kieran flipped a switch. Instantly a signal went out, beaming at a set frequency—the frequency that recalled Madl'r's sensor device.

"I'm detecting movement, Commander," Pattie announced from the sensors. "Small object, picking up speed. The dimensions match those of the device." She checked her readings. "Stevens, I'm showing the device was seventeen centimeters from your projected location."

Fabian grinned but didn't say anything.

Sonya spoke up to keep them focused. "Okay, here it comes. Fabian, how are our shields?"

"Full power, Commander. That thing'll bounce like a rubber ball."

"Perfect. Corsi, you ready?"

"*Standing by, Commander.*"

They all waited, watching the screen. "One thousand meters and closing," Pattie announced, as the dot appeared on the screen's periphery. "Eight hundred. Five hundred. Three hundred. Impact."

Sonya thought she felt the shield ripple, but it was probably her imagination. On the screen, she watched as the device hit the shield and rebounded, then disappeared.

"*Got it!*" Corsi shouted through the link—she had used the impact to pinpoint its location, and had locked the transporters on it, catching and sending it in one quick motion. "*Sending it to—*"

"*I have the device, Commander,*" Soloman announced from the power station. "*It appeared as planned, and I have now removed its command board.*"

"Great." Sonya let out a sigh, and allowed herself a smile. "Okay, team, everybody to the shuttlecraft. Time to get back to our ship."

"It was the failsafe again," Sonya explained to Gold once they'd returned to the *da Vinci*. "Madl'r didn't want to risk any chance of dilithium explosion or damage, so he set the device to avoid direct contact with a deposit. But if it did wind up too close for safety, the device was set to deactivate—

immediate shutdown of all systems—so that it couldn't accidentally bump anything. Corsi transported it into the outpost's power plant, and it shut itself off the minute it appeared. Then we just pulled the plug on it."

"Risky plan," Gold pointed out, "trusting a feature you'd only read about in the plans of a dead scientist whose writing you could barely understand. What if he'd forgotten that feature, or left it out, or altered the programming?"

He glanced down at the device itself, now sitting safely in its cradle. Deactivated, the thing looked harmless enough, its dull metal surface pocked by inset sensors, with ridges swirled about them. Those ridges were cutting surfaces—once the device activated, it began to spin, and the ridges functioned as a drill, corkscrewing through solid rock as if it were paper. Small jets were set about as well, interspersed with the sensors and also inset to avoid interfering with the ridges. The jets were used to maneuver, and with so many of them, the device could change direction at a phenomenal speed. It could even stop and reverse, all in less than a meter.

Sonya shook her head. "The thing already avoided the power plant like the plague when it was first activated. It was just too well-built. Madl'r included every safety he could think of."

"It's sad, really," Gold commented, running a finger absently along one ridge. "If he hadn't built it so well, Madl'r would probably still be alive, and so would the rest of Acid Camp. But he made it so effective it destroyed them all."

"Just goes to show you can't predict everything," Kieran chimed in. "Or maybe that sometimes it pays to do shoddy work."

"Well, don't try that one on my ship," Gold warned, "or you'll be digging through some deep rocks yourself, catch my drift?" He smiled to show he wasn't serious about having to give the warning. He was dead serious about the punishment.

"Yes sir, Captain!" Kieran's salute was only half-mocking, and Gold let it pass. The young man had done some good work here, as usual, and he'd never been one to stand on formalities.

But he did still have a question for his first officer, something that had bothered him since they arrived. "Did we ever figure out how it all started?"

Sonya grimaced. "Unfortunately, we think so."

"Oh?" He waited for her to explain.

"Well, the door to Madl'r's room was unlocked when Corsi first found it—the only one in the building that was. This was his private workspace, and he was obviously serious about keeping things secure, so he didn't just forget. Someone opened it."

"Not Madl'r?"

Sonya shook her head. "His body was near the commissary. But one of the other miners, a man named Stephen Cortez, was found just beyond the building." She sighed, and Gold was reminded again how young she was—and how old he sometimes felt. "Cortez had transferred there eight months ago, one of the last to arrive. According to his records he was a solid worker, specializing in computer operations and remote drilling, but he kept switching from spot to spot, always going for places with fewer people but high potential reward."

"Out to strike it rich, eh?" Gold frowned. "Never works, you ask me. Hard work is the only way to succeed, not hoping for one lucky strike."

"Which is probably why he kept moving on— each place failed to pan out. But here—according to the station logs and our two survivors, Cortez kept prowling around the scientists, asking questions about their work."

"Looking for something he could use, no doubt."

"Exactly. And he must have decided Madl'r had it. We're guessing he waited until Madl'r had just left, then snuck into the building and managed to crack the lock. He found the device, probably poked at it a bit to try figuring it out—and set it off—"

"—and killed himself and everyone else down there." Gold shook his head. "Bad enough he got himself killed, but he took out everyone else along the way. I hate it when other people suffer because one jerk couldn't control himself." He turned back to Sonya. "Good job, Commander—as always." He meant it, too—the young commander had done nothing but impress him ever since she'd taken over the team.

"Thank you, sir. The team gets most of the credit." That was one of the things he liked most about her—like himself, she was always willing to give her people credit. She didn't notice his smile, though—she was glancing at the device instead. "What's going to happen to that thing, Captain?"

He shrugged. "I don't know. I put a call in to Starfleet, letting Captain Scott know we had it. We'll see what they want done. I'd just as soon have it off my ship, to be honest. It makes me nervous." Sonya looked up and met his eyes, and he could tell she agreed. That thing had killed an entire outpost—the sooner it was off the *da Vinci*, the better.

"Be careful with it," Fabian warned as the two Starfleet officers carried the device and its cradle onto their shuttlecraft. "We think sudden changes in air pressure or maybe ambient current could activate it. Not right now, of course—we pulled its circuits before bringing it up. But if it's reassembled, tell them to be careful and to keep it in a shielded room."

"We can handle it, thanks," one of the two replied. Then they were inside the shuttlecraft and the door had closed behind them. Fabian thought they'd seemed in a hurry to leave, but perhaps that was just because they'd been rushed—their ship had been pulled from another mission to detour and retrieve the device.

"It bugs me that Starfleet wanted to see the thing," Duffy commented, standing next to Fabian in the docking bay. "And especially that they wanted the schematics as well."

"I know what you mean," Fabian admitted. "If they just wanted to know how it worked, we could have sent them diagrams. And if they wanted to be sure it was no longer a threat, we could have dismantled it entirely. But to ask for—well, okay, demand—the entire device, and all plans? It's pretty weird."

"More than weird—it smacks of some big plan, and I hate it when we stumble onto those." Kieran didn't have to say what both of them were thinking. Bombs could be placed on ships, and then detonated from within their shields. But bombs destroyed people and materials indiscriminately, and most security sweeps could detect all known explosives. This device didn't use explosives—it wouldn't show on a scan as anything more than a mechanical device of some sort. It was capable of self-starting, and of going dormant for long periods of time. Being within a shield only made it more dangerous, and more effective. And it could be programmed to avoid certain objects or even people—and to aim for others.

"Maybe we should—" Whatever Kieran had been about to say was cut off as both their combadges beeped.

"Everyone, meet in the briefing room at once. We've got a new assignment—and it's going to be a doozy." At the sound of Gold's voice, both men automatically turned and headed for the lifts. Fabian shrugged to himself, trying to put the problem of that device behind him. This mission was over—time to worry about the next one.

HERE THERE BE MONSTERS

Keith R.A. DeCandido

HISTORIAN'S NOTE

Here There Be Monsters takes place shortly after the events of the *Gateways* crossover, specifically after Book 3: *Doors Into Chaos*, Book 4: *Demons of Air and Darkness*, Book 5: *No Man's Land*, Book 6: *Cold Wars*, and the stories "Horn and Ivory," "In the Queue," "Death After Life," and "The Other Side" in Book 7: *What Lay Beyond*.

ACKNOWLEDGMENTS

The author would like to thank Susan Wright, Diane Carey, Christie Golden, Peter David, Marco Palmieri, GraceAnne Andreassi DeCandido, and most especially Robert Greenberger and John J. Ordover, without whom, etc. etc.

CHAPTER
1

"I can't find anything wrong with this thing, Duff," Fabian Stevens said from under twelve tons of machinery.

"There's got to be *something* wrong," Lt. Commander Kieran Duffy said as he peered at his tricorder. "I mean, it's not working."

"I know that, but everything here is checking out."

"Except for the whole not-working thing," Kieran added dolefully.

Fabian climbed out from the hatchway that gave him access to many of the critical systems in the Tellarite generator. "Yeah, except for that." He wiped the sweat off his brow. "I dunno—we've been running around like crazy people for days, and we spent most of the last day repairing this monstrosity. I don't think I'd know a fried EPS conduit if I saw it at this point."

Kieran smiled. "What, you don't like dashing

around half the galaxy mapping gateways and fixing blown-out power systems?"

"Over the course of a month, sure. Over four days? Not so much. The captain wasn't kidding when he said this was gonna be a doozy."

Holding up his tricorder, Kieran said, "Well, in any case, these things don't get exhausted, and it says that everything appears to be functioning normally, too."

"*Gomez to Duffy.*"

Grinning, Kieran tapped his combadge. "Duffy here. You're back, Sonnie?"

"*We'll be flying the* Archimedes *into orbit of Tellar within five minutes.*"

"So the comm relay's all fixed?"

"*Yup. Pattie did most of the work by crawling around the thing's outer hull and replacing the burned-out relays. What I'm wondering is where the* da Vinci *is.*"

Kieran chuckled. "Was wondering when you were gonna ask. They found a derelict ship that apparently fell through the same gateway that blew out the comm relay you were fixing. The captain's towing it to Starbase 12. They should be back—" he checked his chronometer "—actually, any minute now. Didn't realize how late it had gotten."

"*How are you and Fabian coming with the generator?*"

"It's, ah, it's coming."

"*Still haven't figured out what's wrong yet, have you?*" Kieran could hear her smile.

"You know me too damn well, you know that?" he said with mock indignation.

"*Do you want a hand, or would you two rather prove your manhood by fixing it yourselves without any help from us?*"

"Oho, a challenge. Fine, we'll have it fixed before the *da Vinci* gets back."

"*Really?*"

Kieran could hear the dubious note in Sonya's voice. So, apparently, could Fabian, given the guffaw he was trying to suppress.

"Do you doubt me, madame?"

"*No, just wondering if you're willing to put your money where your foot is.*"

"Tell you what, when we have that overhaul at Starbase 96 next month, the winner picks where we have dinner."

"*You're on, Duff. We'll be in orbit if you need us. Gomez out.*"

Fabian frowned. "She called you 'Duff.' I thought that was *my* nickname for you."

"*You* take it up with her."

Holding up his hands, Fabian said, "No thanks. I don't mess around with officers."

It was Kieran's turn to frown. "Fabe, *I'm* an officer."

Fabian snapped his fingers. "Dang. Keep forgetting that." He removed one of the panels from the generator. "I gotta say, I was really worried there for a while. Gateways opening up all over the galaxy, fights breaking out, planets in danger—it was a major mess."

"I wasn't worried."

Shooting Kieran a look, Fabian said, "You weren't?"

"Nope," Kieran said as he opened up another panel. "They put Picard in charge."

"Yeah, so?"

"Soon's I heard that, I knew everything would be fine."

"You're kidding." Fabian was looking at Kieran like he had two heads. "How?"

Kieran opened his mouth, closed it, opened it again, and closed it again. Finally, he said, "You've never served with Picard, have you?"

"No."

"Then you won't get it. He's just got this ineffable—*Picard*-ity. When he's in charge, you just *know* that he's gonna find a solution to the problem."

"Uh, okay."

"Might I add that he *did* find a solution to the problem?"

"True," Fabian said as he peered more closely at the circuitry he had exposed. "Is that—? Oh, no, that's fine. Damn." He closed the panel, then opened another one. "Of course, he wasn't alone. As I recall, certain former crewmates of mine on Deep Space 9 did a nice job disrupting the gateways."

"For all of ten minutes."

"Yeah, but from what I hear, that was a pretty useful ten minutes. Helped expose those fake Iconians for the frauds they were. *And* it was engineered by one Lieutenant Nog. *You* remember Nog, right, Duff? The 'kid' you were so condescending to on Empok Nor? The one whose plan you wouldn't even listen to? The one who made us all look like idiots?"

"Yes," Kieran said in a tight voice, "I remember. It should be pointed out that I did apologize and offer him a spot on the team."

"Actually, it was Captain Gold who offered him the spot on the team, and would *you* take it if you were treated the way you treated him?"

Kieran sighed. "Is there any way I can win in this conversation?"

Fabian looked like he was pretending to consider it. "No, not really," he said.

"Just checking."

"All kidding aside, though, I'm especially glad we didn't find ourselves in the middle of any major wars. I mean, bad enough that the gateway that connected this place to Andor led to that little bit of thievery—"

"What little bit of thievery?"

Fabian turned to look at Kieran. "Duff, we've been on Tellar for a day. All *anyone's* been talking about are the Andorians who came in and stole the colAndor Scrolls."

Kieran shrugged. "It's best to just tune out Tellarites complaining about Andorians. You'll live longer."

"Good point."

"I was more worried about that nonsense between the Carreon and the Deltans. Not to mention the Markanians and the Aeron."

"Who?"

"Couple of former members of the Thallonian Empire."

"Oh, okay. I don't follow all that post-collapse Thallonian stuff. I tried, but it just got too complicated. I lost track. Is Captain Calhoun still dead?"

"As of this week, he's alive," Kieran said with a grin.

"Okay, just checki—" Fabian cut himself off.

"What is it, Fabe?"

"You're not gonna believe this."

"Believe what?"

"I mean, you're *really* not gonna believe this."

"I certainly won't if you don't tell me what it is."

"This is really unbelievable."

"So I've been led to understand."

"You know how the gateway on Tellar started draining power from this generator?"

"Considering we just spent most of the last twenty-four hours fixing the damage done by the power surge, yes, I do know. Get to the point, Fabe."

"Well, when that surge hit, it knocked an isolinear rod out of whack. Not much, only about a millimeter or so."

"So that's why this thing won't work?"

"Yup."

"This entire piece of twelve-ton machinery is dead because an isolinear rod is a millimeter out of alignment?"

"Yup."

Kieran hesitated. "This is the part where I say, 'I don't believe it,' right?"

"It would bring the joke full circle, yes."

Sighing, Kieran put his head in his hands. *I suppose I walked right into that one.* Then he looked at Fabian, who was simply standing there. "Uh, Fabe?"

"Yeah?"

"All we need to do to fix this is put that rod back into place, right?"

"That's right."

"So, uh—why haven't you?"

"I was waiting for your order. After all, you are an officer, second in command of the S.C.E. team, third in command of the *da Vinci*, and all-around important person. I am but a humble engineer, a mere cog in the mighty wheel of Starfleet. I would *never* presume to circumvent the chain of command by proceeding without an order from you."

Okay, it's official, Kieran thought, *we need shore leave, and soon. That damned overhaul at 96 can't come soon enough.* "Mr. Stevens," he said in a mock-formal voice.

"Yes, Lieutenant Commander Duffy, sir?" Fabian said in a like tone.

"Would you be *so* kind as to put the isolinear rod back in place?"

"Yes *sir*, right away, *sir!*" Fabian saluted sloppily, then reached into the generator.

Two seconds later, the large piece of Tellarite machinery hummed to life.

"Congratulations, Mr. Duffy," Fabian said, "it's a generator."

"*Da Vinci to Duffy.*"

Kieran blinked. That was Captain Gold's voice. He wondered when they came in-system relative to when Fabian found the rod—mainly as it would determine where he and Sonnie ate on Starbase 96 next month. "Go ahead," he said, tapping his combadge.

"You two finished down there yet?"

"Just done now, sir. And Commander Gomez and P8 Blue are in orbit."

"I know, the Archimedes *is docking now. I need you two up here pronto—we just got a distress call from Maeglin."*

"Oh God," Fabian said, "not the Androssi again."

"No, it's actually another gateway problem. And they asked for us specifically."

"Nothing like gratitude," Kieran said. "We just need to tell the Tellarite authorities that their generator's finally up and running, and then Diego can beam us up."

"Good. I'll let Corsi know we're pulling out, as well."

"That'll just thrill the heck out of her, I'm sure, sir."

CHAPTER
2

Malk had fully expected to live his entire life without ever seeing a twelve-meter-tall, two-meter-wide green scaly creature with yellow eyes.

Then again, he had also fully expected to live his life as a farmer on Maeglin with all the comforts of twenty-fourth-century living.

This, he thought as he stared up at the twelve-meter-tall, two-meter-wide green scaly creature with yellow eyes walking toward his farm, *will teach me to have unrealistic expectations.*

Things had been bad enough these last few months. Maeglin had been colonized about a hundred years earlier by a group of Tellarites who wanted to "get back to nature." Malk had always found that bitterly amusing in light of recent events.

Maeglin was not part of the Federation, and so when the third straight year of bad crops meant that the colony was in serious trouble, they didn't have an immediate recourse. Some advocated asking the Federation for help, but others were against that. Adding fuel to the fire was the presence of the Androssi, an alien race of technicians who offered a solution to all their problems for a very cheap price.

Ultimately, it came down to a bidding war with Starfleet, in the form of one of their vessels full of engineers, the *da Vinci*. The *da Vinci* offered a method of reenergizing the soil that would take time and mean another difficult year, but with tremendous long-term benefits, and no deleterious side effects whatsoever. The Androssi offered instant gratification, but would not let the authorities (or the *da Vinci* crew) examine the specifications, and they were vague about the long-term consequences.

Despite the lack of consensus, some Maegline went ahead and struck a deal with the Androssi. As a result, they had good soil again—but the equipment used to revitalize the planet's ground also released a duonetic field into the atmosphere. Suddenly, no electronic equipment of any kind could work on the planet. Both Maegline authorities and the *da Vinci* tried to stop the Androssi, but to no avail.

However, the engineers on the Starfleet ship were able to retard the effects of the field, enough so that at least *some* equipment would work. Their crew were regarded as heroes, and they went on their way. Malk, for his part, didn't see them as heroes. If they were *real* heroes, they'd have stopped the Androssi in the first place.

This all served to explain why Malk could only

get his equipment to work about a quarter of the time, and why he'd been reduced to such menial and outmoded tasks as hoeing and weeding and mowing.

It did *not* explain why there was a twelve-meter-tall, two-meter-wide green scaly creature with yellow eyes walking toward his farm.

Then, about three meters from the farm, the creature stopped.

Malk's nearest neighbor was named Dav. When the duonetic field first hit, Dav had dug up an old projectile weapon, saying that he, at least, would be safe. At the time Malk had thought Dav to be insane.

Right now, Malk was wishing Dav was nearby. Malk had a phaser somewhere in the farm, but phasers weren't the most reliable weapons these days. Besides, it would take him several minutes (if not hours) to find the damn thing, and who knew what the creature could do in the meantime?

The creature started making an odd kind of noise and gesturing. Malk didn't understand a word of it.

"Go away!" he shouted, knowing how ridiculous it sounded.

More noises and gesturing.

Again, Malk shouted, "Go away!" Then, for good measure, he added, "Get out of here!"

Still more noises and gesturing.

"Damn you, *get off my farm!*" Malk cried, shaking his fist.

Suddenly the creature screamed so loud that

Malk's ears rattled, and then it stomped forward, right *into* the farm.

Within minutes, Malk's farm, his equipment, his possessions, his food, and everything else he kept in the structure—which was made out of a plastiform that had withstood various nasty weather conditions with nary a scratch for three generations—was shredded.

Malk couldn't believe it. His jaw drooped from his snout. The chair his mother had given him. The clothes he had replicated. The food stores for next week's market. The kitchen. The only-sporadically-working comm and the old-fashioned radio, either one of which he might have used to call for help. All of it was reduced to rubble by the large green thing in the space of about five minutes.

And then it stomped off—heading, Malk dimly noted, in the direction of Dav's farm.

Maybe it's susceptible to projectile weapons, Malk thought with little hope. If it could tear his tough old farm up, he doubted that Dav's silly antique would have much of an effect.

Malk had thought, like most Maegline, that the day the Androssi came was the darkest day in Maeglin history. Now he had to wonder if it would have competition for that distinction.

CHAPTER
3

"*You understand, Captain, that normally we wouldn't send in the S.C.E. for this sort of thing, but Starfleet is still stretched a bit thin and you are in the area.*"

Captain David Gold kept a pleasant expression plastered to his face as he replied to Admiral Koike. "Of course, Admiral. Besides, we do have a history with Maeglin. And they *did* ask for us by name."

"*True, true. The* Malinche *will be there in three days. But, of course, you should go in and do what you can to placate the Maeglin authorities until they arrive.*"

"Of course, Admiral." Gold somehow managed a smile.

"*Good. Keep us posted as to your progress, please, Captain. Koike out.*"

As soon as Koike's face disappeared from the screen, the pleasant face and the smile fell, and Gold let out with a curse or six in Yiddish, concluding with, "Damn desk jockeys."

"Transporter room to bridge," came the voice of Diego Feliciano over the comm.

"Go ahead, Chief," Gold said, getting his voice out of what his wife called "grump mode" and back into what he himself thought of as "command mode."

"Commander Duffy and Mr. Stevens are back on board, sir."

"Good." Corsi and her team had beamed up just before Gold's little chat with the admiral, and Gomez and Blue had already docked the *Archimedes*. He turned to the ensign at the conn. "Set course for Maeglin, Wong, maximum warp."

"Yes, sir."

Turning to the tactical station behind him, Gold said, "Call a meeting in the observation lounge in five minutes, McAllan."

The lieutenant nodded, and Gold got up to get a quick bowl of soup before the meeting. If they were going back to Maeglin, he needed fortification.

Domenica Corsi was exhausted. She had spent the better part of a day coordinating with the Tellarite police force, which had some unpronounceable name or other, to control the looting that was going on in the capital city, which had an even more unpronounceable name. This was a result of the city's primary generator going down.

That, in turn, was the result of some kind of gateway opening up on the planet, one of thousands that had opened all over the galaxy, apparently. Corsi didn't know the details, and didn't much care. She did her job as *da Vinci* security chief, and kept the looting to a minimum until Duffy and Fabe fixed the generator.

As she approached the quarters she shared with the ship's chief medical officer, she cursed at herself. *Duffy and* Stevens, *dammit, not "Fabe." He's just another crewmate. Yes, he was nice to me that night when I needed him, and he's been good enough not to make a fuss about it since, but it's over now. So stop thinking about him that way.*

Cursing Dar for the millionth time, she entered her quarters, and was surprised to see Dr. Elizabeth Lense sitting on her bed reading a padd. "What're you doing here?" Corsi asked.

Lense smiled a small smile. "I *live* here."

"No, I mean Hawkins and Eddy are in sickbay—they got knocked around by some Tellarite kids. Why aren't you there treating them?"

"I'm letting Emmett handle it," Lense said, using her preferred nickname for the *da Vinci*'s Emergency Medical Hologram. "He can use the experience." Unlike the two previous EMH models, Emmett was on a kind of learning curve (and also was a bit less acerbic), akin to a first-year intern. Starfleet Medical thought this model might be easier to deal with.

Corsi considered arguing the point, then decided she was too tired. She walked over to the replicator. "Computer, double espresso."

As the drink materialized, Corsi thought back to that wonderful summer on Earth when she was twelve, going to the Café Roma in New York City. That was the first time she'd ever been to Earth—

her parents were colonials—and also the first time she'd had espresso. She hadn't been able to live without the stuff since. The *da Vinci* replicator had done a particularly good job with it, thanks to some tinkering done by P8 Blue on Corsi's behalf. *Sometimes it's good to serve on a ship full of tech-heads.*

"*S.C.E. team, report to the observation lounge.*"

Corsi closed her eyes. *Damn. Should've known there'd be a meeting. We're being diverted somewhere, that* always *means a meeting.*

Within five minutes, she and Lense had arrived at the observation lounge. Gomez and Duffy were already there, and the others arrived soon enough. Corsi noticed that Duffy and Gomez were staring at each other in a manner that was intended to be subtle, and had the reverse effect of being stunningly obvious to everyone in the room.

Corsi shook her head.

"I take it everything on Tellar went well," Gold said by way of starting the meeting.

"Yes, sir," Duffy said. "The Tellarite High Muckitymuck sent his personal thanks to you and the crew for all the work we did repairing the gateway damage."

Gold frowned. "He's not actually *called* that, is he?"

"Uh, no, sir, but I wouldn't dream of trying to pronounce it."

Bart Faulwell then let loose with a barrage of syllables. At Duffy's sharp look, the linguist smiled and said, "What can I say, Commander, we have different dreams."

Turning to Corsi, Gold said, "We're not leaving Tellar in the lurch security-wise, are we, Commander?"

"I don't think so, sir," Corsi said. "Honestly, the only reason they needed our help was because the generator went down. With that back up, the locals should be able to handle any further problems."

"Any casualties?" Gold asked Lense.

"Just some bumps and bruises. Emmett's handling it."

Gold gave Lense a funny look at that, but said nothing but, "Good. Commander Cho's people at Starbase 12 found a match for the ship we towed—belongs to a race called the Wadi from the Gamma Quadrant. In fact, they were the first race from Gamma to make contact with Deep Space 9 after the Bajoran wormhole opened."

"And it fell through a gateway?" Stevens asked.

Gold nodded. "And had the stuffing pounded out of it at some point, by the looks of it."

Stevens chuckled. "I heard stories about that first contact on DS9. I'm not surprised that they got pounded." He shook his head. "I wish we'd had a chance to check out the gateways before they went down."

"I agree," Blue said, making one of those odd noises she made. "Their power consumption ratios must have been—"

Gold held up a hand, which Corsi was excessively grateful to see. "Speculate on your own time, people. Doping out the gateways is someone else's problem. Our problem, as usual, is to clean up other people's messes."

"The S.C.E., the waste extraction robots of the galaxy," Duffy said with that idiotic grin of his.

"This particular mess," Gold continued, "is at a waste extractor we've been to before, so to speak. Maeglin."

Corsi winced. "Not the Androssi again."

Chuckling, Duffy said, "That's what Fabe said."

Corsi winced again.

"We should be so lucky," Gold said. "No, it's another gateway problem. Apparenty, a gateway showed up on Maeglin, too—and it had no trouble operating in the duonetic field, either."

Gomez leaned forward. "Completely unaffected?"

"That's what they tell us."

She nodded. "Actually, that fits. The gateways have seemed to have a huge power store on their own. It's only the ones that got used heavily—like the ones in the Tellarite system—that started draining power from other sources."

"According to the communiqué from Governor Tak, nobody on Maeglin used the gateway. They couldn't tell what it was, and they didn't want to risk it. Besides, the readings they were able to take on the other side were—weird."

"Weird?" Duffy asked with a smile.

"They're sending us the telemetry now, but that's a minor point. After our old pal Nog did that ten-minute shutdown of the gateway—"

Several people gave Duffy amused glances at that. Duffy seemed to slide farther into his seat. Corsi thought he damn well should look abashed— Nog was a good officer, and he deserved better treatment than Duffy gave him back on Empok Nor. Corsi never liked Duffy much, though he comported himself decently enough against the Tholians, but mostly she thought him a sorry excuse for an officer. She expected that kind of behavior from the noncoms, but Duffy was an Academy graduate.

"—suddenly, the gateway was a hotbed of activity. All sorts of things came running out of it."

"What kinds of things?" Gomez asked.

Gold grinned. "Monsters."

Corsi pursed her lips. The captain could sometimes be frivolous, though never to a fault, but this was just silly. "Monsters?"

"Well, no, not really, but they sure do fit the profile." Gold touched a panel on the table in front of him, and an image appeared on the viewscreen. It was a large biped with scaly yellow skin, and a huge tail. That was followed by an image of a flying creature that vaguely resembled an Earth pteranodon, then another image of something that Corsi swore was a dead ringer for a Vulcan *sehlat*, only—based on the house it was standing next to—about ten times the size.

"My God, they *are* monsters," Carol Abramowitz said as the image shifted to a six-legged creature with compound eyes and massive insectoid wings. "Every one of those looks like something out of a childhood nightmare."

"Speak for yourself," Blue said haughtily. "All of our childhood nightmares on Nasat involve short, skinny bipeds."

Gomez turned to Gold. "How many?"

"So far these four are the only ones they have images of, but the reports indicate at least two more roaming around. No sentient fatalities yet, but they have been consuming crops—and animals."

"That could wreak havoc with the ecosystem," Lense said. "Introducing a host of new predators into the environment—"

"So we need to, what?" Gomez asked. "Help them round up the creatures?"

"And communicate with them, if possible. It'll take four hours to get there from here. Gomez, Duffy, Blue, Stevens, I want you to give us ways to get equipment to work as efficiently as possible in that duonetic soup down there. Get Barnak to help out, and anyone else you need. We don't have much time, and the Maegline have enough problems without half a dozen rabbits stomping through their briar patches. Get to it, people."

Everyone got up. Most made a beeline for the exits. Corsi finished her espresso and went to the replicator to get another one.

Gold went up to Gomez and Duffy, who were standing extremely close to each other. "I'm guessing you two had a lunch date. Sorry to cut it short."

"We'll have other chances," Gomez said with a smile.

"It's not that—I just want you to eat more. You need some meat on your bones, Commander. You almost wasted away to nothing on Sarindar."

Duffy grinned. "I'm trying to fatten her back up, sir."

Chuckling, Gold said, "Get to work."

They departed, leaving Gold and Corsi alone in the room.

"All right, Commander, what's on your mind?"

Corsi blinked. "I'm sorry, sir?"

"You've been drilling your baby blues into my head since the meeting started. What's bugging you?"

Ninety-five percent of the time, Corsi was grateful to have a CO who was perceptive. This particular instant fell into the wrong five percent, however.

To her surprise, words did fall out of her mouth. "I don't think what those two are doing is appropriate, sir."

One of Gold's bushy eyebrows raised. "I beg your pardon?"

"I don't think it's appropriate for the two of them to be involved, given their . . . situation. Regulations—"

"—are sufficiently vague," Gold interrupted, "and generally left to the captain's discretion." His voice grew deeper, which Corsi knew was his more serious tone. "This particular captain has no problems with it as long as it doesn't interfere with the performance of their duty. Both their service record and my observations of them since they've been under my command indicate to me that that won't be an issue. If I'm wrong, I'll deal with it, but there's been nothing to suggest it's an issue yet. Are you questioning my judgment, Commander?"

Corsi knew that there was only one answer to

that question. "No, sir. I withdraw the objection, sir."

"Good." He broke into a smile. "I do value these little chats, Commander. Anytime you have a grievance, don't hesitate to bring it to my attention."

In a much smaller voice, she said, "Yes, sir," and moved toward the doors.

"Oh, and Commander?"

Corsi stopped, but did not turn around. "Sir?"

"Whenever you're ready to tell me what's *really* bothering you, I'll be here."

Definitely the wrong five percent, Corsi thought. "Yes, sir," she repeated, and left the observation lounge.

Damn you, Dar.

CHAPTER
4

Lin had been spending more and more time at the lake lately. Well, her free time, anyhow. She did her chores, of course, and was at the table for mealtimes, but aside from that, she liked the lake better than being around her parents.

It wasn't that she didn't love her parents. She loved them more than anything—except maybe *egrimat* pie. But lately, all they did was argue.

It didn't used to be that way. They used to be nice all the time. But then all the stuff stopped working right. Lin remembered it really well, since it was right after her fifth birthday. It had been her best birthday yet, with lots of *egrimat* pie.

It was also around when those weird brown people came, and then the other weird people— they all had the silliest noses. They were all long and skinny and the absolute strangest things Lin had ever seen.

After they came and stuff stopped working right, Lin's parents started fighting. They had never fought before, but now they couldn't do anything else.

Lin picked up a stone and threw it into the lake. It made a nice splooshing sound. She picked up another stone and did the same thing. This kept her attention for several minutes, until she ran out of stones. So she decided to start walking around the edge of the lake. This was one of her favorite things to do. So far she'd never fallen in.

Well, okay, there was that one time when her father surprised her by calling her name, but aside from that, she'd never fallen in.

Her arms extended to keep her balance better, Lin started walking around the lake. The sun was starting to go down, so when she came around, the sun was in her eyes. She stopped, blinked the glare out of her eyes, then started walking again.

Or she would've, except there was a big furry thing in the way.

Lin screamed, and lost her balance. She twirled her arms in an attempt to get it back, but it didn't work, and she fell in.

Luckily, she had fallen in before, and knew what to do: she swam. It wasn't like the last time, when she almost swallowed all that water. She wasn't a baby anymore, she was smart. She learned how to swim, and now she kicked her legs and stroked with her arms. Within seconds, she was back at the edge of the lake.

The furry thing was still there, staring at her with big, yellow eyes. It was more than twice as big as Lin. It was covered in brown fur and had a long snout that looked like a funny mix of a proper snout and those weird strangers' noses. It also had lots of really sharp teeth, and big claws.

"Uh, hello," Lin said softly. Her parents had always tried to get her to speak more forcefully, but she was shy. She was also cold from all the water, which was dripping on the ground.

It had been lying on all fours. Now it gestured with one of its front paws and then made some kind of weird noise.

"My name's Lin. What's yours?"

It made another gesture, then made another noise.

Then it reached into the lake and splashed some water.

Lin frowned. She wasn't sure what she was supposed to do next. So she did the same thing. Her splash was a lot smaller than the furry thing's, of course.

The furry thing seemed to like this, as it then made a funnier noise and splashed again.

Lin decided to make the same noise—or at least come really close to it—and splashed again. She tried to splash harder so she could make almost as much noise as the furry thing.

"Lin!"

That was her father's voice. "I'm over here!" she cried out.

For some reason, the furry thing didn't like this. It started shaking and making a really awful noise.

"Don't worry!" Lin said. "It's just my father. He's usually really nice. Except when he and my mother are fighting, but still, you'll like them."

Lin's father came over the small hill that led to

the lake. As soon as Lin saw him, she said, "Look! I made a new friend!"

She had thought that her father would be happy to see the furry thing, as he seemed to be nice and friendly. But her father started getting that look he always got whenever he argued with her mother.

"Move away from that, Lin—*now!*"

"What's wrong?" Lin asked, confused.

Her father grabbed a stick off the ground, and waved it at the furry thing. "Get away from her!" he yelled. Lin noticed that the nostrils in his snout were wider than usual.

The furry thing just made another strange noise. But then it surprised Lin by getting up on its hind legs.

Her father then got a weird look on his face.

It took Lin a moment to figure it out. He looked *scared*. Lin couldn't believe it. Her father was *never* scared!

"I said, get *away from her!* Lin! Move away!"

"But—"

"Move *away!*"

Lin didn't move. She didn't understand. The furry thing was just a nice animal who came to watch her walk along the lake. She thought maybe she could explain—

The furry thing waved its arms and made another noise.

"He isn't trying to do—" Lin started to say.

"*Get back!*" her father yelled. Then he threw the stick at the furry thing.

The furry thing batted the stick away. Then it

made another noise. Lin's father grabbed her, picked her up, and ran back toward the farm.

Lin screamed. Not because of the furry thing, but because her father was hurting her. She was just trying to make a new friend!

The furry thing continued to cry out, but it didn't follow them back to the house. As soon as they got back inside their large house, her father finally put her down, and she could breathe properly again.

"Why did you *do* that?" Lin asked. "It was just—"

"What the *brobah* were you thinking?" Her father yelled so loud that the windows rattled. "Don't ever get close to a crazed animal like that!"

"It *wasn't* an animal, it was—"

"*Don't talk back to me!* Now stay inside!"

Her father went into one of the closets. The door to it was always open because the doors didn't always work right. Her mother figured it was better to just leave it open all the time.

He grabbed the nasty gun.

Lin got scared. "You're not gonna shoot him, are you?"

"Damn right I am! Nobody tries to kill my little girl!"

"He wasn't trying to *kill* me! Why won't you *listen* to me?"

But her father still wasn't listening. Instead, he was calling for her mother to look after Lin while he went out with the gun.

Lin was scared. Not so much for herself, but for the furry thing.

She hoped it would be okay.

CHAPTER
5

"Take a look at this, Kier."

Lieutenant Jil Barnak, chief engineer of the *da Vinci,* and the only person who referred to Kieran Duffy as "Kier," for which Kieran had always been grateful, plunked the two boots down on the workbench in engineering. Kieran looked at them for several seconds.

"Those are gravity boots," he said, showing what Sonnie often referred to as his keen grasp of the obvious.

"Yup."

Continuing in that vein, he added, "And they're blue."

"Yup."

"Okay, I'll bite, why are they blue?"

Fabian, P8 Blue, and Sonya all chose that moment to enter engineering. Sonnie had called a meeting to see what progress had been made in what Kieran had been jokingly referring to as "Operation: Mighty Maeglin Monster Hunt."

Fabian grinned. "They're not happy with their lot in life?"

Pattie joined in. "They're long-lost relatives of mine?"

"No," Jil said with an amused shake of his graying head. "It's blue because making it pink would've been silly."

Kieran chuckled. "Of course, that should've been my first guess."

"In any case," Jil continued, "it's a coating of my own design. It'll keep out the effects of the duonetic field."

"You sure?" Sonnie asked.

"Tested it in the hololab myself." The *da Vinci* did not have a holodeck as such, but one lab had been given over to holographic use. The hololab was strictly used only for duty-related matters, much to the chagrin of most of the crew complement, though Corsi would have been just as happy to get rid of it altogether. But it was too useful for bench tests and other applications to not have. Kieran had tried to find a way to finagle using it for a date, but Sonnie shot that down before he could even finish the sentence.

Pattie made one of her tinkly sounds. "That'll work for anything that doesn't have a display or an interface."

"Beats a kick in the head, certainly," Kieran said. "Thanks, Jil."

"*Ina to Gomez.*"

"Go ahead," Sonnie said, tapping her combadge.

"*Commander, I've downloaded the telemetry*

*Maeglin sent us of their probes into the gateways.
You should take a look at this."*

"Pipe it down to engineering, Mar."

"Acknowledged."

Sonnie walked over to a wall console, Kieran
behind her. Pattie, Jil, and Fabian remained at the
workbench, but fixed their gazes on the screen—
*curious enough to look, but not wanting to crowd
the first and second officer,* Kieran thought with a
smile.

Kieran peered at the readouts, but couldn't
make heads or tails of it. Sonnie was looking at it
pretty intently, though. "Mar, is that what I think it
is?"

*"Looks like it, Commander. Whatever was on the
other side of that gateway wasn't in this universe."*

Kieran put his head in his hands. "Oh God, no.
Interdimensional travel always gives me a stom-
achache."

"Actually," Pattie said, "it's not that bad."

Though sorely tempted to pursue that revela-
tion with the Nasat, Kieran knew they didn't have
time. "Mar, have any of the other gateways been
like that? I thought they were just space portals."

*"Way ahead of you, Commander. Apparently
there was an interdimensional gateway they found
in the Sagittarius cluster about a hundred years ago
that might have been one of the Iconians'. There've
also been some reports of some of the gateways
being time portals. So there's some precedent for
atypical gateways, anyhow."*

"Good work," Sonnie said, and Kieran silently
agreed with the sentiment. "Keep digging, see if

you can find any more specifics. Maybe we'll get lucky."

"Yes, sir."

"Ina Mar, research junkie," Kieran muttered with amusement. This was a side to their Bajoran ops officer he hadn't known about.

"She plays a mean saxophone, too," Fabian said.

"How the heck did a Bajoran learn to play the saxophone?" Kieran asked.

"What, Bajorans can't play human instruments?"

"I didn't say *that*—"

"If you two are finished," Sonnie said with an indulgent grin. "Pattie, think we can cobble together a force field generator that'll work?"

"With Jil's paint, absolutely," Pattie said with one of her happier tinkles. "I should have a dozen of them by the time we arrive."

Sonnie turned to Fabian. "What about weapons, Fabian?"

"No joy there," the black-haired engineer said, blowing out a breath. "I've tried everything—yes, Commander, even that scattering-field-negating trick you pulled on the Breen and the Eerlikka—but none of them get past the deadening effect of the duonetic field. We may have to settle for them conking out on us periodically."

Setting her fists down on the workbench, Sonnie leaned forward and said, "We're not 'settling' for anything."

"Why not just use the paint?" Pattie asked.

Kieran shook his head. "Once we apply it, we're

stuck with whatever setting it's on when it gets painted. We don't even know what settings are effective against these things. We have to be able to change it."

"And," Jil added, "if we don't paint the panel, it'll be just as susceptible to the duonetic field."

Pattie made one of her more contemplative tinkles. "Why not use a remote control?"

This time it was Sonnie who shook her head. "No, that won't work either—it'll be just as susceptible to the field."

"Not if I make a force field small enough to fit around someone's hand. I'll make it a wrist unit."

Fabian smiled. "That could work. Whoever's armed can fire the phaser with one hand and change the settings with the remote in the other hand."

Jil rested one large hand on his equally large stomach. "Yeah, but that means they can only fire one-handed, and the other hand'll be useless. They won't be able to do anything except shoot."

Shrugging, Kieran said, "That's the long definition of security guard."

With an amused tinkle, Pattie said, "I dare you to say that in front of Corsi."

"Do I *look* stupid?"

"Kieran, don't ask questions you can't handle honest answers to," Sonnie said with a wicked grin. "Okay," she went on, growing more serious. "So we'll try to herd these guys with light phaser fire and cage them in force fields until we figure out what to do with them. Hopefully, even with the duonetic field, the universal translators will be able to work out their language. And I want recordings of every encounter with these things for Bart, in case the UTs need some help. Now—what about the one that can fly?"

"Or *ones*," Fabian said. "We still don't know what they all look like."

"That's why I asked Jil for the boots," Kieran said. "I figure I can play chicken with the flyboy—or boys," he amended with a look at Fabian, "and lure it to the ground and let one of Core-Breach's flunkies and Pattie's force fields do the rest."

"Isn't that dangerous?" Pattie asked.

Sonnie grinned. "Says the woman who spent the morning crawling around the outer hull of a comm relay. Don't worry, Kieran's got an A-rating with the boots. In fact, I remember a certain holodeck program on Ardana that you were quite adept in."

"As opposed to you," Kieran said, "who kept flying into the clouds."

"I prefer to keep my feet on the ground, thanks."

"Commander," Jil said hesitantly. The Atrean scratched his oversize ear.

"What, Jil?"

"Well, if what Lieutenant Ina said is correct, these things aren't from this dimension."

"Right."

"Well, I assume the reason why you checked the telemetry of the gateway was to see where they came from, and maybe get them home, if they came from close enough. I mean, we can't use the gateways anymore—from what I understand, they've been permanently shut down—but they could easily be from this general area of the Milky Way and we could get them home, then. But if they're from another universe altogether . . ."

There was quiet around the workbench for several seconds. Then Sonnie finally said, "We'll build that bridge when we come to it. Besides, even if this was one of the regular gateways, there's every chance they'd be from somewhere deep in the Beta Quadrant, or the Delta Quadrant, or a part of the Gamma Quadrant that's nowhere near the Bajoran wormhole. Right now, our priority is figuring out a way to minimize the damage they're doing to Maeglin. We'll worry about the possibility of returning them later."

Jil nodded.

Sonnie looked around the workbench. "Fabian, Kieran, set up the remotes for the phasers. Pattie, Jil, make us some force fields. I'll coordinate with Corsi on the security arrangements. Let's go."

Kieran smiled. Sonnie had always been the take-charge type, but there was something different about her ever since she came back from Sarindar.

Of course, since that's also when she decided we should be an item again, I'm probably biased, he thought with a smile as he and Fabian started work on the remotes.

CHAPTER
6

Andrea Lipinski felt ridiculous holding a bright blue phaser in her left hand.

Normally Lipinski liked the look and feel of the type-1 phasers—easy to handle with one hand, able to change settings quickly, and they always hit their target. But normally, the phaser wasn't so . . . so . . . *blue*.

Worse, because it was covered in this blue whatever-it-was, she couldn't change the settings, so she was carrying a remote control in her right hand—*and* her hand was covered with a small force field, so the hand was useless except for holding the remote.

All this because of what the Androssi did to Maeglin.

Lipinski made a mental note to strangle the next Androssi she happened to come across.

She also made a mental note to strangle Corsi. Bad enough she had a blue phaser, but also a blue bug—she had been assigned to accompany the Nasat.

"Are you okay?" Blue asked, causing Lipinski to jump and aim her phaser at the surprise noise. "Easy," Blue added, waving two of her icky arm-like things. "I'm on your side, remember?"

That's easy for you to say, she thought. "I'm fine. I just—"

"You don't like bugs."

Lipinski blinked. "Uh, well, no, I— How'd you know that?"

"Body language. You get that instinctive human jerkiness every time I'm around. Most people get over it after they've gotten used to having me around—well, except Carol when she wants to get into a snit about some imagined slight I've perpetrated in our quarters—but you haven't yet. Every time I come across it, it usually means some kind of entomophobia."

Lipinski actually chuckled. "Figures."

"What?" Blue asked while making one of those weird noises she always made.

"You're an engineer, so of course you've got some kind of technical term for it."

"Of course," Blue said with another funny noise. "It's how we fool people into thinking we know more than they do."

"You mean you don't?" Lipinski said, perhaps a bit too snidely.

"Oh, sure we do. Just not as much more as we let on."

Lipinski honestly couldn't tell if Blue was joking or not, and that just irritated her more.

They kept walking through the underbrush of this jungle in the middle of the main continent on

Maeglin, where most of the Tellarites had set up their homes. It was humid and Lipinski's uniform was starting to stick to her skin. *Why the hell does Starfleet insist on these damn two-layer uniforms, anyhow?*

Blue let out a kind of bell-like noise. "What is it?" Lipinski asked, raising her phaser.

"The *khest'n* tricorder's not working again. Damn duonetic field."

Lipinski tried to relax a little. *Just take it easy, she's not going to crawl all over you or eat you or anything like that. She's a crewmate. Not like those* things *back home on—*

Don't think about it.

They moved into a clearing, Blue tapping commands into a tricorder that responded by making none of its telltale noises.

Why couldn't Corsi have put me with Stevens? He's nice—and cute. Maybe if we were paired up, I'd finally screw up the courage to ask him out.

But Corsi had teamed up with Stevens herself— which was odd, in and of itself. She usually went with officers. Lipinski wondered if there was anything to that.

Nah, not Core-Breach. Heart of duranium, she's got.

Blue made a chirpy noise, scaring Lipinski out of ten years of life, punctuated by an exclamation of, "There we go! Tricorder's working, and we've got a fix. Follow me!"

Then she got down on all eights and started skittering forward at some ridiculous speed. Lipinski struggled, both to keep up and to keep her lunch down. Watching those legs skitter like that reminded her *way* too much of—

Don't think about it.

They ran through some more underbrush, then came out at what Lipinski thought was another clearing, but was in fact a field of farmland. Lipinski hadn't the first clue what any of it was, and at the moment she didn't care, because it was what was in the middle of the field of crops that had her undivided attention.

It was a giant bug.

Dealing with the small bugs from home had been bad enough. *(Don't think about it.)* Dealing with serving on the same ship as a human-size bug had been barely tolerable.

But this—this thing was several meters long, had six icky, spindly legs that were all longer than Lipinski was tall, big wings that looked flimsy for all their size, and huge eyes that bore into her head like—

"Shoot it!"

Lipinski blinked. "What?" She realized that the bug was moving away from them at a speed that even Blue wouldn't be able to keep up with.

"Shoot it, or it'll get away!"

Setting her phaser on light stun with her encased right hand, she fired.

The bug didn't even notice the amber beam that struck its thorax.

Of course not, they're indesctructible, just like—

Don't think about it!

Raising the level to heavy stun, she fired again, just as the bug was going out of sight. However, heavy stun got the thing's attention. It stopped and started to turn.

She fired again.

It made some kind of odd noise, and also raised two of its legs in some kind of gesture. With growing confidence, Lipinski fired again. It made another odd noise/gesture combination, but she didn't let it bother her. *This isn't so bad.*

She believed that right up until it charged at her.

Oh God, I'm going to die, was the only thought that ran through her head as a several-meter-long bug that was roughly the size of the moon she grew up on charged toward her at some obscenely high speed. She couldn't move, she couldn't act, she couldn't breathe, she couldn't think beyond the fact that she was dead meat, and that she was—as she had always feared—going to die at the hands of an insect.

Then, suddenly, the insect stopped moving forward, as if it had crashed into something, just as the air crackled with—

With a force field. Of course. That was the plan, after all. I fire on it to distract it and goad it into coming close, then Blue hits it with the force field.

The insect continued to make odd noises, and gesture a lot.

"Sometimes," Lipinski muttered, "I really, really hate this job."

"Did you say something?" Blue asked.

"Nothing. What now?"

Blue made more of those damn noises of hers. "That's unfortunate."

"What is?"

"The UT can't make heads or tails of this. It's looking more and more likely that these things aren't sentient."

Lipinski made a face. "What, you thought these—these *things* might be?"

"Any particular reason why I shouldn't?"

While she couldn't really read Blue's tone very well, Lipinski realized that the Nasat probably took offense at that statement. "I'm sorry, it's just that—"

"That you're an entomophobe, and you can't imagine insectoid life being sentient."

In fact, that was exactly what Lipinski had been thinking, but Blue made it sound so . . . prejudicial.

That's probably because it is *prejudicial.*

"I'm sorry," she repeated, sounding more emphatic this time. "I guess old habits die hard."

"Usually, yes." She made another noise, then tapped her combadge. "Blue to Gomez."

"Go ahead."

"We've neutralized the large insect."

Blue then gave the coordinates of their location, to which the commander replied, *"Good work. I'll let the Law Enforcement Bureau know, and they'll collect it."*

"According to the reports from the Maegline, we've still got at least five more to go, correct?"

"Four, actually—Jil and Friesner got one also. Duffy, Drew, and I are hot on the trail of the pteranodon-like one, and Corsi and Stevens think they're close to the green one. You two see if you can track down one of the other two."

"Acknowledged." Blue tapped her combadge, reached into the bag she had tucked into her chitinous armor, and pulled out another force field generator. "Shall we?"

Lipinski took a long look at the force-field-encased giant insect as it kept wailing and gesturing.

Wish we had those damn force fields back home.

"Yeah, okay, let's go."

CHAPTER
7

I should've been a bird, Kieran Duffy thought giddily as he flew through the air.

In his life, both as a kid growing up and taking apart the family replicator, and later as a Starfleet engineer, Kieran had encountered all manner of technological devices, but his favorites were always the gravity boots his uncle got him for his sixteenth birthday.

The six months that followed that birthday were among the happiest of Kieran's life—and among the unhappiest of his parents', as they were convinced that he was going to break his neck crashing into something. Or several somethings. He wore the boots so much that Dad was convinced his feet had atrophied.

Unfortunately, where the pleas of his parents and the endless safety lectures from his uncle failed to curb his enthusiasm, biology succeeded. Kieran hit his growth spurt midway through his seventeenth year, and soon the boots no longer fit.

And there was no way in hell his parents were going to let him have another pair.

Then came Starfleet Academy and one of the happiest days of his life: when they *issued* him gravity boots as part of an exercise. After being denied his favorite toy for three years, someone willingly *gave* them to him.

He quickly amazed Professor Hsu with his prowess, and he was instantly recruited for the 3D polo team. He was captain of the team by senior year, and led the Academy to the championships twice.

But all of that was secondary to the sheer joy of being able to fly through the air unfettered like this. No encumbrances, no ship's walls surrounding you, nothing holding you in place. Being able to tell the wind was shifting just by listening to it. And the view was just spectacular.

Kieran particularly appreciated being able to take in Maeglin this way. The last time they were here, he had been too busy dealing with Overseer Biron and his Androssi goons to truly appreciate the natural beauty here. He could see what the Tellarites who founded the colony a century ago saw in it. Growing up in the heavily technological Earth of the twenty-fourth century, getting to see something as magnificently pastoral as Maeglin was a rare treat. Now he wished he'd ordered up more blue gravity boots so the rest of the crew could see what he was seeing.

"Lieutenant Commander Duffy, come in, *dammit!"*

"Yes, Mom!" Kieran said instinctively. "Uh, I mean, sorry, Commander."

"I've been calling you for a full minute." Sonnie sounded rather peeved.

"Sorry," he repeated. "I've been, uh, distracted."

"I'll bet. Well, get your head out of the clouds—"

Kieran couldn't resist. "That's gonna be hard up here."

A pause. *"I walked into that, didn't I?"*

"With both feet, your eyes wide open, and a bull's-eye on your face."

"You know, Kieran, between that and the 'Mom' line, you're cruising for a serious bruising when you come back down to earth."

"Yes, sir. Anyhow," he added quickly before Sonnie could reply, "any sign of the big guy?"

"Unfortunately, the duonetic field has kicked in, so we're not picking up anything. That's why I contacted you, I was hoping you saw something."

" 'Fraid not, but I—"

He cut himself off as he saw the giant orange shape flying right at him—and getting closer by the second.

"Check that, Sonnie, I've got him. I'll lead him to—" He looked around. "Aw, hell, I've lost my bearings. Where are you?"

"Right where you left us. Unfortunately, I have no idea where you *are, since the tricorder's out."*

"Joy."

Kieran immediately started flying toward the orange pteranodon-like creature. Just as it lunged right at him, he swerved downward. Luckily, gravity boots had controls on the inside and were manipulated by pressure made by the toes—Jil's paint had no effect on it the way it did on the touch-sensitive displays on other devices.

Angered, the creature flew down after Kieran, as planned—except, of course, Sonnie and Drew weren't right under him because he'd been too busy reliving his callow youth to pay attention to where he was. *Dammit, Duff, you're an officer now, not a sixteen-year-old. Clowning is one thing when it's just you and the gang horsing around, but we do have a job here.*

As he neared the tree line, Kieran angled his body upward and shifted the boots' acceleration so he'd start flying horizontally. It wasn't the most elegant of turns, but it didn't need to be, as long as he surprised his quarry.

Unfortunately, it was better equipped for flying than Kieran. It recovered quickly—and was gaining on him. *Figures. He's been flying all his life, I've been flying as a hobby on and off. Of course he's better at it.*

He found himself over a lake. *Okay, let's see how he likes this. Hope Jil made that stuff waterproof. . . .*

Again, he angled himself downward, again shifting the boots' acceleration. It was only about six meters down to the lake. *At least, I hope it's a lake. And it isn't a shallow one. Suppose I should've checked that before—*

He broke through the ice-cold water, which was like being repeatedly slapped by a wet towel. He went down about three meters before his momentum lessened enough to allow him to turn around.

No sign of him.

He looked up and saw a water-distorted image of the monster was circling the area of the lake that Kieran had dived into. *Guess he doesn't like the water.*

"Gomez to Duffy—we've got the tricorders again. And—what the hell're you doing underwater?"

Sound traveled just fine underwater, but Kieran was in no position to answer just yet. He watched the creature's pattern of flight around the lake for three revolutions, found a good window, and then fired the boots upward at the right moment so he would (he fervently hoped) surprise the creature and get the jump on it.

He burst through the water and zipped upward. The creature made an odd noise and some kind of motion with its tiny feet, then went up after him.

"Sorry about that, Sonnie," Kieran said, grateful for being able to breathe once again. "Needed to keep this thing busy for a minute. Where are you?"

"Keep flying due west for two hundred meters, then due south for fifty, and you should be right over us."

"Damn. I did stray, didn't I?"

"Just a bit, yeah."

"Sorry 'bout that. I should be in position in thirty seconds."

"Your friend is right behind you," Sonnie said, sounding worried.

Kieran had kind of figured that, though he didn't bother to turn around, as that would slow him down. By flying ramrod straight, he cut down on his wind resistance and was able to move faster through the air. With the monster's speed, he needed every advantage he could get.

After he turned south, he saw Sonnie and Drew pretty quickly. Sonnie was studying her tricorder intently, then looked up and smiled at him. Drew, of course, had his phaser ready like a good little security guard. Kieran immediately veered downward again, counting on the creature to follow.

He couldn't just land, though—he needed to dump velocity or he'd be a smear on the pastoral Maeglin ground—so he immediately veered back up, crying, "Get him!"

Unfortunately, the whole plan was predicated on his quarry following him down, Drew shooting it, and Sonnie slapping the force field on.

The creature, however, was not cooperating. It learned its lesson from the last time it followed Kieran in a downward trajectory and almost got wet. It remained circling over Sonnie and Drew.

Kieran's own trajectory took him back upward, and he slowed the boots down as he rose, then hovered in the air, even with the monster's circling, but from a distance of about thirty meters.

He tapped his combadge. "Okay, *that* didn't work."

"*Brilliant observation,*" Sonnie said dryly.

On one of its go-rounds, it must have caught sight of Kieran, because then it made another screechy noise, waved its feet some more, and flew right toward him.

"Yipe!" Kieran cried, and started flying away.

Drew, bless his heart, chose that moment to fire his phaser, which stopped the flying monster dead in its tracks.

The phaser blast didn't do any harm—it was only a light stun from the sounds of it—but it did force it to reconsider which human it was going to go after.

The hell with this, Kieran thought. He flew upward about fifty meters, then angled himself back downward, and flew straight for the ground—except for the fact that he had placed himself so that the creature was smack between him and the surface.

Which meant that it was rather surprised to find a human crashing into its back. At least, Kieran thought, it sounded surprised when he crashed into it.

They both went careening toward the ground. About half a second before they'd hit, Kieran threw the boots into full reverse.

Unfortunately, while doing so lessened the impact, it did not negate it as Kieran had hoped. They were going too fast, and the boots could only go so far against that momentum. The impact jarred every bone in his body. As he rolled off the monster crying, "Now!" in the hopes that it would prompt Sonnie to put it in the force field, he felt like one massive bruise.

"You okay?" Sonnie asked.

"Fine, did you—"

"Yes, I got the force field up. It's secure. Mind telling me what you were thinking?"

"I was thinking that—ow—we needed to convince it to come down to earth. I figured that would do it."

"You could've broken your neck!"

Note to self, Kieran thought, *do not ever let Sonnie know how much she sounds like my mother right now.*

CHAPTER
8

Bart Faulwell was practically on the edge of his seat in the observation lounge waiting for everyone else to arrive. Captain Gold was first, followed by Commander Gomez, then Pattie, and finally Carol Abramowitz and Dr. Lense came in together. Commander Duffy, Fabian Stevens, and Commander Corsi were missing, he noticed, but as soon as Carol and the doctor sat down, Gold started the meeting.

"Before we get down to brass tacks, how's Duffy doing?" Gold asked Lense.

"Emmett's taking care of him—he's fine, really, just some bumps and bruises."

"Good," Gold said, though Bart noticed that the captain seemed irked at the doctor for some reason. "Where are Stevens and Corsi?" he asked Gomez.

"Still down on the planet. There are two of these things unaccounted for, and they were hot on the trail of one of them—the big green one. The other one seems to have disappeared, but it's one of the ones the Maegline made a visual record of, so we know it's out there. And there could be more."

"Good. Now then, our linguist called this little confab, so—talk to us, Faulwell."

Bart leaned forward in his seat, trying not to sound overanxious. "I've been studying the recordings you've all been making on the planet and running them through my translation programs, trying to see if there's a language there that the UT isn't picking up for whatever reason." He touched a command on the panel in front of him, and the frozen image of one of the creatures came on the screen. "What was confusing was that I found the remnants of a language, but not enough to form a proper translation matrix. Parts of the structure seemed to be missing."

"'Remnants'?" Gomez asked with a frown. "What, they used to know how to talk but only remember parts of it now?"

"That was actually my first thought," Bart said, "but no, that's not it. The thing is, the UT, and all the other translation programs that have been developed over the years, work on either spoken or written language."

"What else is there?" Blue asked.

Bart grinned. "Watch and learn."

He touched the panel again, and the image started to move. It then switched to another creature, then another, then another.

"I don't get it," Abramowitz said, "what are we looking at?"

"I chose these particular images for a reason," Bart said. "They all have something in common."

"Gestures," Gold said suddenly. "They're each gesturing. In fact, most of those are the same gestures."

"Exactly!" Bart said, excited. "Are any of you familiar with sign language?"

"Sure," Gomez said. "I remember people talking about it on the *Enterprise*. It was right before I came on board—there was this diplomat who couldn't hear. When he lost his interpreters, Commander Data communicated with him through American sign language. It's an old way of talking—" she smiled, making the connection "—through gestures."

Bart nodded. "Exactly," he said again. "I remember reading about that mission, actually. Advances in technology made sign language pretty much redundant now, which is why your Commander Data had to dig it up in the archives. But there are some similarities between these gestures and some of the basics of the various sign languages developed by humans, Vulcans, and Bajorans centuries ago—enough that I was able to run it through the computer. I *think* we've got enough that we might be able to communicate with them."

Gold leaned forward. "So you can program the translators?"

Wincing, Bart said, "Probably not, sir. The UTs are geared toward spoken language—combadges don't have optical receptors to pick up the gestures, and their language is a *combination* of the verbalizing *and* the gestures. The UT just isn't equipped to handle that. I'll need to communicate with them directly and act as an interpreter—the same way Commander Data did on the *Enterprise*."

Smiling, Gomez said, "Good work, Bart. Captain, with your permission, Mr. Faulwell and I will beam down and start working on communicating with the ones we've captured."

"Granted," Gold said with a nod. "I'll talk to Governor Tak."

Sonya wished they had had time to stop at sickbay to check on Kieran. But right now the priority was to put Bart's plan into action. If these creatures were sentient, she just hoped they understood why the S.C.E. did what they did to round them up—after all, they *were* rampaging and causing severe damage to a colony that had enough problems. At least they had, so far, accomplished that goal in a manner that did the least harm to the creatures themselves.

Still, a trip to sickbay would've been nice, she thought as she, Bart, and Drew stepped onto the transporter platform. *If nothing else, it'd give me another chance to yell at him for being such a jerk.*

She still wasn't one hundred percent sure how she felt about Kieran. Maybe she did love him—but she certainly cared about him enough to really hate the idea of his taking such ridiculous risks with his person as he did today. *Being captain of the 3D polo team fifteen years ago does not mean you can fly like a lunatic now!*

Alas, that castigation would have to wait until
the mission was over—and would probably be
done in the privacy of one of their quarters rather
than the middle of sickbay. Which would make it
that much easier for Kieran to make it up to
her . . .

She smiled as they materialized on the planet.
As soon as they did, she put thoughts of the future
out of her head to concentrate on the present.

That present turned out to involve standing
around and waiting for Bart to work his magic.
The four creatures that had been rounded up—
besides Duffy's friend, Pattie and Lipinski had captured the insect and one that looked like a furry
orange ball with arms and legs and big eyes, and
Barnak and Friesner had nabbed the yellow scaly
one—were then brought to a large warehouse near
the capitol building. Here, they had been kept captive by a larger version of the force field, emitting
from a bright blue generator.

Bart slowly approached the warehouse, and
started making odd noises and gesturing. This
seemed to surprise the creatures, who all moved
away from him. Then one of them—the insect—
moved closer.

"Commander?" Drew asked, pointing at the
insect. "Who was it who captured that one?"

"Pattie and Lipinski. Why?"

"Hmp."

"What does 'hmp' mean, exactly, Mr. Drew?"
Sonya asked with a smile.

"Oh, it's just that . . . well, Andrea's kinda got
this . . . well . . . this *thing* about bugs."

"Bugs."

"Uh-huh. Don't know the details—something happened when she was a kid—but she *really* hates bugs. I think it's kinda funny that Corsi put her with Blue *and* they wound up corralling the insect, that's all."

"Funny's one word for it," Sonya said neutrally. She made a mental note to have a word with Corsi about Lipinski when this was over.

Bart, meanwhile, continued his dialogue with the monsters, which seemed to be going well, based on the fact that the conversation was fairly sedate, the monsters weren't smashing up against the force field in an attempt to maul Bart, and Bart had on his intense-but-enthusiastic look. He'd had it when he was plowing through the Syclarian journal last week at BorSitu Minor, too, and Sonya enjoyed seeing it.

At one point, the insect was doing almost all of the talking, with Bart only throwing in the occasional comment, then Bart "spoke" for several seconds. *And still not a peep from the universal translators. I guess the gestures really are critical to this language.*

Then, finally, Bart turned and walked back to Sonya with a grave look on his face. "We've got a serious problem, Commander."

CHAPTER
9

Domenica Corsi stared at Fabian Stevens as he smacked his tricorder on the side, and wondered why she had assigned herself to him.

She'd mostly been avoiding Fabe—Stevens—since Empok Nor. It was better that way. Lense knew about their tryst, but she wouldn't say anything, and miraculously, the gossip hadn't seemed to spread beyond some salacious remarks made by Hawkins and Drew. Stevens himself hadn't said a word—he'd done just as she requested, treated it as a one-time thing with no strings.

So why did she choose to spend all this time alone with him now?

She wasn't sure. It wasn't like she took advantage of the time at all, since they only had duty-related conversation while they tried to track down one of the extradimensional things and encase it in one of Blue's force fields.

This one had already destroyed one person's farm—the owner, a cranky old Tellarite named

Malk, had carried on for several minutes on the subject—and had moved on to another farm down the road. At present, they were about a hundred meters away from that house, and getting closer.

Unfortunately, that duonetic field that the Androssi inflicted on Maeglin was now interfering with the tricorder, so they'd lost their mark.

"Aha!" Stevens said suddenly.

"What?"

He held up the tricorder and smiled. "We have achieved tricorder. And our green monster is right up this way."

As he moved forward, Corsi held up the phaser with her right hand, the remote control in her force-field-encased left.

"I just want to say—" she said, then cut herself off.

Stevens, still looking at the tricorder, said, "What?"

"I wanted to thank you."

Now Stevens did look. He seemed confused. "For what?"

"For not saying anything about—about what happened last month."

"You asked me not to," Stevens said with a shrug. "Assuming you really meant it, what else was I supposed to do? You asked me not to tell anyone, and I didn't. You also indicated that it wasn't the beginning of anything, so I don't expect it to be."

Corsi frowned. "What do you mean, 'assuming you really meant it'?"

Stevens stopped and turned to look at her. "Did you really mean it?"

"Of course!" she said angrily.

Again, he shrugged. "Then it's no big deal. I'm not going to betray a confidence. It was what it was, and we've moved on." He peered back down at the tricorder. "It's still in the same spot. Let's go."

Shaking her head, Corsi said, "Right. Of course." *Focus on duty,* she thought. *And he's right, we've moved on.*

So why the hell do I keep harping on it?

They soon came within sight of a large structure that was dwarfed by the much larger green bipedal creature standing over it—and bleeding a yellow ichor from its side. It was also holding a Tellarite in its massive green claw. Corsi noticed some kind of primitive projectile weapon on the ground near the creature.

Indicating the tableau with her head, Corsi said, "My guess is that our friend there shot the big guy with that weapon on the ground."

Stevens nodded. "And the big guy took umbrage."

"He ain't seen umbrage yet," Corsi said as she raised her phaser. She may not have had the best handle on her feelings, but now she was in her element.

"Gomez to Corsi."

"I'm a little busy, Commander—one of our new playmates is about to squeeze the life out of a Tellarite."

"Don't shoot it, Domenica, that's an order!"

"What?"

Then came the voice of Diego Feliciano, the *da Vinci's* transporter chief. *"I'm locked on to their position, Commander."*

"Energize."

Moments later, Drew, Gomez, and Faulwell materialized a meter to Corsi's right.

Before the transporter effect had even died down, Gomez was holding up one hand. "Don't fire, Commander—there's more to this than we thought."

Faulwell started to move closer to the creature and then started bellowing at it and gesticulating madly.

"What the hell—?"

Gomez added, "You and Drew keep your phasers ready, and put 'em on heavy stun. If there's any kind of move against the Tellarite or Bart, go ahead and fire, but *only then*, understood?"

Corsi let out a breath between her teeth. "You're the boss."

Faulwell continued his bizarre diatribe. After a minute, the creature put the Tellarite down.

"It's okay, sir," Faulwell said to the Tellarite, who ran for his weapon. "Please, Afredaspweo-tynerek doesn't mean you any harm. He's just confused."

"That *grabthar* tried to kill me!"

With an anger Corsi wouldn't have expected from the usually easygoing linguist, Faulwell asked, "Was that before or after you shot him?"

"I was defending my home!" And the Tellarite went to pick up his weapon.

Corsi nodded to Drew and they both aimed their phasers at the Tellarite. "Touch it and you won't get the chance to pick it up."

Ignoring them, the Tellarite bent over. The moment his fingers touched the weapon, Corsi and Drew both fired. The Tellarite fell over, stunned.

Stevens looked at Faulwell. "What goes on here, Bart? Is Fred here a good guy after all?"

"And what about the farm he trashed?" Corsi asked. She didn't see any good reason to let the Tellarite shoot the creature again, but she wasn't completely ready to trust this—"Fred" yet.

"Back where he comes from, he's a prisoner."

"What!?" Corsi raised her weapon and aimed it at "Fred."

"A *political* prisoner!" Faulwell said quickly, holding up his hands. "He and the others we captured were rounded up by someone called Grujaerpoiucdwqil—he's like that furry one we still haven't tracked down yet." Corsi noticed that every use of a proper name for one of these creatures was accompanied by some kind of weird gesture. "He apparently rounded up everyone who wasn't like him and put them in prisons. When the gateway opened, these six were sent in to test it out. The feeling was, they were prisoners, they were expendable, so they'd send them in first. Then the gateways shut down, and they were stuck.

"The problem was, nobody could talk to them, and all their attempts at communication failed—obviously, since we couldn't talk to them, either.

They're sorry for the destruction they caused, but they were lost and confused. They want to make amends."

"And you believe them?" Corsi asked, shocked at Faulwell's naïveté.

"Yes. Because they have no reason to lie—and because they could have broken out of the force fields any time they wanted."

Even Gomez was surprised at that. "What?"

"Yes, Commander—they can. We can even prove it now. Fabe?"

Faulwell held out his hands. Smiling, Stevens tossed the force field generator, and Faulwell caught it. He put it on the ground, said several things while gesticulating some more to "Fred," then turned on the force field.

Moments later, "Fred" literally walked *through* the force field.

Corsi felt her jaw drop. "How in the hell did he *do* that?"

"They all can," Faulwell said. "But they realized what was going on when they were being rounded up, and they decided that it would be better if they bided their time until they could communicate properly. Until we started corralling them, they didn't even realize they'd done anything wrong."

Gomez nodded. "Hopefully, we can defuse this and figure out what to do—without all the property damage."

Stevens grinned. "That'll depend on whether or not the Maegline are all as trigger-happy as Farmer Brown here."

Returning the grin, Gomez said, "Governor Tak is more reasonable, I'm sure."

"He'd almost have to be," Drew muttered.

Corsi, however, noticed that Faulwell was still having a conversation with "Fred."

"Uh, Commander?" he said, turning back to Gomez.

"Yes?"

"We've got a bit of a problem."

"What?"

"You know the last prisoner left—the one we haven't caught—is of the same race as the one that's in power in their home dimension?"

Gomez closed her eyes. "I just know I'm not going to like this."

"You're not. The five we've got were all political prisoners. The other one—his name is Natywpaw-erldatqwewob—is a criminal. A psychopath."

Corsi let out a very loud curse.

"Blue to Gomez—Commander, the last creature has broken through the force field, and phaser fire is having no effect, repeat no effect, not even on the highest setti—ooof!"

Gomez tapped her combadge. "Gomez to Feliciano. Diego, lock onto Blue and Lipinski, get them out of there, *now!*"

One second later, Feliciano said, *"Got 'em, Commander. Ay, madre—Feliciano to sickbay, medical emergency!"*

"What's happening, Diego?" Gomez asked anxiously.

"Both Blue and Lipinski are unconscious, Commander—and Lipinski's bleeding like crazy."

"Dammit!" Gomez said.

"Commander," Faulwell said, "Afredaspweo-tynerek says he can take care of Natywpawerld-atqwewob."

"Tell Afredas— Tell 'Fred' we appreciate it, Bart, but—"

"Fred" let out a wail and gesticulated like crazy. Corsi had a feeling that he was pretty emphatic about whatever point he was making.

Faulwell gave a quick reply to the creature, then said, "Commander, we can't stop Natywpawer-ldatqwewob without his help. You heard Pattie— not only won't the force fields work, neither will the phasers."

Gomez frowned. "We'll stop them together. Corsi, set phasers on maximum." She tapped her combadge. "Gomez to Feliciano. Six to beam to the location where you transported Blue and Lipinski."

CHAPTER
10

Afredaspweotynerek knew that this was going to happen. He and the others had tried to reason with the creatures, tried communicating in every way they knew how. They hadn't realized the harm they had done until Bartfaulwell's people took punitive action. True, it wasn't really effective, but Afredaspweotynerek and the others knew it was best to bide their time. Bartfaulwell justified that faith.

But Natywpawerldatqwewob was another problem entirely. Afredaspweotynerek and the others just wanted to be free of Grujaerpoiucdwqil's tyranny. Natywpawerldatqwewob, though, he wanted to kill things. As many things as possible.

"We're about to be transported," Bartfaulwell explained.

"I don't understand."

"Like the gateway that brought you here, only not so big a jump. We can move from place to place."

Suddenly, Afredaspweotynerek felt an odd tingling sensation. When it cleared up, he found himself in a different place.

Truly, Bartfaulwell's people could do wonders. Yes, Afredaspweotynerek decided, he was going to like this place.

Assuming, of course, that they could stop Natywpawerldatqwewob. Afredaspweotynerek saw the killer just as he was slashing through one of the natives of this world.

One of Bartfaulwell's people cried out and fired her weapon at Natywpawerldatqwewob. Unfortunately, it only served to anger him.

Another of Bartfaulwell's people made a noise, and then two of them fired their weapons for a more prolonged period.

Natywpawerldatqwewob's response was to lunge after them. Afredaspweotynerek feared for the lives of his new friends—not to mention the lives of his comrades. They had a chance to start over, make a new life, but if Natywpawerldatqwewob kept up his killing ways, it might never happen.

Afredaspweotynerek would not allow that. He ran toward Natywpawerldatqwewob, saying to Bartfaulwell as he ran, "Tell your people to stay back. Natywpawerldatqwewob will kill them!"

"What are you going to do?" Bartfaulwell asked.

"What I must."

At that, Natywpawerldatqwewob laughed. "Do not be a fool, Afredaspweotynerek. I will kill you as easily as I killed that minuscule life form." He indicated the fallen male native of the world, who was presently being stood over by two females, one his own size, one considerably smaller.

"I will not let you harm these people anymore!"

"You'll have to stop me!"

"Oh, I plan to."

Then Afredaspweotynerek slashed at Natywpawerldatqwewob with his claws.

The clash was an epic one. Afredaspweotynerek was stronger than Natywpawerldatqwewob, but Natywpawerldatqwewob was faster. He ducked under Afredaspweotynerek's attack, and slashed with his own claws. Afredaspweotynerek blocked that and kicked at his foe, but he was able to avoid it.

Afredaspweotynerek was not sure how long he struggled against Natywpawerldatqwewob. The only thing he knew for sure was that he was losing ground. Gathering all his strength, Afredaspweotynerek managed to flip Natywpawerldatqwewob over his head.

But even as he crashed to the ground in a heap, Natywpawerldatqwewob made a grab for one of the bits of flora that Bartfaulwell called "trees" and ripped it from the ground. He swung it at Afredaspweotynerek, who was too fatigued from being shot and from the fight to dodge it.

The impact collided with Afredaspweotynerek's head, and he, too, fell to the ground. He tried to force himself to get up, but Natywpawerldatqwewob got to his feet first, still holding the "tree."

Before Afredaspweotynerek could react, Natywpawerldatqwewob rammed the tree through his chest.

Afredaspweotynerek had felt pain before—particularly during his interrogation at the hands of Grujaerpoiucdwqil's enforcers—but nothing like this. He could feel the life flowing out of him.

Natywpawerldatqwewob laughed. "You are such a fool. Now I will kill everyone on this planet—perhaps everyone in this entire universe!"

Fury gripped Afredaspweotynerek. Bartfaulwell and the others stood no chance. Natywpawerldatqwewob had killed at least one person, possibly more. Afredaspweotynerek could not let this go on, no matter what the cost.

He gripped the "tree" with his talons, his yellow claws digging into the plant's surface. Though pain racked his body, he yanked on it. Unfortunately, it didn't come out. Afredaspweotynerek almost blacked out from the wrenching agony, but somehow he forced himself to try again.

Gripping the "tree" even tighter, he pulled upward—and the plant was free!

Of course now his life was draining from his body at a great rate. He had only a short time to get to Natywpawerldatqwewob before he expired. But he would not die without taking that murderer down, too!

Screaming a cry of anguish, he lunged after Natywpawerldatqwewob, who had moved on to try to kill Bartfaulwell and his people. In fact, Natywpawerldatqwewob had one of them gripped in his talons, much as Afredaspweotynerek had held that native who shot him. She looked like she would be dead in a minute.

"No more deaths!" Afredaspweotynerek cried with the last of his breath as he heaved the "tree" into Natywpawerldatqwewob's back.

Then the world went dark, as he fell to the ground once more.

CHAPTER
11

"Report," Captain Gold said from the head of the observation lounge table.

Sonya tried not to scratch the bandage on her side. She had only just gotten all her movement back from when the monster shii ripped her torso open on Sarindar, and then she got hoisted by *another* monster. "Governor Tak has agreed to take in the remaining four creatures—"

"They're called Yewqapoiueqrpoui," Bart said helpfully.

"—and provide them with homes. One of them, in fact, specifically said he'd work on the farm owned by that man that Nat killed."

"Nat?" Gold asked.

"For simplicity's sake, we started referring to the green one as 'Fred' and the furry one as 'Nat.' Mr. Faulwell's the only one who's been able to properly pronounce their full names."

Gold chuckled. "Fine. Go on."

"In any case, the governor was moved by the

sacrifice that Fred made—basically giving his life to prevent more Maegline from being killed. And he was especially appreciative of the fact that the, uh, Yukes were willing to be captured the way they were."

"The only problem," Bart said, "is communication. The UT won't work with a language that integrates so much with a physical component. So, sir—I'd like to request permission to stay here for a while, to teach the Maegline how to speak to the Yewqapoiueqrpoui and to teach them how to speak Tellarite."

"Unfortunately, we can't stick around," Gold said. "It looks like all the gateways *mishegoss* has calmed down, and we're back on our usual duties—which means we have to pick up some mining equipment at Starbase 413 and then head to Beta Argola." He grinned. "But that's not something that'll require a linguist, I don't think. We'll muddle through without you for a few weeks, Faulwell."

"Thank you, sir," Bart said with a smile.

"Is there any way to get these people home?" Gold asked Sonya.

She shook her head. "They're not interested. They were prisoners, and with the gateways shut down, there's probably no way to get them back home even if they wanted to go."

Gold leaned back. "Well, if the Maegline don't mind having them, and they don't mind being there . . ."

"Sir," Bart said, "Afredaspweotynerek—Fred— died so that the Yewqapoiueqrpoui could have a

new home. I think we owe it to him to do everything to allow that, rather than waste our energy
trying to open a dimensional portal for no good
reason."

"Fair enough," Gold said with a chuckle. "How
we doing on the casualty front?"

"Only one Maegline died—the one Nat killed.
His wife and little girl are a bit bruised. The girl—
her name is Lin—was pretty traumatized, but her
mother seemed to think she'd be all right. Beyond
that, the only real damage on-planet was structural, and, even with the duonetic field, that's fix-
able."

"What about our people?"

Sonya folded her hands in front of her on the
table. "Lipinski and Blue will both be okay.
Lipinski's out of action for at least a week—she got
torn up pretty bad by Nat." Grinning wryly while
gingerly patting her side, she added, "I know how
she feels, believe me. Pattie only needs a day or
two, though."

"What about Duffy?"

"He's fine. He'll be back on duty next shift." *And
he'd better not think he's off the hook for that lame-
brained stunt.*

"All right. Get some sleep, Commander. And
Faulwell?"

"Sir?"

"Good luck," he said with a smile. "And try not
to get too attached to Maeglin—we still need you
here."

Chuckling as he got up, Bart said, "Don't worry,
sir. Farm life isn't really for me."

"Bridge to Gold."

"Go ahead," Gold said as Bart left.

"Message from the Malinche, sir. They'll be here in thirty minutes, and they'll be ready to take charge of the situation."

Gold looked at Sonya. Sonya looked at Gold.

They both laughed for several seconds.

"Sir?"

"Nothing, McAllan. Tell them to take their time."

AMBUSH

Dave Galanter &
Greg Brodeur

CHAPTER
1

"**A**rrrrrgh!" Christian Basile pulled back his freshly bleeding hand. He gritted his teeth and protectively pulled his wrist toward his chest.

"What happened?" Maria came running up the stone corridor. "What did you do?"

Christian grunted. "I was trying to seal a coupling and my hand slipped. The damn backup generator was down again. I got 'er going but—at a cost." He tentatively showed her his blood-covered hand.

"Oh, my." Maria's eyes widened at the sight of the gash on her husband's hand. She took off her scarf and wrapped it tightly around his palm and the base of his fingers. "We need to let the doctor see that."

He shook his head. "Later. Now that the backup is online again I want to make sure she stays that way." With his good hand Christian pulled a tricorder from his overalls and flipped it open.

As it chirped alive, Maria took the tricorder

from him and put it into the back pocket of her work belt. "You're *going* to see the doctor."

He ignored her and pushed past to the computer console at her left. "I think—" He made the mistake of touching the control board with his bad hand. "Arrgh!"

"Don't do that!" She rushed forward and pulled his arm back.

"Excellent advice," he said through clenched teeth, but had finished pulling up the data he needed. "I think we're going to be okay for a while."

Maria tentatively guided him toward the center of the mining complex. "Until it breaks down again."

"Yes, until then." He shook his head and let her guide him. "She's a finicky one."

He sensed playfulness in Maria's mock frown. "Why do you keep calling it a she?" she asked.

"Because she has me up at all hours tending to her every need, and I spend the longest time trying to please her, only to get a tiny bit of happiness in return. She's the definition of 'high maintenance.' What else could she be, but a she?"

Maria groaned. "That's mind-numbingly sexist."

"It's the Ferengi in me," he said, chuckling.

"You're from Alpha Centauri," she reminded him unnecessarily. "Not a very sexist culture. And you do *not* have any Ferengi in you."

"You said you'd never hold my small lobes against me."

She laughed. "Listen to me and get this straight," she said, stopping them both and pulling him to her. "If lobe size mattered, I'd never have married you in the first place." She kissed him.

"I know," he said around the kiss.

"I know you know," she mumbled, touching his lips with hers, then his chin, then his cheek.

"So . . . you don't really think I'm a sexist?" By now he'd mostly forgotten his throbbing hand. He kissed her again.

Maria pulled back just long enough to answer. "You don't taste like a sexist."

"Neither do you," he murmured, then grunted in pain—she had pressed against his hand.

Her brows knitting, she gasped and saw her scarf was now soaked with blood. "We have to get that looked at."

He nodded and they continued walking. "I'm hoping the doctor recommends *bed* rest," he said, and winked at her.

"You're hoping bed, but not rest."

"Yes, I—"

A chirping alert from the tricorder cut off his thought and he quickly stopped to check it, pulling it clumsily from Maria's belt.

"It's the backup generator again." Closing the tricorder, he handed it back to her. "Something else this time. How are we on batteries?"

Maria sighed and brushed a strand of dark hair from her eyes. He loved her hair, her olive skin . . . he should be thinking of the reactor.

"Last I checked we had forty-three percent charge."

"I wish we could increase the rate of charge," he said, "but I think we'd blow the circuits again."

"Can you fix the new problem? What is it?"

"Overload because the mix isn't clean on the reactor. I'm going to fiddle with the mix again and reset."

"Of course." She nodded. "Do you need—?"

"A hand?" He raised his bad paw but shook his head. "Tell the doctor I'll stop by the infirmary when I'm done."

She nodded. He could tell she didn't like letting him work on the generator before seeing the doctor, but she also knew how important it was to keep power running on a class-D planetoid.

"I'll let people know the power will be back soon."

"And see if you can reach the *da Vinci* again," Christian added as he trudged back toward the reactor section. "We've got to get the replacement parts, or we're all going to freeze . . . if we don't suffocate first."

"We'll keep it together," she said encouragingly. "And they'll be here soon."

"Shields!" Captain Gold bellowed from the command chair just as the first volley of phaser fire crackled across the *da Vinci*'s bow. "Red alert."

"They're coming around again," McAllan called from tactical.

Gold nodded. "All hands, battle stations. Evasive action, Wong." He gestured to ops. "Ina, try to hail them."

"They're jamming all the channels, sir," Lieutenant Ina Mar replied.

"Did our message to Starfleet make it out?" Gold asked.

Ina shook her head. "I'm not sure, Captain."

McAllan huffed out a frustrated breath. "Let's hope so. I'm reading two more ships coming in."

"Who the hell are they?" Gold barked.

"Checking configuration." David McAllan's voice was unwavering in the heat of the battle. "Mid-size cruiser . . . design used by the Munqu. We have a file on them, but I've never seen one."

An explosion rattled the bridge and sent a shudder up everyone's spine.

"Well, now you have," Gold said. "With this reception, I could have waited."

"Battle stations! All hands, battle stations! First officer, report to the bridge!"

Not a call often heard on the *da Vinci*, Sonya Gomez thought as she hurried to the turbolift. *Battle stations? Who'd be attacking us?* Starfleet Corps of Engineers ships weren't usually called into battle—hers was the type of ship that went in *after* a battle, to clean up the mess left behind.

The turbolift doors opened to a much more chaotic bridge than Gomez was used to seeing. An aft console looked like so much slag and one of Chief Engineer Barnak's noncoms was already working on it. *Saber*-class ships had cramped bridges to begin with, but for some reason, with the red lights of their alert status blinking and the burned-out console, it felt even more claustrophobic. Like most Starfleet vessels, the *da Vinci* had a circular two-level bridge, with the captain's chair in the center on the lower level, the conn and ops positions right in front of him, tactical right behind him, and various science and engineering stations lining the wall, broken only by the turbolift to the captain's left, a door to the captain's right, and the viewscreen right in front of him.

That viewscreen presently showed what looked to Gomez like a Munqu ship firing on them.

"I thought the Munqu were pretty reclusive. Why are they attacking?"

"They seem to be coming out of their shell," Gold deadpanned as another aft console exploded and they both cringed just the slightest bit.

"Do we know what they want?"

"They're jamming communications," Ina offered.

"We might have gotten a call out to Starfleet, but I'm not counting on it," Gold told Gomez.

It made no sense. *Who attacks such a small ship with a crew of mostly technical experts for no reason?* The *da Vinci* was on a fairly simple mission to restock a mining colony and transport back a mineral important to cure a Horta plague on Janus IV. Not exactly a covert mission to steal new cloaking technology or repair the engines of a disabled dilithium cargo freighter.

"Sir," McAllan called, "shields are down to forty-seven percent. We seem to be more maneuverable, but they're packing more of a punch."

"Do we have any data on these ships?" Gomez asked. "Weak spots?"

McAllan shook his head. "Only what we're scanning now. There's nothing but the basics in the database."

Gomez tapped her combadge. "Abramowitz, report to the bridge."

Gold nodded. "Good call."

Grunting as he pushed the ship this way and that, Ensign Songmin Wong spoke from the conn station. "Sir, I think they're trying to disable us. Multiple shots at our port nacelle, where the shields are weakest."

"Is this about our mission?" Gold thought aloud. "Why would the Munqu want to keep us from the Beta Argola colony? It's the smallest of mining operations."

"I was wondering the same. All I can think of is that we're stocked to the struts with mining equipment," Gomez said. "If they've scanned that, maybe they want it."

"Badly enough to attack a Federation starship?" Yet another explosion racked the bridge, and Gold frowned at Wong. "Ensign, 'evasive' means *evade*."

Nervously, Wong struggled with his console. "Aye, sir."

Cultural specialist Carol Abramowitz entered the bridge and began to ask what was happening. With a raised hand, Gold held off her comment for a moment and turned to McAllan. "Continue to return fire. If we're more maneuverable, let's use that as best we can, people."

"It's three to one, sir," McAllan said. "I can keep it up, but they're gonna hit us here and there."

On cue, phaser fire spread out across the forward viewer. A near miss. "I see that," Gold said.

Best not to distract Wong, Gomez thought, and Gold obviously thought the same as he turned to the ops officer. "Ina, try to break through their jamming. At least to the miners. Maybe we can warn them, *if* this does involve them." The captain then turned to Abramowitz. "What do you know about the Munqu?"

"Off the top of my head, not much, sir," Abramowitz said, her close black hair reflecting orange in the red alert lights. "First contact was around Stardate 43200, and has been limited to minor border disagreements. They've been classified as mildly xenophobic."

Gold frowned and ran a hand through his thin white hair. "I'm thinking that classification needs to be revised."

"That's all I get." Christian sighed. He re-coded the frequency scanner, then did it again, and then one more time. Nothing.

"Replay it," his wife offered, and she cocked her ear toward the nearest speaker.

With his now healed hand, Christian tabbed at the console and replayed the sketchy subspace message.

Static crackled as it spat from the speakers. "*—is the—ship* da Vinci— . . .—*attack—*"

"That's all there is." He frowned deeply and Maria touched him lightly on the shoulder. Sincere if futile reassurance. She was always his strength in times thick with misfortune.

"I think I heard the word attack," she said finally.

He nodded. "Me too." That was why the message was a frightening one. Was *da Vinci* under attack, or was there going to be an attack on Beta Argola? And more importantly, *why?* Beta Argola was a nice mining colony, but there were surely others that were nicer. Heck, the thing was only two thousand kilometers from one end to another, and half as thick. Gravity was artificial—meaning expensive. If not for it having the element the Horta needed, Christian and his team would have chosen any number of others.

Lingering her gaze on what Christian knew was a cheerless visage, Maria finally said, "Let's try and reach the authorities."

Again, he nodded somberly. "Starbase 413 or wide-band to Starfleet?" Should they risk sending out a wide-band transmission if someone was gunning for them after the *da Vinci?*

"Both." She began keying in the messages. "We should reach anyone we can."

He nodded agreement. "What about replying to the *da Vinci?*"

"I've tried," Maria said with a sigh. "No response."

Christian felt as if a sharp rock was jabbing his gut from the inside out—concern for himself, for his wife, and the thirteen others on the small colony. He inwardly chuckled at calling it a colony. It wasn't as if it were a permanent settlement with a lasting infrastructure and shields. They were pretty defenseless. They had nonmilitary-issue hand phasers and a few phaser-rifles, sure, but it was numbers that counted, and those were few. They had a protective dome, but that could be ruptured easily by a ship with disruptors or phasers . . . he didn't even want to think what a photon or quantum torpedo could do.

He let his gaze settle on his wife, then moved it to the rock and dirt floor at their feet. Antimatter blasting had cleared out their habitat caverns in a few weeks and since they moved from the cargo ship to the settlement, they'd made what felt like a home. While there was always a danger living in space, it was easy to become complacent.

But now? Now Christian was having a hard time not thinking they might die out here.

He rubbed the wish for sleep from his eyes. He was tired, very tired, and really didn't want to think at all.

Unfortunately, it wasn't the time to stop thinking.

CHAPTER
2

"Any answer from Starfleet?" Gold hovered over Ina's ops console and peered down at the frequency logs. He saw what she did: a dearth of incoming messages.

"Just static, sir. I think I'm getting feedback from Beta Argola, though. With some work I may be able to make contact." Her hands did a coordinated dance over her console. "It's possible they got the first message, but I can't confirm."

"We need to reach *them*, if no one else," Gold said, pacing toward the command chair. "This attack is no coincidence. And if the colony isn't getting pounded now, they will be soon." The captain didn't know that for a fact, of course, but it seemed the only conclusion. There was nothing civilized out this far but that planetoid and the *da Vinci*. The Munqu hadn't had a lot of contact with the Federation, but Abramowitz had dug up enough in the databanks to let Gold know something like this attack *was* within their ability, both technically and politically.

"Tactical," Gold ordered as he settled into the command chair and looked up toward the main viewscreen. He didn't like what he saw. His shoulders and jaw tightened a bit. He had to keep reminding himself that his ship was more maneuverable, but when outnumbered three to one that wasn't the bee's knees. The *da Vinci* was taking on a lot of damage. Shield generators were showing signs of overload. Warp engines were off-line so they couldn't escape. It seemed their *only* advantage was that they were avoiding more than half the enemy's shots.

After taking it all in, Gold motioned Gomez to his side. "Commander, assuming we didn't get through to Starfleet, how can we increase the damage we're doing to their ships? If we can just disable them long enough to repair warp drive, we can break away out of jamming range, then call for reinforcements and head for Beta Argola."

Gomez's brows knitted in thought. "Yes, sir. Increase the damage, hm?"

"I have a ship full of engineers here," Gold said with a wry smile and a fleeting glance at the twirling starscape view as Wong maneuvered them away from Munqu phasers. "Surely we can put them to use. What materials do we have aboard that could be used defensively or offensively?"

"Nothing that I can . . ." She paused. Gold knew that look in her eyes: drip-drop, drip-drop. Engineers didn't often have a flood of ideas. Their genius was in gathering the dew from leaves of intelligence and experience. "Mining equipment," she said, finally. "The cargo bays are filled with it. They're overflowing, in fact."

"Can you use it?"

Not yet quite sure of just how she'd do that, Gomez nodded anyway. "We'll find a way, sir."

Somewhere a relay noisily blew itself to bits. The lights went out for a moment, and then the emergency lights kicked in.

"Damn! Three against one!" Wong was struggling with his console and the captain could hear the frustration and tension in the man's voice.

"Steady, son, steady," Gold offered encouragingly as he got up from the center seat and put a heartening hand on the conn officer's shoulder. "Don't be afraid to improvise." He glanced to Gomez, who was now holding onto a handrail.

On the forward viewer, as the starscape and the Munqu ships sped wildly this way and that, Gold and the bridge crew watched as enemy phaser fire shot harmlessly away from the *da Vinci.*

Gold decided he had to be a little more proactive. Bloody a nose and make the Munqu think hard about being so aggressive.

"Come about, two-ten mark thirty. Full impulse."

Wong nodded. "Aye, sir."

One eye on the tactical display, another on the main viewer, Gold instinctively leaned right and called out, "Evasive starboard. Phasers, fire at alpha target."

Hot amber phaser lances sliced into the closest Munqu vessel, sizzling against the enemy's shields and pushing her off course.

"That was a good hit," Ina said, bowed over her sensors. "We knocked their fore shields down to forty-seven percent."

"Tack the other way," Gold ordered. "McAllan, fire when within range of gamma target."

After a brief pause, the tactical officer stabbed at his console. "Firing."

The Munqu ships flanked the *da Vinci* on either side as she pursued their sistership. Phaser shots and even a torpedo blast flared past as the Federation starship bit into its opponent.

With that second blow, all three Munqu ships pulled back a bit, opening a large radius in which the *da Vinci* was trapped.

"Captain, we're being hailed," Ina said. "Audio only, sir."

"Looks like someone got the message." Gold motioned toward the speaker above him. "Let's hear it."

"Surrender your vessel, or we will be forced to destroy you." A harsh voice, medium—if hyper—in tone.

Gold waited, not hesitating, but making his adversary stew a bit. "And you are?" he asked finally.

"I . . . I am the one who commands you to surrender."

"Oh, you do, do you?" The captain sneered and made a throat-slashing gesture with his right hand. "Cut this guy off."

"What do they want?" McAllan asked, continuing to punch commands into his weapons computer.

"Like I said, my guess," Gomez began, edging toward the command chair but still holding the rail behind her, "is that they want the mining equipment. And maybe the colony as well."

"I thought the colony was only mining cribintium for us," Ina offered. "The Horta need it to cure a plague."

The captain shook his head. "They also mine topaline and aridium. Not exactly as rare as dilithium—"

"It's possible they're after the cribintium," Gomez said. "It's very rare, and the Federation would be willing to pay anyone rather than let the Horta die."

"So they'd mine it out from under us and sell it back?" Wong was incredulous but didn't turn toward the conversation. His gaze was squarely on the helm.

"More like they'd mine it and ransom it back." Gold nodded at his own estimation at what was the most likely scenario. "By the time another starship could get here to stop them, they'll have strip-mined the place."

"Assuming we didn't get through to the fleet."

"We'll assume we didn't, and so we have to handle this ourselves," Gold said. "They've probably been monitoring Beta Argola's transmissions and know why we're here, with what cargo, and think us easy pickings. Let's show them we're not."

All nodded, but it was McAllan who spoke first with the ray of hope they needed. "I think I have something," he said, calling Gold's attention to the tactical station.

The captain almost leapt up toward him. "Go."

"Their sensor array is basically Paridian technology." McAllan punched up a screen graphic of the Munqu ship's sensor array. As he did this, Gold noticed he was also programming a firing sequence into the phaser control computer. *Talented kid.*

"There's the flaw we're looking for," Gomez said, reading over the captain's shoulder.

Gold nodded. "I've seen the Paridian systems. Neutrino blast?"

"Yes, sir." McAllan's hands were jitterbugging over his console as he looked at the captain and Gomez and still continued to explain. "A highly compressed neutrino blast from our deflector into their sensor array should overload their grid."

"For a while, anyway," Gomez added.

The captain gestured for McAllan to make it happen. "Think positive thoughts."

"Reconfiguring our deflector," McAllan said. "Ina, I'll need your help."

"On it, Mac," Ina called from ops. Another explosion against the shields, and she added, "And I'm hurrying."

A few minutes passed and eventually McAllan looked up, his lips turned up into a smile. "Ready, sir."

Lowering himself into the command chair, his back tight with tension, the captain gestured toward the main viewer. "Engage."

An electrical buzz vibrated the deck plates as the first shot missed the nearest Munqu ship.

"Again," Gold ordered.

A connection with the second shot had McAllan mouthing a joyful *yes*.

Two more shots would fire, before finally the last two attempts connected dead-on.

A cheer rose across the small bridge.

"Excellent, Lieutenant. Nice shooting." The captain gave his tactical officer an approving nod.

"Thank you, sir." McAllan was still grinning but looking down at his console as well. "Without sensors, they are retreating."

The captain nodding knowingly. "They don't want to be hurt. That tells me they lack backup. This probably isn't an operation by the Munqu government. It's only by some of their citizens."

"Pursuit course, sir?" Wong asked.

"Negative. They'll aim optically if we get too close." Gold swiveled toward Ina at ops. "Short-range scan. We need a rock to hide behind."

"Scanning." The young woman studied her computers for a moment, tapped in more codes, then looked up. "At one-one-three mark seven—a small nebula."

Gomez and the captain made their way to ops and leaned to look at the console.

"Very small," Gomez said, straining to see the nebula on the sensor grid. "Too small to give us cover."

"Yes, ma'am . . . but it does have a radiation signature. It may befuddle their sensors as they clear—buy us a little extra time."

"I'll take it." Gold pivoted toward the helm. "Wong, course one-one-three mark seven. Best possible speed."

"Aye, one-one-three mark seven."

The captain then turned back to Gomez. "Commander, get down to engineering. Help out. Let me know how soon we can get warp drive online. If it's not soon, I'll need you to brainstorm some more . . . creative ideas."

She nodded, and rushed into the turbolift. As Gold settled back into the command chair, threads of the nebula became visible on the main viewscreen. Small nebula indeed. Like a cow hiding behind a sapling. He hoped it would do for now.

Chief Engineer Jil Barnak spat himself out the Jefferies tube. Gomez followed him out and down, and both stood on the deck of the engineering alcove, sharing a dissatisfied glance.

"Have you ever seen circuits that fused?"

Gomez shook her head and pushed out a deep sigh. "Not since the Dominion War." She motioned toward the ceiling, indicating the bridge. "You want to give him the bad news, or shall I?"

Barnak took a step aside as if to get out of the first officer's way. "Please, be my guest."

Taking in a deep breath, she steadied herself and then tapped her combadge. "Gomez to bridge."

"*Gold here. Your tone isn't encouraging, Commander.*"

"No, sir. Neither is my report." One of the tougher parts of being an engineer was having to relate the reality of a bad technical situation. Gomez bit her lip for a moment, then continued.

"One of the plasma conduits is melted completely. Several of the warp control circuits are badly fused. We don't have enough replacements, or the power or ability to replicate them."

"*I see.*" Gold's response was even, calm, almost nonchalant. The mark of an experienced captain who knew how to moderate his demeanor for the sake of his crew.

"Impulse power is still intact," Barnak added, shuffling his feet back and forth just a bit. Obviously he didn't like bearing bad news either. "But efficiency has been reduced by coolant leaks. We should have those sealed in twenty minutes' time."

"*About the time the Munqu will be able to see us again,*" Gold said.

Gomez nodded slowly. It was possible it would be up to an hour, but it was more likely it wouldn't be that long. "About that, sir," she said. "Yes. But maybe we'll have more time than we think."

"Damn!" Christian Basile cursed his luck and the equipment around him and the planetoid and everything but his dog back home. He felt as if his world, his life, were collapsing around him. "Power to the subspace array is down," he huffed. "We're falling apart here."

His wife took his hand from the console, the hand that had been injured, and held it close. "No," she said gently. "The equipment is falling apart. But *we're* going to be okay, got it?"

Christian gathered the tatters of a smile and tried to think positive thoughts. It generally wasn't his nature. Thankfully, it was Maria's. "Got it," he whispered.

She is really the stronger one in many ways, he thought. Christian had always played by the rules and didn't like to take chances. If not for Maria, his life wouldn't be half as interesting. Hell, he'd probably be living in a one-room apartment in New Chicago, where he went to school. Or in a holosuite.

The biggest eyes, he thought, locked in a glance with her. *She has the biggest, deepest eyes.* He then chuckled at how corny the thought seemed, let alone would sound out loud. "I'm going to try to fix the subspace array again." He took her hand to his lips, kissed it, then released her as he pushed himself up.

Maria nodded. "Okay. I'll go see if we can pick up anything on sensors."

Smiling, trying to show her just how much she really *had* lightened his mood, Christian winked at her. "Meet you back here in thirty, cutie."

She winked back. "It's a date."

He went his way, and she went hers. Maria had been the one to tell the other miners what was going on. She could soothe them just as easily as she did her husband. The others were mostly single, but there were two other couples. She had told the couples first. She said it was easier to break bad news to more than one person at a time. He'd asked her if that was a two-birds-with-one-stone advantage. She'd hit him and said it was because people tended to support one another.

As she always did him. And vice versa.

Forty-three and some odd minutes later, he had dubbed himself a communications and engineering genius. He'd taken any number of things that had everything to do with mining, or food replication, or bathroom fixtures, and nothing to do with communications . . . and cobbled together their subspace array.

"I did it!" Dropping his tool case on the floor, Christian ran up to his wife in the main control room and grabbed her by the shoulders as she turned from one of the computer consoles. "I got the damn thing working again."

"Just in time," she said, and the moment he saw her frown, his smile disappeared. "We have other troubles," Maria continued. "We've lost containment on the antimatter blasting charges."

Christian's jaw slackened in shock and he thought his face must have flushed—it felt as if it were on fire. "How? That system is completely sep—" He twisted around Maria and intently scanned the monitor screens. "Oh, God. No." He curled around toward her. "Tell me we have transporter power and can beam them—"

She shook her head rapidly. She was scared—and that was rare for her. "Even if we did, with our low power we couldn't beam them far enough away. The shockwave—"

"It would still compromise the dome," he said angrily. "And it sure as hell will from the inside."

"And take all of us with it." She wasn't crying, but Maria's eyes were beginning to tear.

"Call in Sanders and the Ochawas. I think they're the only ones still in the mines. Make sure everyone is here ASAP." Christian moved toward the comm station. "We need the *da Vinci* here in a few hours."

Maria nodded, clasping her own hands tightly. "Let's hope they're okay."

"If not . . ." No. Christian didn't want to think about that.

"Should we break out the EVA suits?" Maria asked.

"I . . . I don't know. Let's wait. Maybe the *da Vinci* . . ." He didn't know what else to say. "If they can't get here—" He didn't finish the sentence, because he didn't want to voice his true thought: *We'll all be dead.*

CHAPTER
3

"We need options, people, or we're all dead." Gold lowered himself into the observation lounge seat at the head of the table, next to Gomez.

"We've come up with some ideas, sir," she said, and motioned to her Bynar team member. "Soloman?"

The delicate alien bowed his large head respectfully and spoke quickly but softly. "The Bynars once investigated a Munqu computer installation and I have the information gathered from that. Theta radiation might disrupt their computer core, forcing them to work on manual overrides."

Nodding his agreement from across the table, Fabian Stevens added, "We don't have a way just yet to deliver a massive theta wave pulse, though—besides which, there's all kinds of other dangers with that. So Soloman and I are working on a way to infiltrate their computers via subspace carrier wave."

P8 Blue, the pillbug-looking insectoid Nasat team member, chirped. "Interesting. How so?"

"They didn't disable their identification beacons," Soloman said. "The data in them is meaningless to us, but the carrier, if its frequency can be decrypted . . ."

Stevens pursed his lips into a thin line. "I'm no Bart Faulwell, but I'll do my best." Faulwell, the team's linguist and cryptographer, was presently on the planet Maeglin, helping a small group of other-dimensional aliens assimilate to their new home.

Nodding once, a clipped gesture, Soloman added, "And I will be able to help with the Munqu computer algorithms."

"Once that's done, we may be able to reverse the beacon and use it to get into their computers," Stevens said.

Gold nodded. Smart people, he thought, but all this was maybes and ifs. It was less comforting than it might seem.

"Lt. Commander Duffy and I also have some work." Gomez tapped a command into the computer before her and a cargo manifest appeared on the screen beyond the table. "Ship's phasers are diminished from battle damage, and one bank has had an irreparable overload. But we're transporting several of these A9667L-lithium phaser-drills." The entry of the drill on the manifest began to blink.

"Aren't they too narrow against a starship?" Pattie asked.

"We're hoping to modify the mount muzzle to

enlarge the beam. We'll work on it." Gomez handed her captain a data padd.

Gold glanced over it. "Very good."

"I have an idea as well," Pattie said. She seemed to lean forward from her specially designed seat, though with her insectoid form and dark exoskeleton her body posture looked different than it actually was. "But I will need to read schematics on the lithium phaser-drills."

"They're in the computer." Gomez smiled and then turned back toward the captain.

"Let's check the rest of the cargo again, too," Gold said. "There may be other items of use that on their own don't seem to be. If you can *build* an item into something useful, even if it wouldn't ordinarily be in this situation . . . well, that would be just what the doctor ordered." He rose, trying to end the meeting on a positive if serious note. "We don't have much time before the Munqu are back at us. Let's get to it, people."

The engineers, each with their own specialties, nodded and there was a chorus of "Aye, sir."

As Gold stepped toward the door, the voice of Ina Mar sounded from his combadge. *"Captain?"*

"Gold here."

"I have a message coming in from Beta Argola, sir. It's very weak."

"Patch it through." The captain twisted back toward the table and pulled Gomez with him before she left the briefing room. He swiveled the computer toward them both and a United Federation of Planets logo appeared on the monitor.

"Audio only, sir. Here it is."

"—is Christian Basile of the Beta Argola mining colony, do you read?"

"This is *da Vinci*. We read you Basile. Go ahead."

"Oh, thank God! We've got them! Maria! They're answering!"

Gold shook his head and strained to hear through the static and an interference that warped the transmission. "You're breaking up, Basile. Are you in danger?"

And if he isn't in danger, would this message put him in danger? Gold wondered. The Munqu could be listening. A private mining colony wasn't privy to Starfleet codes and so there was no way to safely encrypt the communication.

"You bet your arse we're in danger! In a few hours—blown to kingd—come!"

"Repeat that, Basile." Gold tapped his combadge. "Ina, boost the gain."

"Trying, sir."

"Basile, repeat. Blown to kingdom come *how?*"

"Anti-matter blasting caps. Twenty gross of them. Usually containment—" The message broke up, but regained itself just as Gold was ready to call Ina again. *"—but we can't do anything. No power for transporters, and we cannibalized our one shuttle to boost reactor life."*

"How long do you estimate before they become unstable?" Gomez asked.

"Repeat that, da Vinci. We lost that."

"How long before they blow?" Gold asked the shorter, more to the point question. Sometimes engineers talked too much.

"We est—two hours, max." There was chatter in the background of the transmission, and Gold leaned closer to the speaker. *"Hold on, da Vinci. What? That depends on our power usage. We're shutting down life support and breaking out the EVA suits."*

"We have some replacement suits we're transporting to them," Gold asked Gomez. "Do they have enough?"

"Copy that, da Vinci, we have enough. We replace every third cargo trip, S.O.P."

"We'll be there as soon as we can, Basile. Keep your people safe."

Static spat back.

"Basile?" The captain punched the intraship comm again. "Ina, what happened?"

"Jammed, sir."

Gold sighed and shared a glance with his first officer. "Welcome back, Munqu."

She started for the door, and Gold followed.

"Duffy and I will get to work on those phaser drills."

"I'll be on the bridge. Keep me informed of your progress." The captain was already rushing for the door, barking orders into his combadge. "McAllan, I want full power to the shields. We need to get rid of the Munqu in less than two hours." *And if they couldn't . . . it would mean more than just the lives of the* da Vinci *crew,* Gold thought. And more than the lives of the colonists. No one could forget . . . if they failed now, it would be the Horta who would suffer as well.

CHAPTER
4

"Owww! Damn!" Gomez dropped the autotorq wrench to the deck and yanked her right hand away from it with her left. "Stupid, stupid, stupid!"

Kierian Duffy rushed to her side from across the room. "Hey, you okay?" He leaned down to look at her hand, and when she wouldn't present it, Duffy kneeled on one knee and pulled it into view.

"I'm fine, it's nothing." She noticed it was red, but not bruised. Just pinched. Her outcry had been more frustration than anything else. Their refit of the phaser-drills hadn't been going as well as she'd planned, and on top of that, the Munqu had found them. Thankfully, the salvos weren't connecting that often, leaving them all to believe the *da Vinci* had hampered the enemy's sensors more than they had hoped for. "I didn't think this would be quite so difficult, is all."

Duffy nodded his understanding and gave her

hand the very lightest of brushes with his thumb as he released it. "Well, we're trying to fit peg 'b' into slot 'a,' so it's not surprising."

"Of course not. I said I was frustrated, not surprised." Gomez tried to smile but it felt weak on her face, like her lips were probably just a thin line.

"You're thinking about the colonists," Duffy said, and wasn't really asking a question.

"Sure. Aren't you?"

He made his way back toward the outer bulkhead. "Yeah."

"I hate not being able to go fast enough," she said. "And when that happens, I hate things that slow me down."

Duffy chuckled. "Sometimes, you're such an engineer."

"And you're not?"

"'Course I am." He picked up the phaser torch he'd been working with and double-checked the settings. "That's how I know you are."

"You just keep working and—"

An explosion that rattled the deck and jostled the tools in Gomez's case cut her off.

When it died down, just from the sound she knew it was likely another relay overload. And though she couldn't feel the maneuvers, she knew Wong was doing his best to twist and turn around the enemy fire.

She looked over to Duffy. He was going to cut away a hole in the bulkhead, exposing open space in the hull, so they could push the phaser-drill out, giving it access to the enemy. A small force field was the only protection from the cold vacuum out-side the ship. "You know if they fire directly there while you have that field up, it could burn us both to a cinder."

He winked. "I know it. You know it. Just let's not think about it."

This time she chuckled. "Agreed."

Another explosion. This one distant.

"What time is it?" Duffy asked after a few moments of silence.

"Five minutes after the last time—"

"Computer, what time is it?"

"Twenty-two hundred hours, seventeen minutes."

"It's late," he told Gomez. "I skipped dinner."

She heard him, but wasn't really listening. She didn't want to think about dinner. She'd not eaten either, and the last thing she wanted was for her stomach to start growling. Not to mention she'd perhaps start thinking about a romantic, candlelit dinner with Duffy. That's not where her mind was right now. Rather, she was thinking about a colony full of people who were counting on the *da Vinci* to save them. And she was thinking about all those people on Sarindar that she was responsible for who died before she figured out a way to stop the monster shii. She wasn't going to let that happen again. "This isn't going to work. All it will do is scatter the phaser beam and weaken it. We'd have to fire at point blank."

"Well . . ." Duffy shrugged. ". . . that may be an option."

Shaking her head, Gomez shifted the drill to show him. "I have a better idea. If we can set the cannon end to pivot quickly—" She demonstrated by miming the spin of an imaginary joint. "See what I mean?"

"Yeah, I see. Not a bad idea. Increase the arc of fire, rapidly, and you—"

The force of an explosion—from the looks of it, one of the EPS conduits that ran through the outer bulkhead of the cargo bay—forced Gomez against the inner bulkhead. As she quickly recovered and looked up, Duffy was scrambling across the deck, chasing the cutting phaser that had obviously tumbled out of his hand.

"Finish cutting that bulkhead," she groaned out. "We've got to hurry."

Maybe she couldn't modify the drills exactly how she wanted, and what they were doing wasn't brilliant by any means . . . but it was working with what she had. Sometimes that was what being a member of the S.C.E. was all about: working with the cards the situation dealt. *Heck, that's what* life *is,* she thought.

She ran to the nearest replicator and got a list of possible motors that could be created instantly. She scanned the catalog quickly. "No . . . no . . . ah, good enough." With a shimmer and hum the small device appeared. She plucked it close and sprinted back down the corridor.

As she ran in, she stumbled and her vision went blurry. She probably had a mild concussion from when she plowed into the bulkhead. Duffy noticed and turned back toward her.

"Sonnie?"

She shook the cobwebs from her mind. "Fine.

Go on. I'll be ready for that open port in a few minutes."

Duffy's glance locked on her for a long moment, and she nodded again that she was fine. He turned back to his work, grudgingly. Half the size hole she needed had now been burned away, that small portable force field filled the gap, but to her it looked like an open wound in the ship. She could see the stars beyond, and had she looked long enough she might have even seen a fleeting glimpse of one of the Munqu ships that pursued them as it spun past.

Back at it, she thought, and she hooked the small motor, usually used for a type of pivoting holo-matrix emitter, to the phaser-drill's power pack.

A few more modifications and she had what she was looking for. The drill's muzzle now could pivot. It wouldn't be too difficult to link it into the bridge. Not via a direct connection, but a tricorder could probably relay just fine.

As Duffy finished opening the access port in the outer bulkhead, Gomez rigged a connection from the drill's control pad to the transceiver on the tricorder. It wasn't pretty engineering, but makeshift work never was. All she really cared about was whether it would work.

"You ready?" she asked Duffy as he approached.

"Yeah. Need a hand?"

She nodded and rose, hefting the phaser-drill with his help.

"You know, we could have grabbed an anti-grav from supply," he reminded her with a grunt.

"It's only, what? Seventy kilos? We can—ooof—do this."

It wasn't so much the weight as it was the bulk for the unit, and the rattling and shaking of the ship around them as the shields took Munqu phaser shots. The dips in power that were obviously affecting the inertial dampeners didn't help, either.

"Hold on a sec," Duffy said, and Gomez stopped where she was, just a half meter from where they needed to place the drill.

He leaned down, moving more weight onto his shoulder, and with one hand reconfigured the force field emitter. Now they'd be able to push the drill through the shielding and the field would wrap itself around the contours of the casing—without exposing the deck to space.

"It's in," Gomez called as they pushed the drill's muzzle out the port. "Use gravity clamps to keep it in place and seal the crack in the bulkhead with a fast-fusion laser."

Duffy put the last of the small grav-clamps in place and then took a small laser device from a case on the deck. With a bright flash he sealed the drill into place.

"If they hit this direct, it'll blow out the deck."

"Then we better put a few more of these drills in place, so they'll think twice before firing on us." It felt good to get one done. Like she was being more proactive than reactive.

"Where next?" Duffy asked.

"Two more here on portside, then three on starboard, and we can put one dorsal. Then we're out."

"Sounds good. Hope the others are faring well."

Rubbing her temple where she felt a bump had risen, Sonya sighed and whispered, "I know I wish we were."

He pulled her hand from her forehead, kissed her fingertips, then returned it to the bump she'd been massaging. "We are," he told her. "So no worries, okay?"

"Okay."

Captain Gold felt the tension on his bridge, and didn't like it. The battle hadn't been on long, but it was exhausting for his crew, especially for Wong and McAllan.

Then he noticed that Ina was smiling. That had to be good news.

"Captain, Commander Gomez reports one of the phaser-drills is now online. She's transferring firing ability to Lieutenant McAllan."

Gold turned toward tactical. "Got it?"

"Aye, sir," McAllan said. "It's a tricorder link."

The captain pushed himself out of his chair and took a step toward McAllan. "Will it work?"

"It'll have a brief delay, and I'll have to aim manually."

Sparks flew from a rear console and a fire suppression force field cascaded over, dousing the flame and muting the smoke.

"Lieutenant, I suggest we test it now." Gold returned to the command chair. "Tactical display."

As the tactical grid appeared on a corner of the forward viewscreen, the captain thought that while they weren't winning, and they weren't quite

holding their own, for three against one they were
doing well. They'd dealt the Munqu ships some
good licks . . . but without more firepower it
wasn't going to be enough.

"Torpedoes?"

"Fourteen left, sir," McAllan replied. "But one
launcher is malfunctioning. And their shields are
stronger than we thought."

"Wish ours were," Wong said in something just
above a whisper.

Regular battle tactics weren't working anymore.
There are only so many maneuvers one can imple-
ment before they're learned by the enemy and
their computers. Gold was now relying on older,
forgotten tricks. Had they had warp power available, he might have even attempted the old
Cochrane deceleration stunt, or maybe Jean-Luc's
hoary old "Picard maneuver."

"Wong, swoop in starboard and protect the dorsal shielding. McAllan, fire at will. Test our new
phaser-drill. Let's see what she's got."

"Here goes." McAllan tapped into his console
and a loud whine filled the bridge. On the forward
viewscreen, the nearest Munqu ship, flown close
to by Wong's excellent piloting, lit up with amber
phaser flame. After a prolonged blast the Munqu
ship finally fell away, venting a trail of plasma
behind.

"My!" Gold nearly jumped from the command
chair. "That was something!"

"Yes, sir." McAllan was grinning.

Ina reported on what the scanners told her.
"The phaser-drill might not be strong as a phaser

bank, but it *is* tenacious. Enemy vessel has a plasma leak in one of their shield generators. They're moving off for repairs."

"Beautiful. McAllan, keep firing."

As Gold turned back around, Ina spoke up again. "No! Oh, sir. They've already sealed the leak. Their shields are weakened, but still up. Just—up more weakly. But if they sealed the . . ." Ina thought for a moment. "I think it's the frequency of the phaser-drill. It's lower than standard ship's phasers."

"Well, well, well. We may be on to something." The captain dropped back into the command chair and tapped the intercom. "Gold to Gomez."

"Gomez here."

"We need more of those phaser-drills, Commander. They might just save our hides yet."

"Number two is ready to go in, Captain. Give us three more minutes."

The captain rubbed his chin. "Is this something you can teach someone so we can get these deployed more quickly?"

"It'd take longer to explain it than to do it ourselves, sir. We're going faster now. Rest will be deployed in ten minutes."

"Good. Gold out." He looked down at the tactical display and the ship they'd injured was even now returning to battle. "Let's hope that's soon enough."

"They won't be here soon enough," Sanders said, a bit of panic marbling his voice, and Christian wished there'd been some way to organize this without telling his more nervous colleague the exact level of danger. All Sanders ended up doing was upsetting the others.

"Maybe they will, maybe they won't," Dr. Galinski said. "That's why we're taking these precautions. Go on, Christian."

The doctor had always been more supportive, and it was good to hear him put Sanders in his place, as he often did when the other man went off half-cocked about this thing or that.

Christian only hoped his precautions would be of some use. But what else were they to do? Sit and wait to die? That wasn't him. That wasn't any of them. Well, it might have been Sanders. How he became a miner was beyond Christian's imagination. Sure, the mining life was nowhere near as hard as it was even a hundred years ago, but it wasn't easy, either. It was mostly boring, if financially lucrative, but Christian and Maria were good at it, and they'd planned to only do it for a set number of years before they settled down and raised a family, and traveled and . . . none of that might happen now.

He didn't want to think about that. "The plan is to move as far away from the storage area with the antimatter blasting caps, yet still be accessible to the *da Vinci*, should they make it in time," he told the thirteen others. "The lights will go out in about five minutes, and we'll use our flashlights and the emergency lighting. I want all available power going to the containment so we get as much protection for as long as we can. On that note, our subspace array is down again, and I'm not going to bother with it. There's nothing left to say, anyway." He put the helmet to his EVA suit on, and gestured for them to do the same. They all did the same, and when he motioned for them to follow him, the fifteen of them began what was going to be a long procession to the far end of the dome.

After a few minutes of silence, Christian watched his wife code a private channel into the comm pad on her suit's glove.

"Penny for your thoughts," she offered.

He turned awkwardly so she could see him smile. "You even know what a penny is worth?"

"Hundred pennies in a dollar," she said. "We read the same books and watch the same movies. If we had a holosuite here we'd play the same holonovels. You think I don't pay attention to history?"

"Touchy." He chuckled. "No, I mean how much it would be worth to have one today. They haven't been used in centuries."

"Okay," she said, and he knew it was her I'll-play-along voice. "We talking United States?"

"Yes."

"I'll say . . . four hundred strips of gold-pressed latinum."

"I don't know the cost in latinum. In credits, it's about six credits."

Shocked, she almost gasped. "You're kidding me! *That* little? For a coin hundreds of years old?"

He nodded, a movement probably invisible within his EVA suit. "Toward the end of their minting, people were just throwing them away. Or they'd hoard them into jars or toss them into drawers, thinking them too much trouble to keep in their pockets. There are millions still around. Coin shops are stupid with them. I used to collect."

"I never knew that," Maria said, truly surprised.

"Before I met you I sold them all. Was just a hobby as a kid." Fond memories. Is this what people meant by one's life flashing before them when they were about to die? "I thought they'd help pay for a trip to Rigel when I was in college. I found out I only had a handful of really expensive coins."

"No pennies in there?"

"The best wasn't even Terran. Was a Vulcan coin someone gave me, knowing I liked coins. Only reason it was valuable was because the dealer I sold to had no real understanding of off-world moneys."

"Ah."

Christian knew that tone. Maria had checked out of the conversation.

"Boring, huh?"

"Well, it wasn't what I was asking you," she said. "I wanted to know what you were thinking. I don't think it was about coins."

He huffed out a short breath and it steamed his helmet window for a brief moment. "I was thinking about my last anniversary gift to you."

"What about it?"

"I didn't really get you that." He turned toward her, looking to meet her eyes. "I wouldn't get you spindle bearings for our anniversary. I . . . Things were busy and we'd just found the new south vein and I completely forgot. Steve ordered those bearings and I didn't have anything ordered so I just bought them from him and—"

Maria smiled. "I know."

"You know?" Christian's face felt flush.

"Well, not for sure until now, but really—who buys spindle bearings for anyone?"

"You weren't angry at all?" he asked.

She took his gloved hand in hers. "I figure two things . . . one, you gave up your university geology professorship to come here with me . . ."

"And two?"

Glint in her eye, she grinned. "Next year my gift will be enormous and expensive."

Quietly, separated by the walls of two space suits, they laughed.

CHAPTER
5

"**D**amn!" Stevens didn't mean to make his Bynar crewmate jump when he yelled, but with an explosion punctuating the frustration of every other moment, Stevens hated forgetting things.

"What's wrong?" Soloman asked.

At a loss for the word, Stevens mumbled, "I forgot my thingie."

The Bynar looked at him quizzically. "Pardon?"

"My . . ." Hard as he tried, he couldn't think of the name of the tool, but he could picture it in his mind's eye. "My . . ." He closed his eyes, then opened them quickly. "Ah! My Bouse's code distiller."

"Oh," Soloman said, and handed the item to the human from his own case. "I have brought mine. Please, use it if you wish."

"Thanks." Stevens dropped himself into the seat at the computer console next to Soloman and began a download from the main computer into his—Soloman's—code distiller. "How's your part coming?"

Soloman sighed, and for a Bynar that was a quick little huffed-out breath, almost like a scoff. "I do not like the Munqu computer systems, from what I've seen of them. They're inefficient and seem . . . I believe the idiom would be 'cobbled together.'"

A wry smile pulling his lips upward, Stevens chuckled lightly. "Don't you pretty much think that about most non-Bynar computer systems?"

Silently considering that for a moment, Soloman finally nodded. "Most. Yes, I suppose I do. Is that wrong of me?"

Stevens shook his head. "Everyone's entitled to an opinion."

"Then that is mine."

Nodding again, Stevens glanced at the chronometer. "We have to hurry. If anything, shouldn't your superior skill make their system easy to infiltrate?" That came off sounding a bit more snooty than he intended. "You know what I mean," Stevens quickly added, more softly.

"Yes, I understand you," Soloman said, probably missing the subtlety of human tone and thinking Stevens was asking if the Bynar understood the words as the Universal Translator interpreted them. "Unfortunately," Soloman continued, "one can know a great deal about languages but not understand the jabbering of a small child."

"Ah, point taken."

"But," he added, "I am beginning to see an odd scheme to their system. Can you—"

Soloman stopped, interrupted by a severe shudder that ran the deck plates beneath them. When nothing more happened, he continued.

"Can you complete your decryption of their code perhaps using the pattern I've found in their algorithms?" The Bynar handed him a padd.

Stevens took it. "I *really* wish Bart was here . . . but let's give it a shot." For the next few moments he looked from the data padd to his console and back, filling in information and codes and relying on any possible trick he might remember from other, similar encryptions. There were, believe it or not, only a certain number of ways things could be encrypted, even with a computer. He remembered from Starfleet training that there had been noncomputer codes and cryptography by cultures as ancient as Rome on Earth, and the pre-Surak S'loka Empire on Vulcan, but they were simple compared to modern computer encryptions. Well, the Roman ones were. Some of the Vulcan encryptions had been pretty complicated.

Okay, Fabian, get a grip on what you're doing. Talk it through. "Asymmetric patterns in their key encryption . . ." he said more to himself than to Soloman. "That's different, but not unheard of. I think you're right . . . they're using the same pattern. It might even be cultural. I bet Carol would be interested in this."

"Do you have the code key?"

"Not yet," Stevens said excitedly. "But you've given me what I need. With this pattern, I can find the hash value and the hashing algorithm and . . ."

He paused for a long moment and saw Soloman staring at him. "Just a second," he whispered, then his hand hovered toward a monitor. He finally pointed to the screen, and the streaming code that flew by, unencrypted.

"You did it!" Soloman said.

"*We* did it, my friend." Stevens now brought his hand down for the Bynar to shake it, and Soloman took his hand.

"I'll alert the captain." Stevens moved to tap his combadge as Soloman was already working on accessing the Munqu ship's systems via their I.D. beacon. "And you see if all this work will mean anything."

Gomez and Duffy pushed the last phaser-drill into place with a huff and a grunt. She quickly slapped at her combadge. "Gomez to bridge."

"*Gold here.*"

"Captain, the last of the phaser-drills is online."

"*Just in time, Commander. We've managed to pick up some speed on them, but they're catching up.*"

"Sorry for the delay, sir. Duffy and I are going to follow up on some other lines of thought for defensive or offensive weapons. And we'll check on the others."

"Very good. Gold out." As if these people who served under him were his own children, the captain couldn't help but feel some level of pride—what he called *naches*—over their accomplishments. What an amazing group these engineers were. A captain was obliged to know a fair degree about his own ship, and Gold certainly did, but the engineers on his staff had flashes of brilliance that he could barely comprehend. Not that he didn't understand their ideas once explained—but that they imagined them in the first place gave him a sense of awe.

"Lieutenant," he called to McAllan, "let's see just what we can do with this 'mining' ship."

Sounding instilled with new morale, McAllan replied with a hearty, "Aye, sir," and a moment later announced, "I have computer control of the mining phaser cannons."

The captain nodded. "Mr. Wong, let one get close, but try to keep the others away."

"We're within twenty-nine thousand kilometers of the closest, sir," Wong said.

McAllan shook his head. "Range will need to be closer, sir. These drills don't have the scope of our phaser banks."

"I'm aware of that, Lieutenant," Gold said. "Believe it or not, in my time I've had the chance to run a phaser-drill." The captain gestured with his hand, giving his pilot free rein to improvise. "Wong, lure this one in."

"Working on it, sir."

"Easy, son, easy." Gold could see the man's hair was matted with sweat and he was probably one large, tense, knotted muscle.

"That's as close as I can get, sir."

The captain found himself at Wong's side, a hand placed on the navigator's shoulder for support. "A little more . . ."

"He's flying erratically," Wong said. "I can't stay this close and avoid fire."

"You don't need to." Gold smiled. "Close enough. Now, McAllan! Fire!"

A shriek of power filled the bridge and on the tactical display, a small, red line connected the *da Vinci* with the Munqu target. Outside the ship, the light show was probably spectacular—oranges and yellows painting damage in their path.

"Target is arcing away," Ina reported.

Gold pivoted back toward the command chair. "Wong, spin around. McAllan, get him with the portside drills. Fire at will."

"Firing!"

Another whine of noise, and another direct hit.

"Captain, they're damaged. Their shields are down, and . . ." Ina paused, probably making sure her scanners were reporting right. "Sir, their propulsion is off-line."

"One down," McAllan said. "Two to go."

"Excellent, people, excellent." The only problem Gold could see was that the Munqu wouldn't fall for that again. Not unless they were stupid.

And they weren't. "They're staying out of range of our weapons. We're still in theirs." McAllan went from one scanner to another, then back to his tactical console. "We have one regular phaser bank, but power's only at fifty percent . . ."

On the forward viewscreen, a plasma bolt could be seen just missing the umbrella of the shields.

"That's bad aim," Gold commented, mostly to himself. "Worse than it was an hour ago." He straightened himself in his seat and noticed his back was aching a bit—all the strain of trying to stay stable as the ship shook around him. That, and his legendary awful posture. Well, legendary to his wife, anyhow . . .

No time for a visit to sickbay now, though.

"Maybe their weapons lock is still hampered by the sensor disturbance?" Ina suggested.

Gold sighed. "Let's hope so."

The turbolift doors parted, and Gomez and P8 Blue entered, the latter balancing a canister in two of her legs.

"We've got another idea, sir," Gomez said with a triumphant smile.

Gold whirled his command chair around to face them. "Let's hear it."

"I found these among our cargo," Blue said. "Collapse charges."

Gold wrinkled his brows. "Pardon?"

"Gravitic charges," Gomez explained. "They're to be used for collapsing previously used and spent tunnels or caverns so that a structure can be erected above them."

The captain felt a soft chuckle rising in his throat. "And if they went off onboard a ship?"

"It would depend on the internal structure of the vessel," Blue said. "From what we scan of the Munqu ships, two or three decks could be pulled closer together."

"At least enough to wreak havoc with structural integrity," Gomez added.

"Enough to disable one of them?" Gold asked.

She nodded, and beside her Blue made an odd noise that Gold knew qualified as an affirmative. "If placed right."

"Then we need to place it right," the captain said encouragingly.

"It would have to be inside for that, sir," Gomez

said. "We were thinking about beaming it outside the ship and trying to sling it with a tractor beam. It would do less damage, but it might disrupt their warp field."

Gold shook his head. He wanted better than that. He wanted this over—now—before the colonists were "over" with their lives. "What about beaming it aboard their ships—right where we need it?"

Turning her head to one side, Gold could tell Gomez was already thinking of a way to do what he needed.

"Well, if their shields were down—"

"McAllan?" Gold prompted.

"Not as long as they're out of range of those phaser-drills."

"Standard phasers?" Pattie asked.

"Not as weak as they are now."

"We *are* at extreme transporter range," Ina offered.

"Beam through their shields?" Gomez was shaking her head but the captain grabbed her gaze with his and locked on.

"Find a way to make it work," Gold said quietly. "I know you can."

CHAPTER
6

"There's got to be a better way."

All Christian could think was, *Shut up, Sanders.* It was dark, and they were saving their flashlights, and they'd been stuck in uncomfortable EVA suits for too long . . . and Christian desperately wanted to have Sanders sedated or maybe get his butt kicked.

To top it off, the gravity was off in this area, which Christian had planned and expected, but still it irritated him. The planetoid was too small for its own mass to have a noticeable gravity. They all had to be careful not to launch themselves into a bulkhead or the ceiling, or the floor.

"They'll make it in time." He couldn't see her face, but that had been his wife's voice. Still playing the consoler.

"Maybe they'll make it in time," Sanders said. "But would you stake your life on it?"

"We don't have much of a choice," one of the others said—probably Lawson.

"Couldn't you at least have left us lights?" Sanders's voice. Again. And again. If they survived this, Christian was going to get that guy fired. Out a torpedo tube, if possible.

"The emergency lights *are* working," Maria answered for her husband.

"They're too dim. And the peripheral vision in these . . ."

Sanders's voice droned on and on, probably, but Christian had decided to cut audio to the other suits and now only had his wife's comlink open.

"I'm glad we don't have kids," he said.

"Excuse me?"

"I mean everyone here, not just us. We may all . . ." He didn't want to say it again. He wished he could stop thinking it, too. "I don't . . . I don't know if I could take it if there were kids here, you know?"

"Yeah." Her voice was light and almost a whisper, but not quite. "I know."

He knew she was thinking the same thing he was: Why *didn't* they have kids yet? What if now they never would?

"How much longer?" Maria asked.

"I don't know. No way to tell unless we're at the console."

"When it blows . . ."

Christian sighed. "When it blows it blows. Try not to think about it and do what you're always telling me: Think good thoughts."

P8 Blue skittered alongside Gomez as she made her way up the corridor. "Commander?"

"You have something else for me, Pattie?"

"I'm not sure. It may be nothing." Pattie was clicking two of her legs together, and that usually meant she was nervous about something. "However, it might also be something."

Gomez smiled. "Spit it out, Pattie, but you'll have to talk as we walk."

"Spit it—? Yes, of course. In addition to using the collapse charges, I believe if we use the lithium crystals from each of the phaser-drills, we can boost output to one of the drills by one thousand seven hundred percent."

That stopped Gomez in her tracks and she turned to her fellow crewmate. "You've worked this out? How many times would this work? I mean, how many shots could we expect from a drill so designed?"

"At least two."

"Not a lot."

Pattie admitted that with her bug version of a nod. "Yes, but it will be even more powerful than a normal phaser bank. For at least two shots."

"Yes." Gomez liked it, mostly. "However, we'll lose operation on all the drills but one."

"I am sorry if this is not sufficient," Pattie said quietly.

"No, it may be just the ticket. I'll ask the captain, and prepare to make it happen, okay?"

"Very well!" Excited, P8 Blue skittered off.

A few moments later, Gomez joined Soloman and Stevens in one of the labs. "Anything yet?"

As she entered, Soloman turned and nodded, but his tone was discouraging. "We can send a signal back, but all it will allow is access to their communications subsystem."

"Can't you break into their computers from there? We need a way to take down their shields."

Fabian Stevens spoke up. "They have everything but the beacon on a completely different system. We're assuming they at some point realized they had this little hole in their defenses and this was their solution."

Kneading a knot at the back of her neck with one hand—and wishing Duffy was around to give one of his famous massages—Gomez whispered, "Damn."

"If it helps any, we did break their codes," Stevens offered.

"It doesn't. But . . ." She narrowed her eyes and thought for a moment. Just an abstract wondering—an idea seed that might just flower. "The communications array they use for the beacon . . . can you tell it to accept a broader signal?"

"Open up more bandwidth?" Soloman asked. "Easily."

"Enough for a transporter beam?" Gomez questioned with a smile.

"I—I'm not sure," the Bynar said. "I suppose so. Even if there is a limitation, with their codes we can expand them. But we would not be able to get a scanner lock on anyone we tried to beam off."

Gomez shook her head, and continued the sly smile as her idea developed. "Not to beam them off, but to beam something in."

With a chuckle, Stevens nodded his understanding. "You know, that could work."

"I know," she said, that seed now a plant promising fruit, and that small smile now a grin. "So, get on it."

It seemed to be forever before Gomez returned to the bridge, Gold thought. But when she came through that turbolift door, and said those words . . .

"Captain, I think everything is ready."

Gold turned to the main viewscreen. There was no time to waste. None. "Tactical."

Odd . . . it has been two to one for the last twenty minutes and yet there had been a standoff. Why? The Munqu didn't like that the *da Vinci* had dealt one of their ships a harsh blow with the phaser-drills, obviously. But why hold off? The only reason that made sense was because they knew they couldn't take the Federation ship close up. And they apparently felt they had time to wait.

But the captain couldn't wait—not anymore. The mining colony, by their own estimate, had maybe twenty minutes left before their antimatter blasting caps cracked the dome that protected them. It was at least a fifteen-minute journey to the Beta Argola planetoid at high impulse. That was cutting it far too close.

Five minutes, with two ships to one, and twenty minutes before the colony dome was destroyed. The math didn't add up well.

"Pattie's finished," Gomez reported from the auxiliary engineering station.

Gold tapped his combadge. "Corsi? Is your team in place?"

"*We're standing by in the transporter room, sir,*" Security Chief Domenica Corsi replied.

"I'll get down to the cargo transporter," Gomez offered. "We'll want this to be as simultaneous as possible."

The captain nodded. "Wait for my command."

"Aye, sir," she said, and vacated the bridge.

Leaning back, Gold took in a breath and began the end of the battle, one way or another. "Ahead, one-eighth impulse, Mr. Wong."

"One-eighth, sir?"

"That's right. Here." Gold stood and walked to the conn where he played with the impulse inducer controls. "See, coax it back and forth a bit. Like our impulse manifold has a leak."

"Aye, sir, but we're just limping along." Wong looked up at his captain a bit cautiously.

"Exactly."

"But they won't fall for it," the man said. "They won't come close just for this."

"I don't expect them to." Gold shook his head and returned to the command chair. "But they'll be thinking about it. Wondering. Let's get their mind off what we're *really* doing." Again, he tapped his combadge. "Gold to Gomez. Commander, are you ready?"

"*Transporter range of the beta target in five . . . four . . . three . . . two . . .*"

"Energize!"

Corsi materialized next to the Munqu captain—a shortish man with a close beard and a shocked expression. Shocked, because the business end of Corsi's phaser rifle was an inch from his left ear.

"Phasers down!" she barked, and her security team fanned across the Munqu bridge, covering every station and crewman. "No one move."

"You dare—" The Munqu captain tried to lunge forward, and Corsi thought he must be addle-minded. She had two feet and probably twenty kilos on him and swatted him back down.

"I dare, buddy. I dare you to make me use this. Now . . . order your people to power down this ship."

The Munqu captain grumbled, but finally relented. "Do as she says."

"Wise choice." One hand still holding her rifle on her captive, the security chief used her other hand to slap her combadge. "Corsi to *da Vinci*."

"*Gold here, go ahead.*"

"Captain, beta target is secure."

"Now," Gold barked. "Go!"

"Full impulse available."

"Target alpha ship's shield generator."

"Locked," McAllan called, and was almost chuckling about it. After so long on the defensive, he was enjoying being on the offensive. Admittedly, so was the captain.

"We're at extreme transporter range," Ina called. "They're firing."

"Wait—" Gold was on the edge of the command chair. "A little longer . . . we have to get their shields down."

"Ten thousand kilometers, sir."

"Fire!"

The sound rattled the deck plates and bulkheads. A large cylinder of power spread across space from the *da Vinci* and into the last active Munqu ship. It was over in seconds, though it seemed much longer.

"Their shields are down to fifty-two percent, sir," McAllan said.

"Not enough." Gold held onto the arms of his chair as the ship quaked around him.

"They're returning fire."

"I can see that, Lieutenant."

Another explosion and sparks arced between two power cables that fell from a power coupling above the command chair. Gold shielded himself as best he could.

"Plasma charges causing damage. Decks two, three, and five. Hull breach on deck four." Ina coughed around smoke that billowed from her station.

"Wong, come around for another blast from the phaser-drill," the captain ordered. "We can't have them pursuing us. We'll never make it."

"Aye, sir."

They might never make it anyway, Gold thought, glancing at a flashing graphic of current damage. It was a laundry list of just about every ship's system.

"Extreme range again, sir."

"Closer, Wong, closer."

Ina's voice was controlled but could have gone to panic if she'd not been so well trained. "We're losing containment on the breach."

"Evacuate the section," Gold directed. "Lock it off."

"Aye, sir."

"Two thousand kilometers, sir."

"Close enough," the captain yelled. "Fire!"

Another large bolt of phaser lightning sprang forward from the *da Vinci*. Under the weight of it, the Munqu shields sparked and shook and vibrated odd colors.

"Their screens are down to two percent," Ina said, "But our shields aren't much better off."

"Torpedoes?" The captain twisted to McAllan.

"Ready."

Gold nodded. "Point blank! Fire!"

At tactical, McAllan didn't even wait for Ina to confirm it. "That's it! Alpha target's shields are down!"

Captain Gold jabbed his combadge. "Gomez, go!"

"Energizing."

On the main viewscreen, the Munqu ship spun out of control. Lights winked out all over its hull, and as if a giant hand had reached out and grabbed it, the ship crimped in on itself, pinched like a giant drinking straw between massive fingers. Electrical flame zapped this way and that across the ship's skin. Gravity was the weakest of the four universal forces, but still fantastically strong when used the right way.

The Bajoran ops officer gasped and looked down at her console, then back at the forward viewer, then back down at her scanners. "Uh . . . alpha target is . . . bent. I mean disabled, sir," came the sweet song from Ina's lips.

Allowing himself only a moment of awe, Gold almost gasped himself. Bent indeed. He wouldn't have wanted to be the captain on *that* ship when it was returned to port.

"Corsi, we'll be back as soon as we can. Are you secure?" Gold asked over the comm.

"No worries, sir. See you soon."

The captain winced as he twisted and his back pinched, but he shoved the pain away and ordered their escape. "Go, Wong, go!"

CHAPTER
7

First there was the rumble, and Christian knew it had begun. He'd been hoping for the gentle tickle of a transporter beam. This was no tickle.

"Go, go, go!" He wrenched open the door to the airlock and shoved it out of their way. As fast as he could he began hustling people through.

"Where? Where are we going?" someone asked. In the flurry of action and the rumble of decompressive explosion, he only knew it wasn't Maria.

As he continued elbowing people past him, he saw the first sign of a fireball that shouldn't have been coming up the long tunnel. When the anti-matter blasting caps exploded, they should have blown the dome out. And by the sound of it they obviously had—but something else had happened as well, some equipment must have been charged and caused—

It didn't matter. He had only seconds as the fireball barreled toward them all.

"Get in!" he growled at the last one of them, and

by count she was the last. He then desperately looked for Maria and reached out for her. "Maria, blow the doors!"

"Wait," Sanders protested. "If we don't decompress the lock we'll be blown out!"

"That's what I want, you bloody moron!" Christian lunged for the emergency release, and tried to grab Maria's arm at the same time.

He missed her, but jammed his fist into the door discharge and with a crack of light and sound the doors boomed out into space. With them, all fifteen people erupted forward and out into space, chased by a fiery ball of orange-hot plasma.

"We're too late." Ina's voice sank in on itself until it was the softest Gold had ever heard it. "No lifesign readings from anywhere in the dome. What's left of it. No active power. No atmosphere . . ."

Looking over her shoulder, Gold sighed and gave Ina's arm a squeeze. But that probably made her feel no better, and Gold himself had a rock the size of the colony in his stomach. "Maybe they got their shuttle working," he offered.

"No, sir. It's still in dock."

The captain sighed again and crept down to the command chair. He glanced around the bridge, and every station was ghosted by a long-faced crewman. Ghosted. Poor choice of thoughts.

If only they'd been here a little sooner. Five minutes, even. The colonists probably didn't even suffocate. There were signs of a large plasma— *Wait.* "Wait," Gold said aloud, and twisted back to ops. "Ina, scan *outside* the dome!"

"Outside, sir?"

"He said they have EVAs. Scan for external power and—"

Bowed over her scanners, Ina slowly shook her head. "Nothing, sir. No life or power from the planetoid."

"No," Gold said. "No, no, Lieutenant. *Off* the planetoid. If they're in suits, there's not enough mass to keep them—"

Eyes wide and bright, Ina yanked her head up. "Got 'em! Fifteen power signatures. Federation-based!"

Gold almost jumped to her station. "Life signs?"

She breathed a heavy sigh of relief, and the sound and feeling echoed across the bridge. "Fifteen, sir. *Fifteen.*"

Tense muscles melting for the first time in hours, Gold leaned against the ops console as sighs and cheers made rounds on the deck. "Get a transporter lock," he said wearily. "Beam them to sickbay and alert Dr. Lense."

"Aye, sir," Ina said, chuckling an emotional release.

The captain smiled. "And let our fantastic engineers know. They might want to meet just whom they've saved."

"Good evening, Doctor," the Emergency Medical Hologram, version three, said as he appeared in sickbay.

Dr. Elizabeth Lense nodded and tried to look pleasant. "Emmett," she said as she tapped a console that brought the biobeds online. "We have fifteen miners who have been in space suits for an indeterminate amount of time. They may need radiation or even oxygen deprivation treatment."

"Minors?" Emmett asked. "Children?"

"No." Lense chuckled. "*Miners*, as in people who mine."

The EMH nodded his understanding and began pulling out equipment trays just as fifteen columns of sparkle and flash materialized the miners into the center area of sickbay.

"You handle the patients," Lense ordered Emmett as she edged away from the miners and toward the rear sickbay computer console. "I'll set up for cellular scans just in case there are any cosmic radiation concerns."

If only for a moment, Emmett hesitated. "Are you . . . certain you want to handle it that way, Doctor? I could calibrate the computers for—"

"I'm sure, Emmett. Please see to the patients." She turned on her heel and went to the computer.

"Yes, Doctor, of course."

Gold marched into sickbay quickly, having heard yelling from halfway up the corridor. "What the hell is going on in here?" the captain barked.

The EMH was tending to a small group of miners near one biobed, and Dr. Lense was on the opposite side of the room talking to another group who had apparently been examined and were now standing, chatting, the top halves of their EVA suits removed. All the miners, in fact, were in some stage of undress from the bulky space suits.

His glance hanging on Lense for just a moment, Gold quickly turned his attention to the miner who was verbally attacking Gomez. He came up behind his first officer, and asked what the problem was.

"The problem," the man said, "is that your crewmate here has just informed me that more than half our cargo has been destroyed!"

Gomez let out a sigh and rolled her eyes. "Mr. Sanders is disgruntled because we had to cannibalize some of their equipment to save our own lives and his."

"Get gruntled," Gold said.

"And who are you?" Sanders demanded, red-faced.

"David Gold. *Captain* Gold to you, young man. So stow your attitude somewhere before I beam that part of you back into deep space. Got it?"

Sanders took his rant only down a notch. "I appreciate being saved, Captain, but do you know how much we had invested in your cargo hold? Have you any idea of the cost of that equipment you just took to use as if it were your own? I'm telling you right now, Starfleet will need to replace it or—"

"I'm sure Starfleet will listen to your complaints with great interest," Gold said, cutting Sanders off. "But I won't. Now you apologize to Commander Gomez, and while you're at it, apologize to everyone in this room." By now Gold himself was yelling. "This is a sickbay, and you're disturbing patients with *real* problems. Am I making myself clear, Mr. Sanders? I hope we don't need to have this little chat again—so learn to curb your jackass tendencies!"

"N-no, sir," Sanders said. "I mean, yes. I understand. I—I'm sorry." Sheepishly, Sanders turned toward everyone else in the room, and rather quietly repeated, "I'm sorry."

"Good!" Gold thundered. "Anything else I can do for you, Mr. Sanders? Or are you about finished for now?"

His face a bright red now, Sanders pushed himself up on the biobed nearest him. "Finished, Captain."

"Good," Gold said, and twisted around as sickbay broke into applause. All the miners, all except Sanders, of course, were clapping at the captain's tirade.

Smiling, the captain nodded as Gomez, Lense, and even the EMH chuckled. "At ease, people," Gold said. "Commander, a word?"

Gomez nodded and followed him out into the corridor.

"Report," he said as they ventured up the corridor.

"Emmett says they're all in good health based on initial examinations. Signs of stress and such, but that's to be expected, he said. Dr. Lense is talking with some of them."

"I saw that. Well, good that we didn't lose anyone," Gold said as they entered a turbolift. "Bridge," the captain ordered, then turned back to Gomez. "Corsi said the Munqu databanks explained their plan. We guessed right. They wanted the colony and the cribintium to ransom back to the Federation. The mining equipment we were transporting was just the icing on the cake for them. It wasn't part of the original plan, but when they scanned us they thought disabling us would be just as easy as destroying us."

"Is Corsi staying there?"

"Just until the *Sugihara* arrives. They'll take over, and help us with materials for repairs. We might need you to pitch in again, speed things along."

Gomez nodded and she and the captain shared another brief smile.

As the lift door opened onto the bridge, Gold motioned for her to precede him. "Then we should probably get Beta Argola back on its feet. The Horta can wait a little longer, but they'll eventually need the cribintium."

"Big job," Gomez said.

The captain grinned at her. "Commander, I'm pretty sure there isn't any engineering task you and your people can't handle. I'm proud of you— and of them."

"Well, sir, there's one thing I couldn't engineer that you did wonderfully with."

"Pardon?"

A chuckle bubbling from her throat, Gomez followed her captain as he lowered himself into the command chair. "Mr. Sanders, sir," she said. "I couldn't get him to shut up for the life of me."

"Well," Gold said with a wink, "you know the saying, 'different strokes for different folks'? Sometimes it takes a different decibel. Once it's known how loud I can yell, backtalk is at a minimum." The captain looked out across his bridge, met by the knowing glances of his crew. "Right, people?"

Silence responded, and Gold's lips turned up into a wide grin.

"Ahead full, Mr. Wong, to rendezvous with the *Sugihara*."

"Aye, sir," Wong whispered, and what had been a tense bridge in battle just a few hours before, erupted into laughter.

SOME ASSEMBLY REQUIRED

Scott Ciencin & Dan Jolley

CHAPTER
1

Korl Harland kept his eyes fixed on the central monitor, taking in Drei Silveris's voice while he ignored the erratically shimmering photon array over his head, and the steadily growing tremors beneath his feet. His hands flashed across the control array.

"Professor," Silveris said, steadying himself in the lab's doorway, his own eyes glued to a hand-held seismic readout, "it's reached theta pattern! Shockwave impact in less than two minutes!"

"I am aware of our time constraints," Harland said calmly. The photon array, its normally soothing patterns of light swimming and transforming in the air above him, flickered and dimmed.

Silveris stepped hesitantly into the lab and found that, on top of his dread and horror at the approaching catastrophe, his mind still found room for awe and a trace of fear of the immense, mysterious alien machine housed there.

The professor leaned closer to the controls and

spoke, voice barely above a whisper. "I believe you can hear me," he said. "I believe I can talk to you."

Another tremor came, this one more violent; a stack of padds toppled from a nearby workbench and one of the lab's windows shattered. Harland's eight-fingered hands flew across the machine's control console, searching, practically begging the system to respond.

Professor Korl Harland, the Keorgan who had made possible his planet's petition to join the United Federation of Planets by inventing the Keorgan warp drive, had assembled—to the best of his abilities—the huge alien computing system in his own workshop, which occupied space in a building on the outskirts of Yirgopolis, Keorga's capital. Yirgopolis itself, with a population of just under three million citizens, was a coastal city, nestled into a bay on the eastern seaboard of Keorga's most populous continent. Part of a chain of cities and towns stretching both north and south along the coastline, Yirgopolis gleamed as the heart of Keorga, the brightly focused center of Keorgan art—art that had already attracted interplanetary attention . . . art that, along with the rest of Keorgan culture, currently faced a threat of cataclysmic proportions.

Harland worked as fast as he could, tried every control combination he could think of as perspiration beaded on his brow and ran down between his vividly colored eyebrows. He knew it could work. He knew it could be done. He'd *seen* it.

Just after he and several assistants had assembled the machine seven days ago, the big central monitor had flared briefly to life, a brilliant violet energy matrix playing across the screen for precious seconds before fading to black. Since then the screen had come to life on three other occasions, but for no more than a few seconds at a time, and in response to what seemed to be random manipulations of its control console.

Now, with tremors rumbling through Yirgopolis and shockwaves approaching that could easily level the city, Harland wanted nothing more than to see the computer flare to life once again.

So when the first shockwave struck and brilliant violet light flooded the lab, Harland's eyes filled with tears of joy.

Elsewhere in Yirgopolis—roughly one kilometer from Harland's lab—two small children huddled together in the basement of their home. They had been playing a game, but when the earth began to quake and rumble they grew frightened and hid together in a corner.

Rand, the boy, held his younger sister Ria close to him, despite her struggles. "I have to see if Munna's all right!" Ria cried, referring to their pet, which lived in an aviary behind the house.

"Munna's fine," Rand said. "She'll just fly away if anything bad happens." But Ria slipped free of her brother's grasp and dashed across the basement floor.

She never made it to the stairs. In a single movement the earth convulsed and split apart beneath them, a chasm suddenly yawning between brother and sister. Wooden beams and chunks of

metal and glass rained down around them as their
house ripped nearly in half. None of the destruction registered on Rand, though. All he could
see was his younger sister as she teetered on the
edge of the gaping chasm, then toppled backward
into it.

Nor was he aware of a quick violet flicker in one
corner of the basement near the ceiling . . . or of
the small, glittering sphere that abruptly materialized there, hovering, light winking from its surface.

The only thing in Rand's mind, as he dove forward and lunged to grab a scrap of Ria's clothing,
was the fervent, soul-deep wish that the tremors
would stop, that the ground would close, that
everything would go back to the way it was before
the earthquakes started.

The glittering silver sphere revolved, gleamed
once, and a sheet of violet energy exploded from
it, blasting outward from Rand and Ria's house to
encompass all of Yirgopolis, and all of its surrounding countryside, in slightly less than two
seconds.

The shockwaves traveling through the earth
rapidly slowed, then stopped altogether, canceled
out by a strange new vibration through the rocks
and soil. Just as quickly, massive spikes of violet
brilliance erupted from the ground and joined
together, pulling the ruptured earth closed again,
setting aright the toppled buildings, effecting millions of tiny repairs within the space of a heartbeat.

Then, before any witnessing Keorgans even had

time to process what they saw, the violet energy crackled and vanished.

In the basement of their home, Rand found himself holding a sobbing Ria in his arms, crouched on a floor that only revealed its earlier destruction in the form of the tiniest of hairline cracks.

Yirgopolis breathed again, pulled back from the brink of grinding, shattering death.

And as Rand comforted his sister, the glittering silver sphere, still unseen, gleamed once more and faded out of existence, leaving only an odd, deep whispering voice:

"Test Program One complete. Sentients compatible with interface parameters. Readying Test Program Two."

In his laboratory, Harland sprawled on his back on the floor, staring up at the computer's central monitor as the violet energy matrix faded from the screen. It took him a few moments to realize Silveris was speaking to him.

"They've stopped! The shockwaves have completely stopped!"

Harland glanced over at Silveris, who kept looking from his seismic readout to a window onto the city and back again. Silveris rushed to Harland's side as the older man got to his feet.

"You did it, sir! You made the system respond!"

A little shakily, Harland approached the control array, then ran his hand over it. He got no response—the energy matrix had gone. The great machine stood cold and lifeless. But Silveris was correct: The system *had* stopped the shockwaves. It *had* saved Yirgopolis from destruction. And he had brought it to life. Somehow, in some way, he had woken the machine from its slumber, if only briefly.

The ground beneath no longer trembled, but Harland knew it could only be a temporary reprieve.

"I will understand you," he whispered. "I *will.*"

He went back to work, more determined now than ever.

CHAPTER
2

The maximum-security cells on Starbase 27 would not have been described as roomy. Or cozy. Or comfortable, for that matter. A guest of this particular Starfleet detention facility, if he were feeling generous, might go so far as to call the cells Spartan, or possibly utilitarian. But most of the inmates used words like cramped, and claustrophobic, and oppressive, before they started in with the profanity.

Thajus Stone had compiled a list of adjectives he intended to use to describe his own cell, but when his door opened and he got a good look at the Starfleet officer in charge of his case, he decided he'd be better off keeping his mouth shut.

Lieutenant Commander Demosthenes Tull, if he'd followed typical Starfleet protocol, would have sent a couple of junior officers down to bring the prisoner up for interrogation, but he'd found that people tended to become more cooperative the longer they stayed in his presence. So he went to fetch Thajus Stone himself.

As it turned out, Stone looked more or less like an ordinary human male, somewhere around thirty-five years old. Stone's eyes were huge, but so were most people's when they first saw Tull. At nearly three meters tall and more than a meter wide, with dusky skin stretched over muscles like boulders, and human features except for eyes that glowed an opalescent green, Tull was accustomed to being stared at. He was also accustomed to getting swift results without having to do or say much of anything. His physical presence seemed to speak volumes to apes like Stone.

"You're coming with me," Tull said.

In a tiny voice with no trace of bravado whatsoever, Stone said, "Okay."

An hour later Tull sat in his office, waiting for his transmission to go through. He spent the time reviewing footage of Stone's interview on his padd.

"Look, I've put a few of those systems together myself, and *I* couldn't figure out how to work this one," Stone had said, in the very best spirit of cooperation. "So I sold them this thing—so what? If I couldn't get it to work, no chance could *they* get it to work. And what's the harm? Their money's good."

Tull sat up straighter in his chair as Captain Montgomery Scott's distinctive burr issued from his comm speakers. A bad neutrino storm between Starbase 27 and Starfleet Headquarters prevented video from accompanying the signal, but Scott's voice was enough.

"All right, lad," Scott said affably. *"What can I do for you, then?"*

Tull found himself at a loss for a few seconds. He'd studied Montgomery Scott's career through all of its spectacular and bizarre twists and turns, and held the man in considerable awe. He hadn't expected his transmission to be patched through directly to the officer in charge of the Starfleet Corps of Engineers, but here he was, talking to a legend. He swallowed.

"Well, sir, the *Cortez* delivered a man to us yesterday by the name of Thajus Stone. Stone's a scoundrel, half-smuggler, half-ragman, and we brought him in on gun-running charges—"

"Yes? There's more to it, I'm guessin'?"

"Yes, sir. When he realized what a tight spot he was in, he started telling us about other things he'd done, operations we knew nothing about. Things we might not have suspected at all, if he hadn't told us."

"I see. And how does this involve the S.C.E., Commander?"

"Well, sir, Stone says he visited a planet called Keorga a week ago, and sold them a Class 10 computer system. I ran a check on Keorga, sir. They're being reviewed for possible entry into the Federation. A month ago they put in a requisition with Starfleet for a planetary management computer system, but were denied pending the outcome of their petition."

"So the Keorgans got impatient, and went and got one somewhere else. Did Stone say where he found this device?"

"Only that he bought it off another trader, no questions asked. Aside from its purported capability rating, he knew nothing about it, not even its manufacturer. Stone also maintains the system was inoperative when he sold it."

"Inoperative because it was damaged, or because he didn't know how to operate it?"

"Possibly the latter, sir."

"Hmmm. Best run over there and take a peek at what the Keorgans're doing . . . make sure they don't burn their fingers." Scott paused, then: *"Don't you worry, lad. I know just the people who can handle this."*

CHAPTER
3

Bart Faulwell sat in the mess hall of the *U.S.S. da Vinci*, proudly regarding his first true work of art. The ship was a small one and the only place to put his masterpiece on display and invite critiques was here. He waited patiently and soon a steady stream of crewmembers came by and gave their opinions.

Robins from security pointed at the sharp edges at the sculpture's apex and the oddly flowing waves near its base. "What a hideous paperweight. If I were you, I'd try to get back whatever you paid for it. Unless—was that a gift? It doesn't say much about the taste of your friends if it was. Then again, it doesn't say much about your taste if you actually did pay for this."

Orthak from engineering tapped it tentatively with a flipper. He jumped when it moved. "I didn't know you were studying primitive artifacts."

Those reactions, it turned out, were among the most kind and encouraging.

The bridge operations officer, Ina Mar, shook her head. "I can honestly say I've never seen anything like it."

A sigh escaped the beleaguered linguist. "And you hope you never see anything like it again, I'm sure."

The Bajoran said nothing and moved on to the replicator.

Bart's dismay at the overwhelmingly negative reactions to his sculpture didn't stop the floodtide of criticism he had invited. In fact, so long as he sat here sipping his French roast coffee, there seemed to be no end in sight.

Carol Abramowitz now stood before his table. The short black-haired intercultural relations expert crossed her arms over her chest. She looked suspicious. "Did a *child* make this?"

Bart frowned. This was not why he had chosen to make an attempt at creative expression. "No, this is my creation. Something new I'm trying."

Carol simply stared.

Opening his hands widely, Bart said, "It's *art.*"

"Oh. That's what you're calling it."

"This is an expression of my innermost feelings."

"About what? Clutter?"

"It should speak to you."

"I don't think that has anything to say that I would want to hear. Did it just move?"

The ship's medical technician, John Copper, drifted his way. "This? This is what's inside you?" Fearfully, he backed away making a strange gesture, some ancient, arcane ward against ill tidings.

Lt. Commander Duffy came in, took one look at it, grinned, and said, "Blazes! The irony! The sheer wit is astonishing." Then he sipped his quinine water, laughed, and left the mess hall.

Soon, only Bart and Carol remained.

"Actually, I had a specific reason for coming to find you," Carol said.

"Tormenting me wasn't your primary objective?"

"No, just an unexpected bonus. It turns out we're going on an adventure."

"Oh?"

"Captain Gold just received word from Starfleet about two different situations that need to be addressed. One is urgent. The other's not so urgent. Guess which one the puny cultural relations expert, the linguist, and the computer guy are going on?"

"Right . . . details?"

Carol was staring at his sculpture again. She didn't seem to trust it. Maybe it looked shifty to her. Like it was going to do something terrible.

Maybe she wanted to see if it would move again.

"Carol?"

She snapped out of it. "Yes, the mission. Well, while the good captain gets to go off and handle a nice juicy terraforming-gone-wrong, settlement-in-danger, puppies-that-need-saving kind of thing, we're going to see about some business concerning a computer on Keorga."

"Keorga," Bart mused. "As I recall, that world is a haven for artistic types. Good. At least what I'm trying to say with my art should be understood and appreciated there."

"So what is it you're trying to say?"

"If I have to explain it, then what's the point?" Bart asked. "So it's you, me, Soloman—and Fred."

Carol's brow furrowed. "Fred?"

He nodded at the sculpture.

"You named it after that monster on Maeglin?"

"Why not? I thought it'd be a fitting tribute to someone who sacrificed himself for the greater good. Isn't that what art's all about? Expanding the boundaries of expression, indulging in nonlinear thinking?"

"I mentioned the horror part, right?"

Bart smiled indulgently. "Okay, I understand why Soloman is going. Why us?"

"We have to go back a little. The Keorgans requested a planet-controlling computer from the Federation. The request was denied."

"Why?"

"For one thing, they're not part of the Federation yet—their membership application is pending— and for another, the request was made at the same time they attempted to requisition sixteen cubic tons of dark chocolate and a Klingon Bird of Prey."

"A Klingon Bird of Prey?"

"I would have been more concerned about the chocolate. Yes, a Bird of Prey. It seems they liked its contours and thought it would look very pretty in one of their gardens."

"Oh."

"A particularly shiftless trader sold them a

planet-controlling device. It came with an instruction manual. Only, it's in a language no one's ever seen before."

Bart considered this. "Their not being able to read the user's manual sounds like it might be a good thing. Remember what happened when Ganitriul went bad on Eerlik? And that was a world that had had a planet-controlling device for thousands of years. You're saying Starfleet *wants* the Keorgans to have this power?"

"Obviously, Starfleet can't dictate the behavior of an independent world," Carol said. "Choosing to supply or withhold a piece of technology is well within Starfleet's rights. Shopping elsewhere is well within the rights of Keorgans. What's important now is that the Keorgans possess an object of considerable power."

"If they figure out how to put it together and activate it."

"Which they might," Carol said. "Or they may put it together wrong, get it working partially, and not be able to control it. . . ."

"So—our job is to educate and advise. If they're determined to put the system together, we help them to do it correctly and help them to use it safely and efficiently. And with the instruction manual in a language no one's ever seen before, a linguist is required. Very good. So that's why I'm needed. What about you?"

Carol bristled. She looked away. "I'm not exactly sure. The Keorgans have already agreed to accepting our aid. The captain referenced some obscure incident and said he was sending me on this mission because of my sparkling personality. I have no idea what he's talking about. Anyhow, we're supposed to report to the shuttle bay in an hour."

"I'll be there."

"As long as it's without Fred."

She left just as their resident Bynar entered. "Hiya, Soloman," Bart said cheerily. "Do you know about our mission?"

"I do, yes. And I'm very much looking forward to our journey."

"Ah," Bart said, nodding toward his sculpture. "A fellow art lover, are you?"

His heart sank as he watched Soloman take in the lumpy, sometimes twitchy thing before him. "Is that what that is? I thought it was an anti-personnel device."

Bart sighed.

Everyone was a critic.

CHAPTER
4

Bart, Carol, and Soloman made the trip to Keorga on the *Archimedes* mostly in silence. Bart spent the entire time reviewing a copy of the alien user's manual on his padd and attempting to decipher its never-before-seen language; Carol passed the hours by listening to her favorite music (through a pair of earphones, to the others' intense relief); and Soloman, who piloted the shuttle, seemed content merely to study the instrumentation and gaze out the viewscreen.

Exactly on schedule Soloman said, "Approaching Keorga. We'll be leaving warp space in . . . sixty-two seconds."

Carol pulled off her earphones, allowing Bart to hear a couple seconds' worth of *drad* music—just as it hit a spectacularly screechy note—while he put away his padd. She caught the expression on his face and narrowed her eyes, nailing him with a stare. "Not a word," she said.

Bart feigned total innocence. "A word? From

me? About what?" Carol cocked an eyebrow as Bart continued, "Surely not about your taste in music, since, as you know, I have absolutely no opinion about that." They kept up the pantomimes, Carol's stare and Bart's pretended ignorance, for several more seconds before Bart failed to suppress a chuckle and Carol grinned.

Soloman said, "We have arrived."

The sight waiting for the S.C.E. crew as they dropped out of warp was nothing short of breathtaking. Keorga, if left to its natural state, would have closely resembled Earth in size, composition, and atmospheric patterns—but the Keorgans had most definitely not left it to its natural state.

Keorgan artists had perfected a way to energize the planet's wind currents with low-level, controlled photon streams; as the shuttle descended, the Bynar and the two humans gasped at the softly glowing, constantly shifting multihued streamers and waves of light that encircled the planet.

"Mother of mercy," Carol whispered. "It's . . . it's like the aurora borealis, over the entire planet!"

Bart stared, openly floored. "The lights, they'd—they'd have to be diffuse enough not to interfere with air traffic, the closer you get. It's— it's astounding, do you see what they've done? They've created art designed to be appreciated from a distance. From off-planet! They've turned their entire world into a work of art."

Soloman squinted at the flowing, swirling light patterns, then back to the controls. "What they have done has made it virtually impossible for me to operate the sensors," he grumbled. "Far too much interference. Fortunately, I have the landing coordinates already programmed. . . ."

If Bart had had to choose one word to describe Yirgopolis, their destination, he would have chosen "vibrant." The city burst with colors, from the huge tapestries that adorned the sides of whole buildings, to the free-standing sculptures on each street corner, to the dazzling, floating light shows that seemed to appear and disappear in random locations—Carol commented that they looked like super-advanced lava lamps, then had to explain what a lava lamp was. She then said that these were actually called "controlled photon arrays," or, more commonly, "dreamwaves."

The citizens of Yirgopolis were no exception to the rule, either. Their long, loose-fitting clothing ran through every color of the spectrum, and many of them wore their hair in large, elaborately styled coifs that seemed to be sculptures in and of themselves. With their gentle amber-colored eyes and soft, robin's-egg blue skin, the Keorgans were a people who celebrated color in every way possible.

And the music! As soon as the S.C.E. crew stepped out of the shuttle, which Soloman had brought down on a landing pad atop a governmental building in the center of the city, subtle, deeply affecting strains of song reached their ears. The Keorgans had mastered ambient sound; try as he might, Bart couldn't spot any speakers.

"Now *that's* music," he said mischievously to Carol, who studiously pretended not to hear him.

The joyous colors of the city seemed to permeate the bright-eyed young Keorgan male sent to guide them. His brilliant red clothing billowed in the breeze and his vivid yellow hair swept behind him. He introduced himself as Drei Silveris, presidentially appointed aide to Professor Korl Harland.

"We are told you have come to assist us with our computer system," he said. "We're very grateful and we're delighted to welcome you to Keorga."

The emissary smiled, lowered his gaze, and spread his arms open wide in a gesture of welcome and benevolence. Carol emulated his movement perfectly.

"Please, come with me. I'll take you to the professor." He turned and led them across the roof to a waiting elevator.

Carol angled her head toward Bart as the trio respectfully walked a good five paces behind their guide.

"Well," Carol said, quite pleased. "I'd say we're off to a good start. These people are pleasant and civilized. And I hardly think they're facing any great crisis with the computer, considering Silveris's demeanor."

Bart didn't immediately respond, as his eye was caught by an emerald green dreamwave nearby. She sighed theatrically, and Bart turned to her and smiled. "Sorry. Was distracted."

"From now on I'll keep further observations to myself. At least that way I'm assured of an appreciative audience."

"Hardy har har."

As they descended aboard the elevator, a video monitor on one wall lit up, and they found themselves watching a prerecorded greeting from the Keorgan president, a man by the name of Thibor.

"I regret that I cannot come to speak to you in person," Thibor's image said after introducing itself, "but my presence is needed elsewhere. We are told you have come to assist us with our computer system. We're very grateful and we're delighted to welcome you to Keorga."

Bart felt a sudden and odd sense of alarm. The president's words were identical to those of his emissary. Word for word. They had even been delivered with the exact same inflections, the exact same rhythms and cadences. The repetition struck him as ungenuine and raised red flags in his mind.

The president's image was about to speak again when the recording suddenly clicked to static and the elevator trembled. The ambient music shut off, too, and its abrupt absence seemed momentarily deafening. Grabbing a railing for balance, Bart asked, "What was that? An explosion?"

Silveris also had a solid grip on a rail. "No. That was one of the earth tremors."

As the elevator doors opened and they exited into the building's lobby, Carol eyed Silveris closely. "One of the earth tremors? You've had more than one?"

Silveris's calm expression never changed. "Yes." He nearly stumbled as another tremor made the entire building shudder.

Soloman was about to speak when the tremor rapidly escalated into a full-blown earthquake. Yirgopolans scattered in panic around them as a massive shockwave tore through the city. Silveris motioned for them to follow him, but then the lobby floor lurched and they were all thrown off their feet—and before Bart's eyes, the street outside split in half, one huge block upthrust more than four meters. Twisted and sheared pipes protruded from the pavement, spilling water and some kind of gas into the air—

—and even as another shockwave struck, a colossal explosion came from just down the street, blasting the remains of the lobby's front windows inside in a hail of broken glass.

Carol gasped as she saw a rippling river of flame moving up the broad avenue outside, forcing its way along with a new explosion every thirty or forty meters.

"The earthquake has severed our fuel lines!" Silveris cried. "They've ignited!"

The worst of the earthquake seemed to have passed as Silveris and the S.C.E. crew got to their feet again—but the fire raging through the ravaged street outside seemed to be getting worse by the second.

Bart grabbed Silveris by the shoulder. "What about your fire control system? Can it handle this?"

"It already should have! The whole city is equipped with extinguisher nodes, but the quake must have damaged them."

"Can they be activated manually?" Carol asked, staring at the growing conflagration.

Silveris's brow furrowed in concentration. "Yes . . . yes, there should be a manual hub—" He stared around them, then pointed to a narrow door very close to the front of the building. As they ran toward it they could feel their skin begin to tighten from the heat as the fire on the street built in intensity. It had already begun to spread to buildings on the street's other side.

Silveris threw open the door, then let out another cry of dismay; the quake, or the blast, or possibly both, had smashed through the outside wall into the small room where the manual extinguisher controls were; not only did a sheet of flame on the floor separate the Starfleet people from the wall-mounted console, but a fallen beam had smashed through the controls, leaving only exposed circuitry and wiring.

Bart turned to face the others. "Do we have a plan B?"

But Soloman, staring at the damaged console, said, "I do not think we will need an alternate course of action, Bart—if one of you can get me to that console."

"Just wait a second," Carol said, pulling out her phaser. She set it to its widest dispersal and lowest setting, aimed it at the floor of the extinguisher control room, and pressed the trigger.

It worked; the fire, along with about a quarter centimeter of the floor, vanished between them and the console. Soloman rushed to the controls and ran his fingers across them for a few seconds. As he worked, a string of incomprehensible, high-pitched sounds came out of his mouth. Bart knew this was the Bynar's way of communing directly with the computer system.

Within seconds, nozzles sprang up out of previously concealed ports in the pavement outside and sprayed thick gray liquid in long, sweeping waves, targeting the fire perfectly. Within seconds the blaze was extinguished completely.

Bart, Carol, and Silveris all stared around them. Bart was shocked by the sudden calm. Soloman came back out of the control room, and, after a few moments of silence, Carol turned to Silveris and spoke in a no-nonsense tone.

"You knew about the earthquakes," she said. "What we just witnessed is tied in to the computer system, isn't it?"

"Yes," Silveris said, as calm and composed as ever.

He didn't elaborate, so Carol pressed further. "You need a planetary system—because of the earthquakes? Is that it?"

"Yes, that's correct."

Soloman stepped forward. "What kind of a threat are you looking at, from the seismic activity?"

Still perfectly composed, Silveris said, "There is a combination of seismic forces—tectonic shifting, as well as a large geothermal vent emergence—converging on Yirgopolis. If we cannot stop it, Yirgopolis, along with most of this continent's eastern coast, will be destroyed."

None of the three S.C.E. crew could hide their amazement. Quietly, Bart said, "That wasn't in the report, was it? I didn't just overlook that part?"

Finally, Carol said, "And you didn't tell Starfleet about this when you asked for a system earlier? Why?"

Silveris's pleasant expression never changed. "No one ever asked us."

CHAPTER
5

Silveris sat on a bench several meters away from the S.C.E. crew as the bullet-shaped monorail whisked the group to Professor Harland's facility in the capital city's western sector. The trio wished to talk privately—as privately as one could on a monorail with seats for at least fifty Keorgans that was two-thirds filled to capacity. Silveris sat contentedly with folded hands, waiting to tend to the visitors when and if his services were required.

Carol put forth three different conspiracy theories to explain the odd behavior of the Keorgans. She was in the midst of a fourth when Bart took out his padd and went back to studying the strange alien language of the user's manual for the Keorgans' new computer. Soloman sat motionless beside her, also paying no attention whatsoever to her tirade. Carol didn't seem to notice that her audience had, for all intents and purposes, fled from her ranting.

The monorail ride was smooth and pleasant.

The slight hum of the track had been attenuated to produce a subtle musical accompaniment that altered depending on temperature, wind direction, and velocity, and many other factors. Bart listened to the sounds and was reminded of wind chimes.

Carol's face was set in a grimace. "But the *real* reason I think these people act so innocent is—"

"We're going to need help," Bart said, stopping Carol in midstream. Soloman snapped to attention and turned to look his way.

Bart ignored Carol's flustered expression. "They need the computer to calculate exactly where to plant explosive charges, so that the immensely destructive forces building within Keorga can be safely redirected and dissipated. And there may not be much time left before a true cataclysm occurs."

Carol was already tapping her combadge. "On it."

Bart waited as Carol continued to tap—then *stab*—her combadge. Nothing happened. The *da Vinci* certainly should have been within contact range. However, their signal was not reaching the ship.

"There must be some kind of atmospheric condition blocking our transmission," Carol said. "Maybe that swirly artsy thing we passed through."

Bart shook his head. "The shuttle's computer made contact with Keorga to get landing instructions just before we entered the atmosphere. It can't be that."

Soloman cocked his head to one side inquisitively. "Perhaps energies within the atmospheric field somehow affected our communicators as we passed through the disturbance." The Bynar took out a small set of tools and went to work on opening and examining the inner workings of his combadge.

"Maybe Silveris will have some idea of what's going on," Bart said. He waved to the man and motioned for him to come over.

Silveris smiled and repeated Bart's hand signals. Other Keorgans on the shuttle did the same. Soon, dozens were waving and making the strange motion, many looking confused, each amused.

"They're acting like ten-year-olds," Carol muttered. "Their world could be destroyed at any moment and they want us to believe they're off in their own little universes, living in the moment with no regard for anything else. Unless . . . unless it's *true* and there is no guile, no subtext with these beings. And I mean *none*. That would make these people the most childlike in existence." She shuddered. "Blazes, it's even worse than I thought!"

"I think that evaluation's a bit harsh," Bart said. "They're an *alien race*. We can't expect to understand them so quickly. I suppose I should just be grateful that my hand signals weren't in any way offensive to them. A simple wave in some cultures could signify a marriage proposal or a desire to engage in a death duel." He frowned at his companion. "And shouldn't *you* be the one telling *me* these things? This is your specialty, after all."

"I gave you my evaluation. They're like children. I can perform the ritual greetings, dances, salutes, and even mating calls of a hundred other cultures, but I have *never* had any luck fathoming the inner workings of a child's mind."

Bart raised an eyebrow. "I take it you don't like children?"

"They're small. You can't look them in the eye without getting down on their level. This information is known to them and they use it to their advantage. You can't trust them. And they smell bad."

Bart laughed. "They do not. Honestly, Carol, kids are not that bad."

"Maybe not to you. You were one of them, once. I was spared that horror."

"You were never a child," Bart said with a raised eyebrow.

"I have vague memories of being vertically challenged for a brief period of time. But, no, I was never a child."

"Far be it from me to argue the point. I wasn't there. You may well have been hatched at the point of maturity for all I know."

Carol ignored the barb and said, "You know what the worst part about them is? You can't talk to them. Communication is absolutely impossible."

"It's never been a problem for me."

"Of course not. You're a codebreaker. You're used to unraveling bizarre nuances in language."

"And you study other cultures. How can you have a full appreciation of the way another race behaves when something so sweet, innocent, and without guile as the actions of a happy child not only eludes, but actually threatens you?"

"I'm not threatened," Carol said defensively. "I'm simply happier when they're not around."

"Maybe that's why the captain chose you for this mission," Bart said. "This way, you can expand your horizons, broaden your repertoire."

"I think it had more to do with a perceived insult of his wife's recipe for matzoh ball soup, frankly," Carol said.

"Really?"

"I can't help it that on Bramman IV they add ingredients that make it indescribably delicious," Carol said. "Ingredients, I might add, that his wife's recipe could only benefit from. What was I supposed to do? Tell a white lie and say it was the best I'd ever tasted?"

Knowing that he'd never convince Carol that the answer to that question was "yes," Bart stood up. "Silveris, please join us. We have questions for you."

The attaché nodded happily and rose. The other Keorgans were still exchanging waves and making "come over here" gestures while they laughed and played.

Silveris sat down across from the engineers.

Bart smiled. "Is there anything else you're not telling us?"

"Of course," the attaché said.

"Such as?"

Silveris scratched his ear. He looked perplexed. "You would like a recitation of all the knowledge I've acquired over my lifetime? I'm not sure I can remember it all, but I'd be happy—"

"No," Bart said, realizing he had to be much

more specific with his questions. "Is there more you can tell me relating to the planet-controlling device?"

"Yes," Silveris said.

Bart waited. Then he realized his error. "And would you give me that information?"

"Of course."

Again, silence. Bart refused to become flustered. This was, after all, his own fault. He now had an idea of the kind of people with whom he was dealing. Still . . .

Soloman interceded. "Please. Allow me. The directness of these people is akin to speaking with a computer. It requires precision."

"Be my guest," Bart said.

Nodding, Soloman turned and locked gazes with Silveris. "Please give me the additional information about the planet-controlling device now."

Silveris spoke. He recited facts and figures relating to the transaction, how the merchant who sold them the system was found, the number of crates it arrived in, the precise dimensions and weight of each piece, the way the machine seemingly powered up and created energy constructs that reconstructed the damaged city, the precise color of each light on what they took to be the control panel, the particular smell—

"Wait," Soloman said. "Tell me more about these energy constructs."

Silveris did. The level of power he described was off the charts for a simple planet-controlling device.

Bart listened intently—and found the information chilling. He turned to Carol and Soloman. "We are *definitely* going to need help."

Soloman held up his disassembled communicator. "There is nothing wrong with our communicators. However, we cannot use them to reach our ship. Have any other communication difficulties occurred since we arrived?"

Silveris nodded. "There was the disruption of the president's message to you."

"I thought that was because of the earth tremors," Bart said.

"I do not think so," Silveris said. He tapped a small palm computer that rested in his lap. "I have been unable to send or receive messages to the president since that time. I have also been unable to receive updates from any government branch or news service. Oh, happily, however, the last communication from Professor Harland indicated that he had made some breakthrough with the global communications software of the planet-controlling device. I have every hope that all will be well shortly."

Bart ran his hand through his thinning brown hair—which was getting thinner the more time he spent with Silveris. "Wait a minute. Are you saying it hasn't occurred to you that Professor Harland's latest tinkering with the computer may actually have *caused* this blackout?"

"No, I did not make any such connection. Why would I?"

Bart buried his face in his hands. "Thank you, Silveris. That's enough for right now."

When he looked up, the Keorgan was still there.

"We would like a moment alone," Bart said.

Silveris smiled and nodded. "Yes. Solitude can be a pleasant experience. So can having companionship."

Bart gave a pleading look to Soloman.

"Please go back to your original seat," Soloman said.

Silveris rose, nodded, and departed.

"This is wonderful," Soloman said, sighing with contentment. "Everyone on this world says exactly what they mean. No more, no less!"

"It's *maddening*," Carol said. "Exactly like dealing with children. No socialization. No inhibitions. Just pure id."

Bart scratched his beard. "Maybe we can set the shuttle on autopilot, have it broadcast a distress call from orbit, then return at a preprogrammed time."

"One of us would have to return to the craft to do so," Soloman said. "Our communicators cannot reach the *Archimedes*."

"Give me instructions and I'll handle it," Carol said. "I don't seem to be much use on this mission otherwise."

"Let's see what the situation is at Professor Harland's lab, first," Bart said. "If, indeed, Harland caused the communications difficulty and we can find a way to fix it, we can contact the shuttle from his lab and there won't be any need for your going off alone. It *is* a planet filled with children and childlike beings, after all. Wouldn't want you to face that kind of horror alone."

Carol looked away imperiously. "Whatever course is most logical."

There was nothing left for them to say. Long minutes passed as the monorail car rushed toward its next stop.

Bart thought about going back to his attempts at translation, but the inner calm he needed to do his best work on such matters had been shattered. If he had any hope of finally making a breakthrough, he would need to take a moment to meditate—or, at least, to focus his mind on other matters—before returning to that important duty.

He noticed a pair of Keorgans, a male and a female, handcrafting a beautiful shawl. The shawl glowed with brilliant swirls of color. As Bart watched, ever-changing patterns of energy appeared in its weave. His own entree into the special world of self-expression sat beside him in his bag. Rising, he carried Fred, his sculpture, to the artisans, and humbly asked permission to display his creation. They gave it happily.

The male artist examined the sculpture closely, turning it in his many-fingered hands several times. He giggled when it moved.

"May I keep this?" the artist said. "My son would enjoy playing with it. And so would I."

"Oh, yes, me, too!" the female artisan added.

A toy. They think my sculpture is a toy. Ah, well. At least Fred was being appreciated on some *level. . . .*

"Take it, please," Bart said. Even here, his work wasn't understood. Maybe he just wasn't cut out to be an artist.

Bart returned to his seat. Carol was looking out the window, staring at the beautiful spires of the city. It almost looked like a fairy-tale kingdom, Bart thought. But he seriously doubted that Carol saw it that way. He wondered what her childhood had been like. He knew she had joined Starfleet for family reasons. Her mother, grandmother, and great-grandmother had all served in Starfleet. She once admitted that she felt a great sense of obligation to keep the family tradition. But that was all he knew. Not one story of a wild prank she'd committed when she was younger, not one heartfelt tale of a schoolgirl crush, not even a single mention that any current interest she held was a holdover from her youth. Nothing. For that matter, he had no idea why she became an intercultural specialist, as opposed to an officer like her other family members.

Maybe she *had* hatched fully mature, after all.

Bart turned his attention back to the Keorgans. It was odd. He'd always held the belief that those with artistic bents also had a high capacity for abstract thought and reasoning. But the Keorgans were the most literal, factual people he had ever met. They made Vulcans and android life-forms appear to bristle with subtext and machinations in comparison. Yet they produced wonderfully imaginative works of art: beautiful paintings and holos of places never before seen or imagined, amazing flourishes, nuances, and new concepts in architecture and design, and their *music* . . . it practically reached into one's soul.

They seemed to have no imagination, but they were intensely creative.

It was a mystery, that much was certain. But he

260 Scott Ciencin & Dan Jolley

enjoyed mysteries. When the immediate crisis was under control, he would see if he could solve the riddle of the Keorgans and their many contradictions.

The monorail slowed as it approached a station.

When the immediate crisis was brought under control? Bart considered the threat shrouding this planet and its people—and that they were cut off from outside help.

If seemed much more likely.

CHAPTER
6

Carol, Bart, and Soloman stood in Professor Harland's lab, gazing up at the gargantuan computer system before them. Harland had his back to them, conversing quietly with Silveris.

"Either of you ever seen anything like this before?" Carol asked.

Bart simply said, "Nope."

Soloman made a soft little sound in his throat before answering. "It is much smaller than either Ganitriul or the master computer on Bynaus. But I have never seen one precisely like this. I must confess that I'm anxious to begin work upon it."

Professor Harland appeared dismayed, based on Soloman's reading of his facial expression. According to Harland's records he had, within seconds of beginning work on assembling the computer system, calculated every possible combination and configuration of the machine's seventeen individual components. Along with his assistants, he had perfectly assembled and reassembled the computer to fit each scenario, and he had tested it in each configuration in a complex battery of well-thought-out operational trials. Even Carol seemed impressed.

"I don't understand," Harland muttered. "When the first true crisis arose, the system met the challenge. I thought I had something to do with it. But none of my actions provoked a response within the system during the second crisis. Then, when I was out of the room, the system flared briefly, and all communications were disrupted. All this on its own. Perhaps I really had nothing to do with solving the first crisis, after all."

Silveris was consoling the scientist. Soloman asked permission to examine the system and both Keorgans gave their enthusiastic assent. His first task would be to try to locate the cause of the communications failure and deal with that.

In seconds, he was communing with the central control array, speaking in Binary. Nothing happened. None of the strange alien symbols Harland had recorded appeared. Crouching, Soloman let his fingers trace lightly across the smooth metal surface of the computer's housing—and popped a hidden panel loose.

Harland gasped, but didn't say anything. Bart murmured, "My word."

The interior of the alien computer seemed to be alive—not alive in the sense of a living, breathing, organic organism, of course, but alive nonetheless. Streams, waves, and individual particles of violet light swam and flowed inside the machine in intricate, hypnotic patterns, pumping and pulsing as if with a heartbeat of its own. Soloman lifted one hand, flexed his fingers, and slowly, very slowly, reached inside the computer.

A violet burst of energy sent the Bynar flying back. He smashed against the lab's rear wall and slumped to the floor. Bart and Carol raced to his side, but he was shaken, not hurt. They kindly helped him to his feet.

"I tried to interface with the system," Soloman said. "It defended itself. My friends, I have reason to think the system is an—"

He stopped as he noticed something alarming. Every shadow in the room was fading. Gazing out the window, he saw that the day had grown overcast, and stunning clouds that shifted from ruby red to a soft, pale yellow now obscured the sun.

The building suddenly shook with another earth tremor, hard enough to make everyone in the room fight to stay on their feet—

—and with a brief, shrill whine, the massive computer system came to life again. Harland cried out happily, but quickly lost his smile when he got a good look at the central monitor; the violet energy matrix was there again, but this time it seemed chaotic, firing across the screen in random, jagged patterns.

Bart grabbed Carol's arm and pointed. "Look at that!"

Carol and Soloman both turned and saw it: the power cables running from the wall to the back of the computer, thick as Carol's wrist, shimmered with the by-now very familiar violet radiance.

"What's it doing?" Carol asked, staring. "Traveling on power lines?"

And then the whole world became a glare of blinding blue-white, followed a nanosecond later by a clap of thunder like a catastrophic meteor impact that shook the walls.

"What is happening?" Silveris called fearfully. "What is this?"

More eye-burning glares burst through the windows in an explosive display, while the deafening thunderclaps began rumbling together into one long, bone-rattling basso crash.

Soloman ran to the window and looked out—and saw what only he could see, with his eyes unaffected by sudden shifts in light intensity. He let out a high-speed, untranslatable burst of the Bynar language, loud enough for Bart to hear as he stumbled to Soloman's side.

"What's out there?" Bart shouted, keeping his eyes turned away from the window. "What do you see?"

For a few moments Soloman had no words to describe it. Rolling out from Harland's lab in every direction was a wave of lightning strikes, slashing from sky to ground in a savage cascade of electrical fury.

Squinting, Soloman thought he could see the computer's energy signature traveling along the city's energy grid—yes, *there*, as he watched, a crackling violet arc jumped from a lightpost to a powered sign above a store window . . . and less than a second later, a massive bolt of lightning obliterated the sign.

Yirgopolis's vegetation began to burn, ignited by the thousand-degree temperatures of the lightning strikes—trees exploded with each strike, their sap instantaneously boiled to steam—and though the automated fire systems were now back on-line and functioning, the devastation escalated rapidly.

Signage, transports, bridges, buildings themselves, all sustained heavy damage even as Soloman watched.

The Bynar turned his back to the window and looked up into Bart's and Carol's eyes, raising his voice to be heard over the constant peal of thunder. "Lightning—lightning is striking everywhere, following the power routes and circuitry." He looked over at the computer, which still seemed to be going haywire. "I do not know how, but the system's malfunction is calling down lightning all over the city!"

Bart stared at the computer's power cable for a second, checked to see where Harland and Silveris were—both of them were frantically, and unsuccessfully, trying to accomplish something with the computer's controls—then pulled his phaser. "So we disconnect it," he said, and was about to take aim when Carol grabbed his arm.

"What are you *doing?*" she cried.

Bart's eyebrows shot up. "Making the lightning stop?"

Carol growled in frustration. "What, Corsi's not here, so you're going to be the idiot? Listen to me—we don't know what cutting off the power like that will do to the machine, and at this point we can't afford to damage it. With the communications out and no guarantee we can get help in time, this system may be our only chance for survival."

"Well then, I'm open to suggestions." Bart put away his phaser and held up empty hands. "I'm just the linguist."

"Wait a moment," Soloman said. "Lightning strikes are caused by positive charges building up on the ground. They then attract lightning from negatively charged clouds."

Carol frowned. "So, for some reason, the computer is positively charging all of the city's wiring—"

"—and we need to get rid of that imbalance," Soloman finished. He looked around, thinking quickly, and his eyes fell on Bart's phaser. "Bart, give me your weapon. Maybe we can use it, after all."

Bart and Carol followed Soloman to the wall where the thick power cable disappeared into it; the Bynar had already taken out his own tricorder, and he plopped down on the floor, his hands nearly blurring as he disassembled both devices. He spoke without looking up.

"Get me access to the wiring, please? Bart? Carol?"

Working together, Carol and Bart quickly removed the faceplate from the wall socket, revealing softly glowing green, blue, and gold circuitry inside the wall. Bart shook his head, winced at another super-loud thunderclap, then said, "Leave it to the Keorgans to make their wiring aesthetically pleasing."

Harland noticed their activity and came dashing over. "What are you doing? Can I help?"

Soloman spoke, again without looking up, as he placed the combined tricorder and phaser against the wall and connected a small relay to the power cable junction. "I have stripped down the phaser's emission range and adjusted it. If this works as I plan it to, your city's power system will soon be flooded with negative ions."

Before Harland could say a word, three things happened simultaneously: the loudest thunderclap yet smashed over the building like a physical wave, causing everyone except for Soloman to clap their hands over their ears and squeeze their eyes shut; the searing glare of the lightning intensified to an unrelenting assault of light like a billion magnesium flares; and Soloman activated the modified phaser, rocketing its signal into the Keorgan circuitry.

The sudden silence left their ears ringing.

Brilliant spots danced in front of their eyes as they all blinked, trying to restore their vision.

And with a whirring sigh, the computer again went dark, the jagged energy matrix fading from the screen. Outside, a gentle rain began to fall, drops hissing as they landed on superheated pavement and charred foliage.

It all ended so suddenly that Carol felt like laughing. She exchanged elated grins with Bart and Soloman, and would have laughed out loud, if not for a distant, threatening rumble up through the floor: another earth tremor.

The S.C.E. scientists got to their feet and turned

to face the computer. Professor Harland and Silveris stood nearby.

"You were about to voice a theory," Harland said. "Something about the system's nature, I believe?"

Soloman nodded. "I think this is far more than a planet-controlling device. It's displaying self-awareness. I think it is—"

A booming voice from the center of the room cut him off. *"Energy grid established. Test Program Two will now be engaged."*

Soloman's voice was low and hollow: "—an artificial intelligence."

CHAPTER
7

"At least it's speaking in a language we can understand," Bart said. "I've tried everything I know, but I can't get anywhere with the alien language of its user's manual."

"Now all we have to do is get it to listen," Carol said.

Soloman boldly approached the system. "Why did you need to establish an energy grid? What are you testing?"

The machine's only response was a burst of violet energies, a swirling matrix of light that nearly blinded everyone looking its way.

Covering her eyes, Carol growled, "Give me the instructions for the *Archimedes*. We need to get a distress signal out to Starfleet *now*."

Soloman hastily prepared all the data she would need.

"You may want to consider going with it," Bart said.

Carol's nostrils flared in fury. "Because I'm no use here? Or because—"

Bart didn't have time for this. Something about this mission was causing Carol to allow her personal issues to cloud her judgment. He turned from her. "Silveris, I think you should go, too, and report to your president that as wide a planetary evacuation as possible should not only be planned, but placed immediately in operation."

"Such measures are under way," Silveris said. "That is why the president was unable to meet with you."

"Again, information that would have been useful *before* we were summoned to a deathtrap masquerading as a tea party!" Carol fumed.

"Quite enough," Bart said. "Carol—*go.*"

Silveris accompanied Carol as she left the lab. She saw Bart poring over the alien user's manual with Harland and Soloman looking into the blinding light of the computer, as if considering another attempt to interface with it. Then she was being hurried toward the rail station and she quickly took a seat.

"We have very few ships for evacuation," Silveris said. "By going with your shuttlecraft and ensuring that the distress call is sent from orbit and received by Starfleet, you will indeed be performing a valuable role in helping to save our people. I thank you."

Carol suddenly felt ashamed for her behavior. Here was a being facing the possibility of death and the destruction of his world, and his priority was to make sure that she did not feel sad or useless. It was just . . . Well, the very idea of a race totally without guile had been unsettling to her. From the moment she had been able to speak, she had always tried to extrapolate every possible meaning behind every word and gesture she observed. She had always believed that beings such as these *could not exist*.

Her time among the stars, however, had taught her that all things were possible.

Carol smiled at Silveris. "No," she said. "I thank you."

Suddenly, another tremor shook the rails of her shuttle. Several Keorgans cried out in surprise and alarm. Before she was even fully aware of what was happening, the rail ahead split apart and her shuttle was sent careening into empty air. Carol felt her heart rise into her throat as she was tossed from her seat and the spires of the city stabbed toward the shuttle's nearby windows.

Crushing, jarring death was seconds away. . . .

Then it all stopped.

Carol's eyes opened wide as she took in the sight of a giant, glowing, purple hand wrapped around the shuttle. Then the car was gently lowered fifteen stories to the ground, and she joined the stunned Keorgans as they filed out to get a look at their savior.

A twenty-story-tall violet energy construct in the form of a smiling, gentle genie stood high above, his arms crossed over his massive chest. He stood in the middle of a large park. Buildings and walkways surrounded the clearing. The Keorgans gathered around Carol.

"Human woman, I read of this being in the Earth document entitled *Arabian Nights*," a young Keorgan boy said. "Are you familiar with him, too?"

Carol bristled because of the informality of his approach and the manner in which he addressed her, which she could easily have taken as sexist or superior, but she couldn't deny that she was intrigued by his statement and so she took his words at face value. She was human. She was a woman. He honestly had said nothing insulting. "Were you . . . thinking about him when we went off the tracks?"

The lad shook his had. "No. I was frightened and not really thinking at all. It happened so quickly."

"But you were wishing the monorail wasn't derailing, weren't you, *wishing* something would save you?"

Carol felt excited. Perhaps she had begun to get at the purpose of the computer system's tests, perhaps even the true purpose of the machine itself: Granting wishes. Making hearts' desires come true.

Again, the lad shook his head. Carol frowned. She *needed* to feel that she was truly contributing to the mission, and she certainly wanted to quantify the impossible figure standing high above, to whom she owed her life. Unknown quantities always set her on edge. "How did you feel about *Arabian Nights* when you read it?"

"The document seemed odd to me. It contained events that conflicted with known historical facts regarding the planet at that time, such as anti-gravity throw-rugs and such."

She smiled. She was speaking to a child *and* smiling.

At least Bart wasn't here to see it. Then she'd never hear the end of it.

The energy construct of the genie looked around. He cocked his head to one side as he spotted something in the distance.

"Hey, you up there!" Carol shouted. "Genie guy!"

The energy construct did not look down. Instead, he turned and moved off, the bottom half of his body, a trail of smoke, barely touching the ground.

"Wait up, I've got three wishes for you!"

The energy construct didn't slow. Weird. This thing was made of the same energies that had helped to reconstruct the city before the S.C.E. crew's arrival, and of the same energies that took control of the city's power grid. It was linked to the computer, to the "test" it was performing, *and* it was in the form of a being whose sole existence was to grant wishes. Yet he ignored her.

She looked at the faces of the Keorgans. They didn't appear to be bothered or upset to have an energy construct that was twenty stories tall and shaped like a figure out of Earth mythology in their midst. It was a thing they could see, a thing that clearly operated in the physical world, a thing that was not harmful. And that appeared to be sufficient information for them to keep from being alarmed by it.

Carol, despite her bravado when calling out to the genie, had felt terrified of it, though she couldn't quite put into words why that should be so. . . .

Silveris touched her arm. "What is . . . is that Tirellan's third symphony? No, it's something else. A composition even richer than I would have thought possible. . . ."

At first, Carol didn't know what he was talking about. Then she heard it: a vast, rich trill of music, even more beautiful than other Keorgan works they'd heard—and rapidly increasing in volume. She looked up, in the direction of the sounds, and her jaw dropped.

Enormous energy-construct musical instruments stretched across the sky, playing themselves—the music was so beautiful, so perfect . . . even to her.

A weeping Keorgan male stepped out from the small group of fellow travelers. "My symphony . . . complete and perfect, exactly the way I had always dreamed it. I had abandoned it years ago because I could never solve the many problems inherent in its structure. I haven't even given it a conscious thought in months, yet . . ." The expression on his face was of sheer bliss. "What I've always wanted, more than anything, is to share this work with the world. . . ."

Suddenly, the music rose in volume. In seconds it became so loud that Carol gritted her teeth and plugged her ears with her fingers. For a few moments the sounds softened, but then increased again, coming in teeth-rattling bursts and waves. She heard explosions, and turned to see windows shattering under the barrage.

She grabbed the arm of the Keorgan composer. Such a gesture went against all her training, but somehow, that didn't seem to matter right now.

"Make it stop," she said.

"How?" he asked.

"The same way you made it start in the first place. Wish for it to come to an end. Wish it out of existence."

The composer tried. Carol had no doubt of that. She studied his face and saw the intense mental effort he devoted to following her command. But the symphony only grew louder.

Then *other* constructs winked into existence. From where she stood, she could see chaos erupt throughout the city.

Building blocks made of violet energies appeared, some creating massive damage to buildings as they wedged themselves between them and piled higher and higher, creating newer, and even more towering buildings that were ultimately unstable. The blocks fell to the ground, causing injury or possibly worse to screaming Keorgans who fled in fear. The blocks reshaped and piled themselves in ever more complex geometric patterns, creating more and more damage.

Elsewhere, bright violet streamers appeared. They danced and streaked throughout the city, causing accidents by obstructing the view of Keorgans operating machinery, blinding others while they were at the controls of transports, and making still others dizzy by twirling around and around them—sending some falling off roofs or out of high windows.

Amazing violet flowers grew up from the ground and uprooted and overran several blocks at a time.

Yet, the most amazing thing of all was that while some people were injured, the constructs always managed to intersect one another or somehow create a buffer or safety net to catch falling people or cushion blows. Carol flashed on memories from her younger days, in which her parents allowed her to fall and get hurt, but only mildly so. It was the only way she would ever learn anything, they said.

"Second test completed," a booming voice said from everywhere and nowhere at once. *"Secondary level interface with inhabitants achieved. Primary systems now activated. System function may now be achieved."*

Suddenly, Carol understood what was going on. At least part of it.

"These *tests*," Carol said to Silveris. "The first was to see whether or not an interface could be established with the conscious mind of this world's people. The second was to gauge if a deeper connection to the Keorgan subconscious could be established. That's why the system needed control of the power grid—to create all these constructs."

Silveris nodded.

"I want you to get to the president using any

means necessary," Carol said, jamming the small portable padd Soloman had given her into his hands. "Explain the situation, then assign one of your pilots to study the directions on the padd and take the *Archimedes* to deliver our distress signal."

"What about you?" Silveris asked. "Will you be safe?"

"I'm more than safe," Carol said, smiling as she grabbed the arm of the composer and hauled him off in the direction of Harland's lab. "I'm a woman on a mission!"

CHAPTER
8

Harland looked up from his portable seismic monitor. Bart could see the panic rising in his eyes as the ground heaved and vivid purple light beamed in through the windows from the chaotic energy constructs outside. The sky-symphony's music grew even louder, and what little glass remained in the windows began to crack.

"How much time do we have?" Bart asked, gesturing to the monitor.

"I—I am not sure," Harland answered, again consulting the diminutive screen. "Not long. A powerful shockwave just ran through an outlying town, about twenty kilometers from here, and . . ." he glanced up at Bart, trying to stay calm, "I see indications of lava emerging in a drainage canal."

Bart turned to Soloman, who was again studying the computer. "It looks like we're about ten minutes away from getting turned into charcoal."

A commanding voice sounded from the doorway as Carol appeared, a Keorgan at her heels. "Oh, *now* who's being the negative one?"

Carol quickly related all she had experienced and the conclusions she had drawn.

"All right," Bart said. He nodded toward the Keorgan composer. "But why bring him here?"

Pointing to the window, Carol said, "That construct came from his conscious and subconscious mind. If the A.I. is a genie that's just been loosed from its bottle, well, here's one of the people it's granted a wish."

Soloman nodded. "I see. The A.I. will not allow me to interface with it, but it has, in some way, interfaced with this Keorgan. And if that interface is still active, which it appears to be from the noise outside, perhaps, through this man, we can find some way to communicate with the system and have it build constructs that will help us avert the natural disaster about to befall this area."

"Bingo," Carol said.

Keenly aware of the short time available to them, Bart approached the composer. "Your desire was to complete your symphony. The A.I. took that desire, that wish, and fulfilled it, it made your dream a reality. What did you feel was holding you back when you attempted to finish your great work? What was it you felt you needed to complete this accomplishment?"

"Knowledge," the composer said softly.

"Is it knowledge you now possess?"

The composer paused for a moment. He looked off, his head nodding, his eyes vacant, as if he had, with a thought, transported himself to a solitary place in which he might mentally compose an opus. Then he returned, his eyes filled with tears.

"It is," he said. "I now understand exactly my failings in creating my symphony in the past, and how easily they could be addressed. I also understand how to replicate that feat, why—listen!"

He looked up and suddenly, the thunderous music from without changed completely. What had been a furious attack was now a quiet meditation. In the sky, the instruments themselves changed shape.

"He's in . . . he's in control of the construct," Carol said.

"I see that," Bart said. Now the question was how to use that knowledge to their advantage. "The A.I. did more than simply fulfill his wish. It gave him the tools to accomplish the goal himself. It helped to evolve him."

Carol again thought of the scenes of chaos she had witnessed in the city, and the way the energy constructs kept the Keorgans from sustaining more than minor injuries, just as her parents had done. And she thought of the "toys" she had seen throughout the city. Particularly the out-of-control building blocks.

"They're learning toys," Carol said. "It's not wish fulfillment or even evolution the A.I. is after, it's *learning*. It taps into the conscious and unconscious mind to help craft tools that will facilitate learning."

"But these objects are running amok, causing mass destruction," Bart said. "Why?"

Professor Harland pointed at the computer. "I think only *it* can tell us."

Bart touched the composer's arm. "I want you to concentrate on a desire for knowledge of a particular subject. What we need to know is how to communicate directly with the A.I. It speaks in a language we can understand, but it will not respond to any of our direct questions."

"Yes, Keorgans are always direct, this should be no problem for you," Carol said.

The composer swallowed and attempted to do as he was instructed. Outside, his construct changed shape several times, and his symphonies became a chaotic jumble of unfinished compositions. Nearly a minute passed before the man crumbled to the ground, clutching his head. He couldn't do it. Harland raced over and helped the man to the corner.

"They're direct on one level, but not on others," Carol noted.

"Yes," Bart said. "It must have something to do with how they can create such imaginative works when they seemingly have no imaginations. The secret to unlocking that contradiction may be the key to reaching our goal." Bart knelt beside the composer. "Tell me: What are you trying to express with your music?"

"Express?"

"What is its meaning? What statement are you attempting to make?"

The Keorgan stared at him blankly.

"All right, how did you feel when you composed it? And how do you want it to make other people feel when they hear it?"

"I . . . felt pleased. There was synchronicity.

Balance. An equilibrium to the equation. That is what I hope all will feel when they hear any of my works."

"Indeed," Bart said. He turned to Carol and Soloman. "The A.I. is interfacing with the minds of the Keorgans, attempting to decipher what it is they wish to learn through their conscious and unconscious thoughts and desires. The ultimate desire of the Keorgans seems to be to create art and music, yet they're also very skilled at the sciences. They have no form of fiction, no holos, no books, no myths, because they have no capacity for subtext. Yet they create pictures of places they have never seen, places that have never existed. They create symphonies and styles of musical expression unlike anything ever before encountered in the universe. But how can any of this be? Solve one puzzle, and it might just solve them all."

Soloman said, "He said they wish to achieve synchronicity. Equilibrium. Balance. Are these not common factors between science and the arts? Could one not argue that music is simply a matter of math, the same with painting, and so on? A randomizing of certain variables while holding to certain structures with others?"

The Bynar rose and quickly crossed to the computer's open control panel. Before anyone could stop him, he thrust his hand into the glowing array of violet energies once more.

This time, it looked as if he was being electrocuted—his whole body spasmed—but, gritting his teeth, Soloman whispered, "We need you to stop the seismic and geothermic activities here."

Another burst of violet energy sent him reeling away from the computer as more of the strange characters materialized on the screen, and the computer's voice boomed out again. *"Incorrect protocol."*

"I do not understand this," Soloman said. "It has helped to save the lives of Keorgans before. Why won't it listen now? Why won't it help?"

"I don't think it's interested in protecting the Keorgans per se, that's not a part of its programming," Bart said. "It did, however, protect them in the city when they were being threatened by their own conscious and unconscious mental projections run amok. The seismic and other difficulties facing the planet are not being caused by the Keorgans or the energy constructs that act as learning tools. That's why it's not concerned about the danger."

"What if it understood that it was in danger?" Carol asked. "It's acted to protect itself before. And look at all those constructs it made before we arrived, the ones that unmade all the damage the city had suffered."

Bart shook his head. "Those creations came before the A.I. was fully activated. It first created constructs that acted on the conscious mind. Then it made those to act on subconscious desires. But that's over with. Those tests are finished. Now its mission is to teach, and nothing else."

Soloman struggled to his feet. "I have to try again."

The Bynar went to the machine and again attempted to interface. Immediately, Soloman was obviously in severe distress—the muscle spasms were growing more severe—but he repeated his words. "We need you to stop the seismic and geothermic activities here."

The computer's response was immediate. *"Incorrect protocol."*

The defensive energies swept out once more, but this time Soloman withstood them. He forced his hand deeper into the machine, then, with a strange, unearthly scream he sprang away from the machine, staggered to the nearest wall, and collapsed.

Carol rushed to him, Bart right behind her.

"Soloman! Are you hurt?" Carol cradled his head. "What happened?"

Bart had never seen such a haunted look in Soloman's eyes. The Bynar gasped, "Too much—too uncertain, too . . . arbitrary . . ."

Bart and Carol exchanged looks. Bart said, "Soloman, we don't understand. What are you saying?"

The Bynar shook his head as if trying to clear it. "All the . . . all the complexities . . . the computer . . ." He took a few deep breaths and sat up, tried again. "It is not a computer. Not in the traditional sense, anyway. It performs calculations, yes, but . . . but it fully understands *subjective thought*. Shades of meaning, irony . . ." He shuddered. "It *hurt*. Not physical pain, exactly, but . . . it felt as though my brain were about to burst."

As the two humans watched, speechless, Soloman got to his feet and took a few steps toward the alien computer again. Outside, the sky began to darken, but not because of beautiful multi-colored clouds: airborne volcanic ash had begun to blot out the light. The ground tremors growled out a long, steady vibration.

Harland went to his portable seismic monitor. "It's a matter of minutes now. Four at the outer-most."

Bart ran his hand over his mouth. He was closer to figuring out another piece of the puzzle. He could feel it.

Suddenly, the codebreaker's eyes flashed open wide. "Subjective thought! Yes. Now I understand: the symbols on the control panel and in the user's guide, these are not characters that comprise words. They're pictographs. Images that represent concepts and the progression of ideas, all related to the realm of the conscious and subconscious mind. Universal ideas and themes, such as the house, or dwelling place, as the residence of the psyche, keys as opportunity, water for emotions, are all represented here."

"That might explain why the constructs are out of control," Carol said as Bart hurried to the user's manual. "The A.I.'s first two tests were successful, but only to a point. The Keorgans have conscious thoughts and unconscious desires, but they are all arranged in a literal motif. There's no dreaming, no symbolism, not as the A.I. understands it and is searching for it, but its testing parameters were not well enough defined for it see that until it was too late and its systems were fully engaged."

Bart was sweating as he looked up from the user's manual. "It's too complex. I can do it. I can break this code, I can decipher these symbols, but the manual itself is not user-friendly. There's no indexing, no cross-referencing, and that's probably so that a novice could not just jump ahead and take shortcuts to learning. But it's not helping us right now. It would probably take a day to read it thoroughly."

"We have two minutes," Harland said nervously.

Soloman put his hand on the composer's shoulder. "Can you bring your construct here? Reduce it in size and volume so that it would fit inside this room and not deafen us?"

"I'll try," the composer said.

Outside, the cacophony steadily became more orderly, once more organizing itself into a single symphony. But instead of growing softer, it became louder, and soon, blinding violet light flooded in from without as the "instruments" came crashing through the wall, raining glass and debris on everyone. The object then grew smaller and quieter, hovering at a height the others could easily reach.

Soloman touched the construct, and there was no pain, only a hauntingly familiar sensation of unity that he had not experienced since the death of his mate. He walked to the computer, one hand surrounded by the now silent energy matrix that swelled and altered in its crackling violet forms as it adjusted to Soloman's thought patterns.

"First interface achieved," Soloman said.

"It's true," the composer said. "I can't feel it anymore. I'm not one with the construct any longer."

Again very slowly and carefully, Soloman reached inside the computer, this time better prepared for what he would experience, but still his back arched horribly as his body shook in spasms of mental agony—

—then suddenly relaxed somewhat, allowing him to slump forward against the housing. Again the computer's voice spoke to them: *"What do you want to learn?"*

Soloman spoke out loud, his voice shaky, his eyes squeezed tightly shut. "I . . . we . . . want to learn about . . . the ferrous asteroids orbiting throughout this system. We need . . . a controlled electromagnetic projector . . . to bring one or more of them here to us."

The computer's "circuitry" flared a tiny bit brighter for an instant. *"Crafting necessary tool now."*

It took maybe three seconds. The energy surrounding Soloman's hand shimmered, flickered, and transformed into a glittering cone, maybe thirty centimeters from base to point. Soloman stood, looked up at the cone, and it flared a stunning shade of green.

"Can you—" Carol started, then swallowed. "Is it . . . working? Can you tell how to control it?"

"I can *feel* it," Soloman said. "It's—intuitive. It's as though I've always known how to use it."

Bart asked, "Can you make the learning tool do what you want?"

Soloman gazed at the object in awe and wonder. "I think I can."

The building shook violently, forcing them all to

stagger to keep their feet. "You'd better go ahead, then," Carol said urgently.

Soloman nodded, stared down at the cone, closed his eyes—and lifted his arm to hold the object above his head.

No light sprang forth from it; whatever action it took was invisible to the naked eye. But they felt the effects immediately, and on a level that no sentient creature on that planet had ever felt before.

The earth moved.

Not the random, violent thrusting and destruction of two tectonic plates grinding against each other, or the long-brewing, explosive upheaval of an erupting volcano. It was much smoother than that, and yet at the same time much more affecting and profound. Wind suddenly rose and whipped against the building, clouds rushed toward them and smashed apart, and outside along the coast, the ocean's waters rippled and receded before flowing back up to the beaches . . .

. . . and then it was over. The earth tremors that had become a constant murmur in the background had ceased entirely; for the first time in what seemed like an eternity, the ground beneath their feet was stable.

But Soloman was still connected to the machine.

"You did it!" Bart cried in delight. He approached his friend, but Carol put a hand on his arm, stopping him.

"What did he do?" Professor Harland asked meekly. "What just happened?"

Slightly distracted by the sight of his friend still

fused with the A.I. and in obvious pain, Bart said, "Soloman created a magnetic tool powerful enough to reach millions of kilometers into space and bring back asteroids to study—"

Carol finished the thought for him. "And he used it to shift your planet's crust. Very, very carefully, he stabilized the plates along your coastline, and then shifted Keorga's crust so that the budding volcanoes will now erupt on your ocean floor. Your whole world just moved about ten kilometers to the left."

Harland looked confused. "But . . . if the crisis is over, then why is Soloman still interfaced with the computer?"

As if in answer to the question, a booming voice rose about them. *"Learning tool used incorrectly. Stated objective to bring asteroids closer for study not attained. Intervention required. Assistance will be given."*

The "top" spun even higher, lifting Soloman's arm, and activated once more. Again, its effects were invisible to the naked eye. But the computer filled them in on the details of what had just occurred.

"Fifteen asteroids located. All fifteen will breach planetary atmosphere in five minutes and be close enough for study fourteen seconds later."

Bart paled. "Close enough for study? How close is that?"

"Ground level."

"Wait!" Bart called. The machine was actually responding to his queries. "What about the safety overrides? You're programmed to protect those who use the learning tools."

"The rules of learning were manually overriden. Automatic safety feature no longer engaged. Discipline must be maintained. A lesson must be learned. Thank you for using Learning Mech."

The voice fell silent. Bart hollered questions but they went unanswered. Fifteen asteroids striking the surface of this planet at once? In five minutes, where they were standing would be ground zero for an extinction-level event.

"We have to shut this thing down," Carol said. "All we've managed to accomplish is to trade a continent-threatening crisis for one that could destroy this entire planet!"

Bart snorted. "Maybe where it comes from, the impact of fifteen asteroids to a user is the equivalent of a scraped knee." He looked to the user's manual. If only there were more time . . .

Soloman finally spoke. "I have to let it know I've changed my mind. I have to convince it I don't care about studying ferrous asteroids—"

Bart stopped him. "But—is that true? The A.I. will know."

Soloman lowered his head. "I have that interest, yes. Perhaps I can make it send me to them."

"I think I know a way of terminating the system," Professor Harland said. There was pain in his voice. The pain of willing sacrifice. "But Soloman must not hear. He is still interfaced with the computer. What he knows, it will know. That is probably why it won't release him until he has learned his lesson."

Harland told the others his plan.

*   *   *

Soon, Bart and Carol were beside the trapped Bynar.

"Do you really understand what you're getting yourself into here?" Bart asked. "Carol, it should be me."

She shook her head. "One has to lead. One has to follow. There's no way I can lead in this. I only pray I can put aside my ego so I can follow."

Taking a deep breath, she thrust her hand into the energy construct. Waves of energy surged through her, but there was no pain, only a strange sense of surrender that she had rarely felt in her life. She felt the A.I.'s programming combing her mind and struggled to let down the defensive walls she had erected to protect her thoughts and inner-most feelings since childhood.

Beside her, Bart talked softly and quietly, using a technique he had studied called hypnotic regression.

"Find your earliest and happiest memories," Bart said. "Find them and melt into them, let them become your world. . . ."

Carol tried, but there were so few, and so many negative instances to move beyond. . . .

Outside, raised voices that might have been thunder crashed through the city, deafening, ever-rising roars of anger and frustration. The sounds of her youth—of her childhood.

And in one corner, Harland stood near the wrecked wall, nervously watching the readings of his portable seismic monitor. "I'm detecting disturbances. Shifts in the waves. Objects of great size are approaching. It is the asteroids. . . ."

"You must go back farther," Bart said softly. "Find a time when you were contented, when the world was fresh and new."

She considered her childhood, perhaps, as it might have been. As she had so richly imagined it. Then it came to her: A single day when she had been visiting her aunt and she had been left alone on the woman's estate. An entire afternoon of freedom, of racing through fields, of not thinking or worrying, but simply enjoying life as only a child could. . . .

"System error detected," said the A.I.'s booming voice. *"Previous interface test results in error. Maturity Level Five not attained. All failsafes engaged. System shutdown imminent."*

"The readings are changing!" Harland said. "The asteroids are being recalled!"

Bart looked to the shattered wall to the city beyond. "And the constructs are fading from existence. We've done it!"

But Carol couldn't hear any of it. She was lost in that moment of her youth, a single afternoon in which she had found contentment and could laugh and play and dream without consequence.

It was her world now—and a part of her never wanted to leave.

CHAPTER
9

The remaining two weeks before the rendezvous with the *da Vinci* passed quickly. Communications had been immediately restored, but with the A.I. shut down and the planet's seismic and geothermic difficulties under control, there was no longer any need for urgency.

Bart watched as Professor Harland told the story of those last few minutes to a group of children.

"You see, when the A.I. ran its preliminary tests to see if it could interface with our race, it also scanned for certain factors that led it to interpret the level of maturity of our people to be acceptable for the learning tools it would craft. Our lack of what the humans call imagination, subtext, or guile, coupled with our intellectual sophistication, caused the computer to believe that we were mature enough for its lessons. But when the human woman joined the interface with the Bynar, she allowed the machine to comb her earli-

est and happiest memories and see that the level
of maturity needed had not indeed been attained.
Thus it recalled its learning tools and shut itself
down. The system has since been disassembled.
And our new friends have agreed to give us books
and plays and holos to help us understand these
new concepts. There is peace and goodness in
unity."

"What about the human female?" a girl asked.

Harland shrugged. "She is . . . recovering."

While Bart sat on a nearby bench in the park,
Carol came racing up to him. With a silly giggle
she said, "Tag! You're it!"

"Again, am I?" he asked. He was now midway
through the translation of the computer's user
manual. The machine, of course, was far too dangerous to ever be reactivated, but the mystery of
the machine's creators and their strange language
continued to fascinate him.

"I dunno," Carol said, her hands behind her
back, alternately rocking and pivoting.

"Well, when you figure it out, you let me know.
'Kay?"

" 'Kay!" She ran off—and immediately ran back.
"It's funny, that thing that happened with our shuttle. I remember talking to Mr. Silveris. And you
know what?"

"What?" Bart asked patiently.

"He said 'a small group of artists found many of
its components aesthetically pleasing and so they
used a construct to disassemble it.' And you know
what?"

"What, Carol?"

"I think I'm going to spin and spin and spin!" With a laugh, she spun herself around until she was dizzy. Then she collapsed on the ground, laughing. A sudden, serious expression came over her. "I went off again, didn't I?"

"Don't worry," Bart said. "You'll be back to normal before too long. You'll be adult and serious and crabby just like before."

"And suspicious. I'm suspicious, you know."

"Yes, I know."

Then her voice was high and childlike once more. "And you know what else?"

Bart smiled. "No, but I'm sure you're going to tell me."

"Your art made me think about a poem I read once," Carol said, her voice distant, neither childish nor mature. "It had something to do with always seeing life through the eyes of a child." Her eyes glazed over. "And it was squiggly!"

"That was its greatest feature, yes," Bart said.

Carol hopped to her feet, wobbled a little from the dizziness, then ran off to play with a group of children.

Bart considered that if he were another kind of person, he might take a holo of this extraordinary event and keep it on file in case Carol ever got so full of herself again.

Then he pushed the thought aside, thankful that he was not.

He did, however, know what the subject of his next letter to Anthony was going to be. . . .

ABOUT THE AUTHORS

Scott Ciencin is a *New York Times* best-selling author of adult and children's fiction. Praised by *Science Fiction Review* as "one of today's finest fantasy writers" and listed in the *Encyclopedia of Fantasy*, Scott has written over fifty novels and many short stories and comic books in a variety of genres. His recent work includes the novelization of *Jurassic Park III*, *Survivor* (the first in a series of original *Jurassic Park* adventures for young readers), *The Journal of Anakin Skywalker*, *Buffy the Vampire Slayer: Sweet Sixteen*, several original properties, and an *Angel* novel (also in collaboration with Dan Jolley). He also wrote a sort-of sequel to *Some Assembly Required* entitled *Age of Unreason*, which was recently published in eBook form. Scott has been a favorite author in the popular *Dinotopia* and *Godzilla* series, and his other books include *Shadowdale* and *Tantras* (as Richard Awlinson); the six-book *Dinoverse* fantasy adventure; *Gen¹³: Time and Chance* (with Jeff Mariotte); the *Vampire Odyssey* trilogy; and the comic books *Superman: Metropolis Special Crimes Unit*, *The New Gods*, and *Star Trek: The Next Generation: The Killing Shadows*. Scott lives in Fort Myers, Florida, with his beloved wife, Denise.

Keith R.A. DeCandido isn't just the co-developer of *Star Trek: S.C.E.*, he's also a client, having written or cowritten four previous installments in the ongoing saga (see the prior volumes *Have Tech, Will Travel* and *Miracle Workers*), and with three more published in eBook form in 2002 and 2003: *War Stories* Books 1-2 and *Breakdowns*. Keith, a frightening font of *Trek* trivia, also composed the "S.C.E. minipedia" that ran in the back of *Miracle Workers*. When he isn't immersed in the Starfleet Corps of Engineers, he writes other *Star Trek* fiction, ranging from the novels *Diplomatic Implausibility* and *Demons of Air and Darkness* to the comic book *Perchance to Dream* to the award-winning novella "Horn and Ivory" to the cross-series duology *The Brave & the Bold*. In late 2003, he will unleash the *Star Trek: I.K.S. Gorkon* subseries on a panting reading public—the first time a novel series has focused exclusively on *Star Trek*'s most popular aliens, the Klingons—as well as a novel in the *Star Trek: The Lost Era* miniseries. Keith also writes in universes both media (*Buffy, Farscape, Andromeda, Xena*, Marvel Comics) and of his own creation (the upcoming *Dragon Precinct*, which melds high fantasy with police procedurals), and edits the anthology of original science fiction novelettes *Imaginings*. He lives in the Bronx with his girlfriend and the world's two goofiest cats. See how pathetic he really is by going to his official Web site at DeCandido.net, then justify his pitiful existence by joining his official fan club at www.kradfanclub.com.

Dave Galanter and **Greg Brodeur** have penned four other *Star Trek* novels (*Foreign Foes*, *Battle Lines*, and the two-book *Maximum Warp*), and would appreciate it if you bought several copies of each—they make lovely stocking stuffers. Both natives of Michigan, Dave and Greg have never been arrested, and believe this is because their hearts are pure. Greg, who also writes with his wife Diane Carey under her name, has co-authored many best sellers. Dave has only written books with Greg, but hey, those haven't sold poorly, you know? Dave, fond of Canadian Southern Fried flavor Shake 'n' Bake, will continue to write with Greg for reasons that mystify the both of them, including an upcoming *Star Trek: The Next Generation* duology. Greg and his wife Diane have been married over twenty-two years. They have three great kids, a cat, a dog, and yes—believe it or not—a house with a white picket fence. Dave is fenceless, wifeless, kidless, and dogless. He has cats that help him in his search for Miss Right by lying around and sleeping a lot. Dave co-owns the Web sites ComicBoards.com and TVShowBoards.com and also works a day job as a Network Administrator. He's always hardworking and very busy, as opposed to Greg, who uses the Internet sometimes, and mills around smartly so people *think* he's busy. Dave also wrote this bio, and hopes Greg doesn't read this far.

Dan Jolley has been writing comics for every major publisher in the industry since the early 1990s. Among the characters Dan has brought to life are cult darlings like *Vampirella*, licensed film creations such as *Aliens*, and pop culture icons like Superman, Batman, and Wonder Woman. Dan achieved wide critical acclaim for *JSA: The Liberty File*, an alternate-universe story set in World War II starring Batman and several Golden Age heroes, and for *Obergeist*, published by Top Cow, a sci-fi/horror story of a Nazi butcher scientist seeking redemption for his crimes. Dan's other projects include a *Sabretooth* mini-series for Marvel and a collaborative *Angel* novel with Scott Ciencin. *Some Assembly Required* is his first published novel. Dan lives in Macon, Georgia.

Originally from New Jersey and New York, **Aaron Rosenberg** returned to New York City five years ago after stints in New Orleans and Kansas. He has published short stories, poems, essays, articles, reviews, and nonfiction books, but for the last ten years the majority of his writing has been in role-playing—he has written for more than eight game systems (including *Vampire*, DC Universe, *Witchcraft*, and *Star Trek*) and is the president of his own game company, Clockworks (www.clockworksgames.com). Aaron has also taught college-level English and worked in corporate graphics. His novelette "Inescapable Justice" will be appearing in *Imaginings: An Anthology of Long Short Fiction* and he is presently hard at work on more *S.C.E.* material.

Look for STAR TREK fiction from Pocket Books

Star Trek®

Kahless • Michael Jan Friedman
Ship of the Line • Diane Carey
The Best and the Brightest • Susan Wright
Planet X • Michael Jan Friedman
Imzadi II: Triangle • Peter David
I, Q • John de Lancie & Peter David
The Valiant • Michael Jan Friedman
The Genesis Wave, Books One, Two, and Three • John Vornholt
Immortal Coil • Jeffrey Lang
A Hard Rain • Dean Wesley Smith
The Battle of Betazed • Charlotte Douglas & Susan Kearney

Novelizations

Encounter at Farpoint • David Gerrold
Unification • Jeri Taylor
Relics • Michael Jan Friedman
Descent • Diane Carey
All Good Things . . . • Michael Jan Friedman
Star Trek: Klingon • Dean Wesley Smith & Kristine Kathryn Rusch
Star Trek Generations • J.M. Dillard
Star Trek: First Contact • J.M. Dillard
Star Trek: Insurrection • J.M. Dillard
Star Trek Nemesis • J.M. Dillard

#1 • *Ghost Ship* • Diane Carey
#2 • *The Peacekeepers* • Gene DeWeese
#3 • *The Children of Hamlin* • Carmen Carter
#4 • *Survivors* • Jean Lorrah
#5 • *Strike Zone* • Peter David
#6 • *Power Hungry* • Howard Weinstein
#7 • *Masks* • John Vornholt
#8 • *The Captain's Honor* • David and Daniel Dvorkin
#9 • *A Call to Darkness* • Michael Jan Friedman
#10 • *A Rock and a Hard Place* • Peter David
#11 • *Gulliver's Fugitives* • Keith Sharee
#12 • *Doomsday World* • Carter, David, Friedman & Greenberger
#13 • *The Eyes of the Beholders* • A.C. Crispin
#14 • *Exiles* • Howard Weinstein
#15 • *Fortune's Light* • Michael Jan Friedman
#16 • *Contamination* • John Vornholt
#17 • *Boogeymen* • Mel Gilden
#18 • *Q-In-Law* • Peter David
#19 • *Perchance to Dream* • Howard Weinstein

#58 • *Gemworld, Book One* • John Vornholt
#59 • *Gemworld, Book Two* • John Vornholt
#60 • *Tooth and Claw* • Doranna Durgin
#61 • *Diplomatic Implausibility* • Keith R.A. DeCandido
#62-63 • *Maximum Warp* • Dave Galanter & Greg Brodeur
    #62 • *Dead Zone*
    #63 • *Forever Dark*

Star Trek: Deep Space Nine®

Warped • K.W. Jeter
Legends of the Ferengi • Ira Steven Behr & Robert Hewitt Wolfe
Novelizations
Emissary • J.M. Dillard
The Search • Diane Carey
The Way of the Warrior • Diane Carey
Star Trek: Klingon • Dean Wesley Smith & Kristine Kathryn Rusch
Trials and Tribble-ations • Diane Carey
Far Beyond the Stars • Steve Barnes
What You Leave Behind • Diane Carey

#1 • *Emissary* • J.M. Dillard
#2 • *The Siege* • Peter David
#3 • *Bloodletter* • K.W. Jeter
#4 • *The Big Game* • Sandy Schofield
#5 • *Fallen Heroes* • Dafydd ab Hugh
#6 • *Betrayal* • Lois Tilton
#7 • *Warchild* • Esther Friesner
#8 • *Antimatter* • John Vornholt
#9 • *Proud Helios* • Melissa Scott
#10 • *Valhalla* • Nathan Archer
#11 • *Devil in the Sky* • Greg Cox & John Gregory Betancourt
#12 • *The Laertian Gamble* • Robert Sheckley
#13 • *Station Rage* • Diane Carey
#14 • *The Long Night* • Dean Wesley Smith & Kristine Kathryn
    Rusch
#15 • *Objective: Bajor* • John Peel
#16 • *Invasion! #3: Time's Enemy* • L.A. Graf
#17 • *The Heart of the Warrior* • John Gregory Betancourt
#18 • *Saratoga* • Michael Jan Friedman
#19 • *The Tempest* • Susan Wright
#20 • *Wrath of the Prophets* • David, Friedman & Greenberger

Enterprise®

Star Trek®: New Frontier

Star Trek®: Stargazer

Star Trek®: Starfleet Corps of Engineers (eBooks)

#13 • *No Surrender* • Jeff Mariotte
#14 • *Caveat Emptor* • Ian Edginton & Mike Collins
#15 • *Past Life* • Robert Greenberger
#16 • *Oaths* • Glenn Hauman
#17 • *Foundations, Book One* • Dayton Ward & Kevin Dilmore
#18 • *Foundations, Book Two* • Dayton Ward & Kevin Dilmore
#19 • *Foundations, Book Three* • Dayton Ward & Kevin Dilmore
#20 • *Enigma Ship* • J. Steven York & Christina F. York
#21 • *War Stories, Book One* • Keith R.A. DeCandido
#22 • *War Stories, Book Two* • Keith R.A. DeCandido
#23 • *Wildfire, Book One* • David Mack
#24 • *Wildfire, Book Two* • David Mack
#25 • *Home Fires* • Dayton Ward & Kevin Dilmore
#26 • *Age of Unreason* • Scott Ciencin

Star Trek®: Invasion!

#1 • *First Strike* • Diane Carey
#2 • *The Soldiers of Fear* • Dean Wesley Smith & Kristine Kathryn Rusch
#3 • *Time's Enemy* • L.A. Graf
#4 • *The Final Fury* • Dafydd ab Hugh
Invasion! Omnibus • various

Star Trek®: Day of Honor

#1 • *Ancient Blood* • Diane Carey
#2 • *Armageddon Sky* • L.A. Graf
#3 • *Her Klingon Soul* • Michael Jan Friedman
#4 • *Treaty's Law* • Dean Wesley Smith & Kristine Kathryn Rusch
The Television Episode • Michael Jan Friedman
Day of Honor Omnibus • various

Star Trek®: The Captain's Table

#1 • *War Dragons* • L.A. Graf
#2 • *Dujonian's Hoard* • Michael Jan Friedman
#3 • *The Mist* • Dean Wesley Smith & Kristine Kathryn Rusch
#4 • *Fire Ship* • Diane Carey
#5 • *Once Burned* • Peter David
#6 • *Where Sea Meets Sky* • Jerry Oltion
The Captain's Table Omnibus • various

Star Trek®: The Dominion War

Star Trek®: Section 31™

Star Trek®: Gateways

Star Trek® Omnibus Editions

Star Trek® Short Story Anthologies

Other Star Trek® Fiction